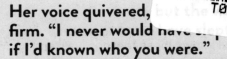

Her voice quivered, but the rest was **firm. "I never would** have slept with you **if I'd known who you were."**

"Where's the fun in that? It was good sex. I haven't stopped thinking about it. But in one of those ironic twists of fate, that next morning, my brother Edmund decided to take a new role in the company and my dad passed the reins of the winery division to me. So, if it helps your sensibilities, at the time we met, I was unemployed. Now that the whole corporate office is relocating to Beaumont, I'm here at least a year. I told my dad I'd give him that."

Her stomach rolled with the implications. She felt queasy, somewhat sick. "I don't hook up. I don't fraternize with hotel guests. This is so awkward. I let myself break my rules for one night."

"I broke mine, too." He rested a hip against the table. "And I'm not a guest. I wasn't that night, either."

"No, you're the boss. That makes what I did worse."

"I wasn't the boss then," he pointed out, using his foot to swing her chair around. "I was a man who wanted you very much."

"Except we weren't supposed to see each other again."

Dear Reader,

Have you ever wanted to start fresh? To become someone new? Lexi knows these feelings well, and she's finally found peace away from the celebrity limelight that dominated her childhood. Then she accidently spends one night with Liam—who turns out to be her new boss. Liam has a protective streak a mile long, so when he discovers his and Lexi's actions have consequences, he'll do everything in his power not to lose someone else.

Room for Two More takes us back to two of my favorite places—the fictional town of Beaumont and the very real Estes Park, Colorado. I hiked in Rocky Mountain National Park when I was a teenager, and while I haven't climbed Longs Peak, members of my family have. I've found hiking, even if as simple as walking a trail at the local park, is a way to connect with nature and discover things about myself. While climbing the world's tallest mountain will never be on my bucket list, I'm fascinated by stories of Mount Everest and have long wanted to incorporate the mountain that represents the ultimate achievement of man yet claims so many into one of my works.

I hope you love Liam and Lexi as much as I do. Let me know by visiting my website, micheledunaway.com, where you can also subscribe to my newsletter.

Michele

ROOM FOR TWO MORE

MICHELE DUNAWAY

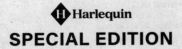

SPECIAL EDITION

If you purchased this book without a cover you should be aware that this book is stolen property. It was reported as "unsold and destroyed" to the publisher, and neither the author nor the publisher has received any payment for this "stripped book."

Harlequin®
SPECIAL EDITION™

Recycling programs
for this product may
not exist in your area.

ISBN-13: 978-1-335-40218-9

Room for Two More

Copyright © 2025 by Michele Dunaway

All rights reserved. No part of this book may be used or reproduced in any manner whatsoever without written permission.

Without limiting the author's and publisher's exclusive rights, any unauthorized use of this publication to train generative artificial intelligence (AI) technologies is expressly prohibited.

This is a work of fiction. Names, characters, places and incidents are either the product of the author's imagination or are used fictitiously. Any resemblance to actual persons, living or dead, businesses, companies, events or locales is entirely coincidental.

For questions and comments about the quality of this book, please contact us at CustomerService@Harlequin.com.

TM and ® are trademarks of Harlequin Enterprises ULC.

Harlequin Enterprises ULC
22 Adelaide St. West, 41st Floor
Toronto, Ontario M5H 4E3, Canada
www.Harlequin.com

Printed in Lithuania

MIX
Paper | Supporting
responsible forestry
FSC® C021394

In first grade, **Michele Dunaway** wanted to be a teacher. In second grade, she wanted to be a writer. By third grade, she decided to be both. Now a bestselling author, Michele strives to create strong heroes and heroines for savvy readers who want contemporary, small-town adventures with characters who discover things about themselves as they travel the road to true love and self-fulfillment. Michele loves to travel, with the places she visits often inspiring her novels. An avid baker, Michele describes herself as a woman who does way too much but never wants to stop, especially when it comes to creating fiction, or baking brownies and chocolate chip cookies. She loves to hear from readers at micheledunaway.com.

Books by Michele Dunaway

Harlequin Special Edition

Love in the Valley

What Happens in the Air
All's Fair in Love and Wine
Love's Secret Ingredient
One Suite Deal
Room for Two More

Visit the Author Profile page
at Harlequin.com for more titles.

For Nat, Harper, Karissa, Caro, Avery, Ali, Maya,
Zeriuah, Emily and Lillie. Can't wait to see
what the future brings. Go forth and conquer.

For Jill Marsal, my agent,
and the entire Harlequin Special Edition team,
who made this book possible.

For Dave and Jennifer of Fearsome (fearsomeis.org),
who hiked the entire Appalachian Trail, and for all my
other friends who post pictures of their various hikes
(and things like helicopter flybys of Everest).
Your adventures inspire me daily.
Thanks for making the world a better place.

Chapter One

Her stilettoes should be illegal. Or at least against hotel policy.

Four inches high. Black leather. Scuffed red bottom. Hint of clear polished toe. Liam Clayton frowned with prickly, unwanted awareness as he assessed how long, shapely legs covered in flesh-colored stockings skyrocketed and disappeared under a black, A-line, knee-skimming skirt. Curvy hips swayed as the brunette edged around the ballroom. Even without those heels, he could tell she was tall, at least five-nine.

A white oxford, long-sleeved shirt covered thin, dancer's arms that toted a medium-sized cardboard box. The silky black vest indicated she was a Beaumont Chateau staff member, but Liam hadn't seen her before. Dark hair pulled into a French knot revealed a face that could stop men in their tracks: perfect nose, full bow lips and high arched brows. Liam was too far away to see her eyes but imagined them to be soft brown and full of intelligence. She didn't appear to take notice of any grand opening gala guests. She strode forward with complete confidence, despite the fact her steps became increasingly wobbly the closer she was to the exit. When she shifted the box, her right ankle twisted and bobbled, but she righted herself before he could cross the room and offer assistance. Then she disappeared like a figment of his imagination. Maybe she had been. Just a ghost from another time, back when he'd had a heart and a libido.

Curious as to why the woman had caught his attention, he began to follow. "Not so fast," Eva said, putting a hand on the sleeve of Liam's tux. "Where do you think you're going?"

"Anywhere but here?" Liam peered at his little sister. Since she was five-two, he topped her by ten inches. Still, she succeeded at pushing him around.

Eva arched a brow. "Ha. Ha. Aren't you the jokester. No, seriously."

As Eva folded her arms, Liam frowned at her. "What? It's the truth. I've put in my time."

"Is that what you see this as? It's a party. With your family. At the grand opening of our latest hotel. You should be having fun." Eva pointed at his chest. "Lighten up. Enjoy yourself. You have to get back into the world sometime. Might as well be tonight. Stop wallowing."

Even though she hadn't jabbed him, Liam rubbed a spot on his chest. "You know these events aren't my scene." That was one reason why he'd sold his tech start-up two years ago, a few months after the accident.

"Look, we all know you'd rather be in some developing country doing something noble, but you're needed here. And it's time." Eva caught herself before she waved a finger.

"I don't like the BS of doing things like this." And the sale of his firm had netted him enough money to allow him to concentrate on his charitable works, most of them being done anonymously.

"Boo-hoo. Look, we all know you'd rather be hiking—"

"I haven't done that in two years." Liam interrupted more harshly than he intended. He felt guilt rise both for snapping at his baby sister and for his decision to forgo his favorite hobby. The accident had not been Eva's fault. She meant well. She simply didn't understand, which she made clear when she continued to speak, ignoring his discomfort.

"Maybe it's time you should get back on a mountain. Anya wouldn't have wanted you to stop doing what you love. You've been a walking dead man for two years. A shell. Enough's enough."

As Edmund, Liam's older brother, took the stage to make his grand opening speech, Liam thanked the gods for their fortuitous timing. Edmund's planned remarks saved Liam from dealing with Eva and her further nagging. He wasn't ready, and she didn't need to keep pressing.

Liam half listened as Edmund, who served as the VP of Clayton Holdings, welcomed everyone to the Chateau. When the heir apparent began to thank the mayor, Liam tuned his older brother out. Edmund, the king of ambition, had followed in their father's footsteps in wanting to build the Clayton Holdings empire. Minus the Roman nose Liam and his brothers shared, and the gray eyes all four siblings shared, Liam took after their mother more than their father. He wore his dirty blond hair far longer than his siblings' black locks. He hated the proverbial rat race. He wanted wide open skies, not steel towers and concrete sidewalks. Wanted to give back, not conquer, unless it was a mountain summit.

Maybe his philosophy came from being born second— the heir spare to the dynasty. His father and uncle wanted Liam to join the family company, but Liam so far had said no. After immense pressure from his mother, Liam had caved and agreed to be present and accounted for tonight. He wished he could loosen the bow tie or at least take off the tuxedo jacket. Hating the penguin suit, he ran his finger under the shirt collar and murmured noncommittally to those who stopped to make conversation.

Now that the opening remarks were done, Edmund began to make his way through the crowd. When he stopped to greet their parents, Liam used the opportunity to plan his exit. Before he could escape, he watched as Margot Van Horn cornered his older brother. Edmund had been trying to acquire Van Horn Hotels for at least two years, but he hadn't been successful. Liam hated the wheeling and dealing part of the family business. Edmund had had to go undercover to try to win the hotels, but he'd failed. However, everyone was smiling. Strange.

Whatever was going on, Liam took it as a good sign that he could finally disappear without being missed. And when Edmund suddenly made a beeline outside and into the French gardens, Liam decided he wouldn't begrudge Edmund his getaway. Perhaps his brother was finally going to try and win back the woman of his dreams. If so, Liam wished him well. Edmund deserved some happiness.

Besides, logic said that if Edmund got to leave this fancy party, so did Liam. He glanced at his parents. He loved them, but after already dealing with Eva's opinions on his lack of dating, Liam had no desire to talk to anyone else tonight. He nudged his sister and showed her his empty glass. "Here comes Mom and Dad. Divert them, will you? I need another drink."

"Liam!" Eva protested, but he blew her a kiss and pivoted in the other direction. He moved swiftly, weaving through the crowd toward the open bar. Then, once he'd put enough people between him and his family, he slipped into the hall.

Several people mulled in the corridor, but Liam kept walking. He'd put in enough face time. He'd smiled for the requisite family pictures, publicity photos that would be circulated online and in the mainstream media, the culmination of Eva's PR work to launch the opening of the Beaumont Chateau. Liam didn't care the hotel was the crown jewel in the family portfolio. He was ready for escape. But before he could reach the exit, he saw his cousin Jack and his wife, Sierra. They hadn't seen him yet, giving Liam time to avoid another long conversation about the family business. He pivoted and stepped through the first opening he could find, which led into the softly lit hotel bar.

And there she was.

Lexi Henderson wasn't the type to be impressed easily. But everything about the Beaumont Chateau was perfect. Absolutely, gobsmackingly, fantastically perfect. She'd been working at the luxurious boutique hotel since the April 1 soft open. Now that the official grand opening weekend was here, Lexi wasn't regretting her decision to take a bartending job in Esprit de Bonne Vie, which she'd learned meant "spirit of a good life" in French. Her job certainly was a way toward a good and normal life. In the past two weeks since she'd arrived at the Chateau as an associate bartender after a stint at the Beaumont Grand, Lexi had doubled her tips. That boded well for her finances, especially as the Chateau was completely booked for May and June. At this current rate, in eight weeks, she'd be in a strong enough monetary position to afford classes at the local college. She'd also have a minuscule nest egg in the bank, which was fine, for her mother always said a bird in the hand was worth two in the bush. Thinking of her late mom made Lexi's heart pang, so she focused on the positives. She was lucky she'd learned to bartend so fast, and that she'd managed to snag an opening at the coveted Chateau. She still wasn't sure how that miracle had happened but was extremely grateful.

Clayton Holdings had outdone itself. The Chateau was a beautiful six-story hotel, built to exacting standards. French settlers had founded the town of Beaumont in 1769, and castles such as Versailles, Fontainebleau and Chambord had served as the architectural inspiration for the Chateau's exterior. The interior consisted of thirty-seven guest rooms, most of them suites. With full banquet facilities and meeting rooms, indoor and outdoor pools, a world-class spa, two fine dining restaurants and the French bar where Lexi worked, visitors never needed to leave the grounds. Although, if they wished, they could take a complimentary shuttle to all six of the nearby Clayton wineries.

No expense had been spared, as if Edmund Clayton III had been channeling his inner Vanderbilt when he'd approved the plans. Earlier in the evening, she'd seen Edmund, his father, uncle and sister, Eva, moving about like local celebrities during the grand opening festivities. But Lexi wasn't working any of the bars in the ballroom or even the one on the terrace. As one of the newer bartenders, and because she was still in training, tonight she unloaded boxes and manned Esprit, which admittedly had seen zero patrons since everyone was at the gala. The bar, while open, was an afterthought, which was why her boss had assigned her this venue. Despite her confidence, she was the newest hired.

Using the bar towel, Lexi wiped down the glossy, polished wood surface normally covered by drinks. Best to be prepared. One never knew when someone might wander in.

Like him. The most gorgeous man with shoulder-length hair her fingers itched to run through slid onto the bar stool. She felt the impact of his wide smile in her knees. "What can I get you?"

"One finger Old Forester 1910. Neat."

"Good choice." One rule of bartending she'd been taught at the Grand—make the customer feel valued and smart by offering a compliment. Not that she'd ever sampled the bourbon he chose. Lexi rarely drank what she poured. She retrieved the bottle and grabbed a short glass. As she slid over his drink, she gave him what she hoped passed for a professional smile. He was good-looking in that rugged, sporty kind of way, as if he might be a professional athlete of some sort. He had wavy hair, with those blonder highlights that were caused by the sun, not the salon. He wore the style longer, to the nape of his neck. Maybe he was a musician. No, she decided. He wasn't. She'd met enough of them to know their vibe. His was completely different. He had an innate confidence of someone who knew exactly who he was and what he wanted.

Firm, strong fingers lifted the glass. He had the kind of hands with blunt, real nails that were clean but not manicured weekly. As he sipped, she worked to calm a heart that shouldn't be racing because of a sexy voice, a smooth, chiseled chin, or smoldering gray eyes. Guests were off-limits, even if he'd melted her insides. Besides, at this point in her life, the last thing she needed was Mr. Hot and Steamy. She wanted Mr. Nice Guy, not someone who wore innate, let-me-take-you-to-bed sexiness like a second skin. She wanted Mr. Slow and Steady, not Mr. Fast and Furious. Or Mr. Settle Down, not Mr. Set Me on Fire.

She had no idea if the man seated in front of her was any of those things, but it didn't matter. What was that old saying? Fool me once, shame on you. Fool me twice, shame on me.

Once around the block in a long-term personal and business relationship with Mr. Wrong had sent Lexi scampering for the anonymity of Beaumont, a town one of her so-called "friends" had mentioned in passing. After doing some online research, Lexi had decided to give Beaumont a try. The historic small town located outside of St. Louis was Lexi's second chance, a way to disappear into the woodwork, a place to start fresh. A place for metamorphosis, same as the Chateau, which had risen from an old farm field. She'd literally shed her persona. Become someone new. That's who'd poured Mr. Dreamy's bourbon and who watched his throat move as he sipped.

"Is it always this slow in here?" He had a rough voice, the kind that sent those cliché shivers down a woman's spine.

Maintaining outward control, her shoulders rose and fell in a tiny, nonchalant shrug. Bartenders were chameleons, becoming servers, companions, therapists and nurturers depending on what the person sitting on the stool needed. "Actually, it's usually very busy, but most guests are here for the gala. It's a whole weekend worth of events, you know."

He pointed toward the nearly full bottle sitting near her right hand. "Since it's just us in here, pour yourself a glass. Keep me company. Put it on my tab."

"I'm not able to drink with guests." Which was the truth. "Even if it's an open bar like it is tonight." Also the truth. "Hotel policy, you know." And her personal one.

"A pity." He pushed the empty glass toward her, which she refilled. "I hate drinking alone."

"There's an entire party full of people drinking in the ballroom."

His lip curled as he lowered his glass. "Yeah, that's the last place I want to be."

"Forgive me if I don't understand why but—" She grabbed a glass, filled it with club soda and took a sip. "Glamorous people. Delicious food. At least it looked good." Her stomach rumbled its protest for missing dinner. Cheese and crackers purchased from a vending machine didn't quite cut it, and her body wanted more than the club soda she drank to settle her stomach.

He motioned with his left hand, indicating her middle. "Do you want me to go get you a plate? The food's pretty good."

Heat rose in her cheeks. He'd heard her stomach growl. "I'm fine but thank you. I'm off soon. But surely you'd have more fun inside."

"That's what my sister implied. But that party is like being in a lake filled with piranhas. I might not get out alive. I hate these things."

"Then why are you here?" She was genuinely curious.

His mouth twisted wryly. "Family. Decided to keep the harmony, so here I am in this monkey suit."

"I can understand family expectations." Her entire childhood consisted of constant family pressure to perform. And she had, caving to her father's will until six months ago, when she'd walked off the job. In a surprise move, she'd engaged lawyers and drained her entire bank account to buy out her contract. Melynda Norfolk was no more. Lexi could still hear her father's scathing words of "You'll never amount to anything again." She focused and pointed at Mr. Beautiful's glass. "Another round?"

"I'm good. Two's plenty after the champagne toasts from earlier."

Since she'd helped unpack and ice the bottles, Lexi knew what he'd had had been actual champagne, not sparkling wine. Champagne could be labeled such only if it came from the region in France that gave the bubbly its name. The gala had served attendees both Dom Pérignon and Cristal, another indication that no expense had been spared. The rest of the wine had come from the Clayton Holdings wineries located in both Washington State and Beaumont, Missouri.

Since her customer was finished, Lexi reached for the whiskey glass at the same time he pushed it toward her. As they touched, electricity coursed through her veins, and nerve-endings short-circuited into delicious tingles. "Sorry about that."

A sexy eyebrow arched and a hint of a grin spread. "What, the zing? Most fun I've had in a while, and especially the most fun I've had tonight."

The burst of flirty smile was as tempting as a swimming pool on a hot day, and her mouth dried to paste as her gaze traced over his tux. He'd loosened the bow tie. His sexy presence made her want things. It tempted her to violate the hotel's no fraternization with coworkers and guests policy. She purposely kept her voice light and her demeanor casual. "Then it's clear you should get out more."

"You're right. Maybe I should." He stood and dropped a fifty on the bar top. "Thanks for good conversation. Have a nice night."

"Good night, and try to have some fun," she called after

him, earning a back hand wave. As if willing him to turn around, she watched him leave. He never looked back and soon the bar was empty again. She pocketed the money and wiped down the place his drink had rested. Probably for the best. He was a temptation she didn't need.

Ever since she'd walked off the set six months ago, after finishing Damon and Melynda's latest music video, she'd had one goal—to live a normal life. Bartending was a means to an end. Five months ago, when she'd arrived in Beaumont, she'd lucked into having a great teacher over at the Beaumont Grand. Tania Gulledge had taken a chance and hired a girl with no experience. Tania had promised Lexi that should she work hard, the lead bartender would teach her everything she needed to know about serving drinks and keeping customers happy.

Tania, who hadn't wanted to move to the smaller-sized Chateau, had taught Lexi that people had different reasons for sitting in a bar. Some wanted to socialize. Some wanted entertainment. Some wanted to simply de-stress, while others didn't want to feel alone, or go home to an empty house. Under Tania's instruction, Lexi had mastered the art of knowing exactly how to provide what a client needed besides booze, all while maintaining an arm's distance. She had no idea what the previous guest had wanted, minus an escape from the party.

Despite his earlier vibe, she knew nothing about him really—whether he was married, single, straight or not, or what he did for a living. Maybe he'd come into the bar because the party was overwhelming and he had social anxiety. Nothing wrong with that. These type of events could be draining. She knew that firsthand. She used to attend galas like tonight's, in what seemed like a lifetime ago, instead of half a year. Those outings where she'd had to be perfectly dressed and smile nonstop had been back when she'd been someone else, a celebrity managed by not only the studio and record label, but by a controlling father-manager who'd overseen every aspect of her music career since age eight.

That's why succeeding, all by herself, mattered. Last September, when she'd started this do-over, even a bartending job had seemed an impossible reach. She'd had tutors, not public schooling. Having a team of people surrounding her who made all the decisions, she hadn't learned things like money management. Or how to cook. Or clean.

Who would have predicted she could escape the past and stand on her own two feet? Or that she'd share a house with a roommate she'd found online, a place paid for with her own money and deposited into her own bank account? Milestones for someone who'd never had the traditional school/college experience.

Lexi shifted from foot to foot as she washed and polished glassware. She hadn't intended to wear the expensive heels from another life, but she'd had little other option upon finding that her roommate, Dawn—who technically was also her landlord—had moved the ballet flats Lexi had accidentally left out instead of putting them away. Because she'd forgotten that house rule, Lexi attempted to wiggle toes that had long gone numb. She stared around the vast, TV-free space that felt even more empty since he'd left. The gorgeous man who'd sat in front of her had been rugged. Tempting. Far too good-looking. Dangerous as the tingles that one brief touch created. The shivers still traveled giddily down her spine.

Who was he? Had he been a test of her character, of her adherence to hotel rules? One such test had happened over at the Beaumont Grand. Within the first thirty days of her employment there, Lexi had discovered a wallet laying in the middle of the hallway. When she'd quickly turned it in, her boss had told her she'd passed and reminded her that the Claytons expected their employees to adhere to the highest of ethics.

Whoever he was, he was gone now. Lexi checked the watch on her left wrist—the thin leather band already beginning to fray. She had an hour left on her shift.

"Hey, we're still going to La Vita è Vino Dolce later, right?" Loretta breezed through. Twenty-eight to Lexi's twenty-six, she and Loretta had become fast friends once Lexi had arrived in Beaumont five months ago. Loretta worked the front desk and had no clue about the celebrity Lexi had once been.

Then again, Lexi no longer looked like Melynda Norfolk. She'd lost the platinum blond and returned her hair and eyebrows to their natural darker brown color. She'd cut away six inches, allowing her hair to go back to its naturally curly state. She'd kept it long enough to pull into a knot or ponytail, but she'd lost the bangs and gotten rid of the false eyelashes and lip filler. When she looked in the mirror, she saw brown eyes surrounded with natural makeup—that was when she bothered to wear any—not the heavy caked-on crap that had taken hours to apply. She saw a girl who was a healthy weight, not one so thin a light breeze might blow her over.

She smiled at Loretta. "Yes, we're still going to the wine bar. It's Saturday night, after all. And I'm not closing." And for once, Lexi had somewhere to be other than the bedroom she rented in Dr. Dawn Dulle's house.

Alvin, the Chateau's head bartender and manager, would

close Esprit. While tonight's gala went until midnight, as the night wound on and the number of guests dwindled, fewer bartenders would be needed in the ballroom, so they would transfer to Esprit. Lexi was looking forward to a night out. The outside world wasn't as scary as her father had implied, especially Main Street Beaumont. Besides, she knew how to take care of herself. She'd been naive once. Trusting. Gullible. Dependent on her father's will. Never again. One more step in moving forward—socializing with real friends.

An hour and a half later, Lexi sat in La Vita è Vino Dolce, a two-ounce pour of Riesling strategically placed on the bar top in front of her. While still in her uniform, she'd unbuttoned the top of her shirt and stuffed the vest in her purse. Loretta was ten minutes late. Nothing too worrisome as Loretta rarely was on time for anything other than work. Lexi felt perfectly comfortable sitting by herself and saving a bar stool. The self-serve wine bar had a low-key, relaxed vibe. The hundred-year-old former storefront had been gutted. The exposed brick walls rose a story and a half, making the smaller interior seem spacious. Most of the tables were full, with patrons serving themselves by using chip cards in the temperature-controlled, glass cases that contained four bottles of wine each. Her phone pinged with a text: Something came up. Can't make it. So sorry!

Lexi stared at the sad face emoji Loretta had added. Well, being stood up sucked in more ways than one. Because of the plans she'd made with Loretta, Lexi had carpooled to work with another coworker. Had she known Loretta might cancel, Lexi would have driven herself instead. Taking another Uber at peak time would eat into her budget. She reached for her purse and readied to leave.

"Excuse me, is this seat taken?" A deep voice washed over her, creating prickles of awareness.

"Not anymore." Lexi turned and froze. "You."

A delicious grin widened on the man she'd served earlier. "Me. And I promise I'm not stalking you. This is simply a lovely chance of fate. Call it my lucky day that I get to see you again. Now you can actually have a drink with me."

No longer wearing the tux, he'd changed into well-fitting jeans and a long-sleeved polo, perfect for the pleasant spring night. Hard to believe there'd been a hard freeze a few weeks ago.

Mr. Dreamy pointed to her near empty glass. "Can I get you another? Want to share one of the flatbreads they have? You did eat, didn't you?"

Lexi warred with indecision, her body zinging electrons and her stomach grumbling. This man was lethal temptation, and he called forth a primitive desire to be reckless. "Thank you, but no. I was leaving." She drained the last sip.

"Boyfriend stand you up?"

Nice fishing, Lexi thought. "I was meeting my best friend, actually. She just texted that something came up and she can't make it. I'll eat at home."

"Where's the fun in that? Join me, I'll do my best to try and keep you company. If I'm boring, you can go. Deal?" His deep smile called a moth to explore the flame, and she found herself tempted to do just that. If she waited, the rideshares might get cheaper.

"I don't see why not. Deal." She wished she'd gotten a larger pour of wine, but decided against going to get one now. Two ounces had been enough, especially on an empty stomach.

"Excellent. Good choice. This is a fun place. Have you

been here before? I was here the other night. I'm staying down the block."

"You're not at the hotel?" That surprised her. So many people had flown in for the gala that the guest overflow had almost completely sold out the larger Beaumont Grand. Accommodations in the Chateau had been so coveted, they'd been near impossible to book.

He removed the wine bar's chip card from his pocket. "I'm at the Blanchard Inn. I might have had to attend the party, but that didn't mean I wanted to stay there."

"Oh, but it's such a gorgeous hotel." It struck her that, as a gala guest, he'd probably seen dozens of high-end, exquisite hotels. She had once, too.

"It is, but I like things quieter. Local. More off the beaten track." He extended his hand. "I'm Liam."

Touching him was like the start of a NASCAR race, like that one time when she'd once yelled "Drivers! Start your engines" and felt the vibration of forty-three cars each with 670 horsepower cranking and reverberating.

"I'm Lexi. Nice to meet you." She pushed her empty glass aside. "I'll be right back. Restroom."

"I'll be right here."

She slid off the stool, onto feet trapped in too-tight heels. Her right foot wobbled and he was there instantly, standing and sliding his arm around her waist, his thumb pressing against her spine as he steadied her. Muscled forearms flexed, and she made the mistake of putting her hands on his hard chest, where her fingers froze. Heat pooled between her thighs. Never had she experienced the overpowering force of instant attraction, or the hunger to linger, sample and enjoy. His mere touch created little explosions, each one blowing massive holes in the wall of her self-imposed "no men" policy. The dimples in his cheeks deepened, the indentation in the center of his strong jaw begging to be touched. His hair swooped back from a high forehead and dark blond strands curled around his ears. He traced a line from her elbow to her wrist, branding her skin. She took a much-needed step back. "Thanks. I'll be right back."

Her feet cramped as she walked to and from the bathroom. He was still sitting at the bar when she returned. In front of him was a margherita flatbread. He inched the board toward her. "Your stomach's been grumbling since Esprit. Eat something."

"If you're sure." It looked delicious, like him. At his nod, she lifted a piece. "I'll have just one."

He gestured toward the wooden serving board. "Take half. I ate at the gala and normally don't eat this late. I only wanted a nibble or two. And it seems I was born with my mother's need to feed people."

Lexi put three additional slivers onto her plate. Ingrained habits were hard. She'd always maintained a carefully curated diet, one that had devastating consequences as she'd tried to maintain the correct weight. Salvaging her mental and physical health had been one reason she'd quit being Melynda. The bartender came by and set a glass of water in front of her, and Lexi nodded her appreciation. "Okay then. As long as you tell me how much my half is. I insist on paying for my fair share."

Liam bit into the flatbread, which made a crunching sound. "I don't want your money. It's on me in exchange for some good conversation. Will that work? No ulterior motives." His smile threatened to undo her.

"That's kind. Thank you." She'd leave once she'd eaten something. "I appreciate you sharing. It's really good."

He tilted his head, giving her a perfect view of the sexy little dip in the center of his chin. "I'm glad you like it. Didn't figure you for a vegetarian, but went with that option anyway."

"It's perfect. I'm not a finicky eater." At least not anymore.

Because the bar served more than wine, he'd ordered a finger of bourbon, and the bartender set the glass in front of him before moving away. He wiped his hand on a napkin and took a sip. "I'm glad you're staying," he told Lexi. "It's been a while since a beautiful woman graced me with her presence. I'm enjoying your company."

No way would she believe that. He was a sexy, big bad wolf. He'd eat her alive, and she'd enjoy every minute. Innate sensuality radiated, along with a powerful undercurrent that roused the butterflies in her stomach and made them flit about. When he smiled, the action lit up his whole face, softening the angles that begged for a woman to trace. "Surely not. Women must throw themselves at you."

"That doesn't mean I want to date them. I was in a long-term relationship and since then…" He shrugged. "Even though I'm straight, women have held little appeal. Until you."

Disbelieving, she fingered the stem of her empty glass. "It can't have been that long. You're joking."

He held her gaze. "I never joke."

Three words delivered like cannonballs. Her eyes widened and she sucked in a breath. "Never?"

"No. I'm the serious one in my family. They say I'm too serious. Too fuddy-duddy. If you need someone to bring down the mood, they say I'm that guy."

"I can't believe that."

Those wide shoulders shrugged. "It's one reason I escaped and left the party early. I'd rather be here by myself than in the ballroom with hundreds of people."

"I see." But she didn't. He was an enigma. His irresistible aura had kept her sitting here, hadn't it? Sucked into his shimmery web? She found herself compelled by an unseen force to get to know him. "Surely you do something for fun?"

He conceded that point with a brief nod. "I like being outdoors. Hiking. Mountain climbing. Another reason I hated that fancy gala. But I went to keep the peace."

"Sometimes that's important." How many times had she done just that? She sipped some water and tried to focus on something positive. "Have you hiked anything I'd know? Not that I'm a hiker. I probably wouldn't know anything you mention. I'm just trying to make conversation."

"Which I appreciate. How about the entire Appalachian Trail?"

"Okay, I've heard of that. All of it?" She pushed her empty plate forward. They'd finished the entrée.

He grinned and pushed his own plate forward. "All of it."

"How long does that take?"

The corners of his mouth inched up as if he could tell he'd impressed her. "Five to seven months."

She leaned back, stunned. "You must really be into hiking."

When he grinned, his smile was infectious. "I was. Racked up quite a few summits. The Matterhorn. Denali. Longs Peak. There are others. Made it to Camp One on Everest but…" His face clouded. "Circumstances on the mountain changed, so the quest was abandoned. Doubt I'll ever go back. I stopped climbing after that."

"I've read lots of people die on that mountain." She gave a small shudder.

Liam took a sip of his bourbon, calling her attention back to his tantalizing lips. "It's unforgiving, that's for sure. How about you?"

"Well, I'm not a mountain climber. Not even a social climber." Much to her father's disgust and disappointment, she'd hated the celebrity lifestyle.

Liam chuckled, good humor restored. "Good to know. But hobbies? Things like that? Are you from Beaumont?"

"Are you always this inquisitive?" Not wanting to go too deep and threaten exposing her past, she turned the question back around on him.

A strong forefinger absently tapped the top of the bar. She liked his hands. They appeared strong yet not necessarily calloused. As a brief silence fell, she worried if she'd offended him, but then he spoke, as if choosing his words carefully.

"Actually, I'm not normally like this. I've quite surprised myself tonight. I'm amazed by how interesting I find you. It's been a while since I've even wanted to talk with anyone, much less a woman. But here we are."

Unsure of what to read into that statement, Lexi shot back, "Well, six months ago I swore off men, so maybe I sort of understand where you're coming from. I'm assuming you're like me, once burned, twice shy. Wondering why we're sitting here but not really ready to move away."

"Something like that." The bartender removed the empty flatbread board, catching both of their attention, providing a small break. When the bartender stepped away, Liam pushed his empty glass aside and turned his full attention to Lexi. "Do you want to get out of here?"

Chapter Two

Lexi swallowed. Her libido roared to life and screamed a resounding "Yes!" Instead, all she could manage was a simple, stammered "Uh."

He instantly understood her hesitation. "We can sit in the parlor of the inn. It's quieter." He pointed to her feet. "You can at least get out of those shoes for a while. You've been rubbing them against the bar stool leg the entire time we've been sitting here."

He clearly had great observation skills. First her stomach and now her shoes. "Yeah, today was not a good footwear choice on my part. I really should just go home." Part of her didn't want to do that either, and that part won out. "Okay, we can leave. As long as we stay on the first floor. I've always wanted to see the inside of the inn. I've heard it's marvelous."

"It is and of course. I am a gentleman. You can call a car whenever you're ready."

She believed him. Her gut told her she'd be safe with him, even on the short walk.

Liam had already paid the bill, and they grabbed their coats. She slipped her arm into his, taking comfort in his strength as her stilettos traversed the uneven cobblestone sidewalk that lined both sides of Main Street. They reached the historic Blanchard Inn, a three-story Victorian building with a wide front porch and heavy wooden double doors covered by spring wreaths.

Liam entered a code to unlock the front door. They stepped into a high-ceilinged foyer that showcased a grand staircase. "Wow." The more than two-hundred-year-old inn lived up to Lexi's expectations, especially with its parlor fitted with comfortable period pieces. "I love it."

Liam pointed toward some sofas in the room to the left. "Take a seat. Kick off the shoes. I'll run upstairs to my room. The inn supplies slippers, and I'll bring down a bottle of wine."

The promise of comfortable slippers tempted. Slippers were safe, and a chance to soothe her rebelling, tortured, aching feet. She'd worn these designer shoes once before— for less than an hour. They were killing her. The door opened and a group of people entered and moved into the parlor. Lexi frowned at the intrusion.

"I have a sitting area in my suite," Liam said. "If that's not too forward. You can trust me."

Having dealt with so many who'd betrayed her, she knew he hadn't lied. His gaze hadn't darted from side to side. He hadn't blinked or swallowed needlessly or fiddled with something. She nodded and wordlessly followed him up the huge staircase. He opened the door. "It's a bit much, I know, but I like it. I've stayed in everything from tents to log cabins. Even I had to admit this room is pretty cool. It's like going back in time."

Lexi entered the room and gasped. When she'd delivered items to guests, she'd seen the inside of several of the Chateau's suites. Each had been designed to be slightly unique and different, but all had contemporary finishes including huge walk-in showers with oversize rainwater nozzles and multiple jets.

Liam's room at the inn was old-fashioned and quaint. A Victorian-style love seat and two high-backed chairs surrounded a gas fireplace that flickered. The room's centerpiece was a huge canopied queen bed. The comforter was turned down, red-and-white-striped mints placed strategically on the fold. Butterflies suddenly took flight in her stomach. What was she doing? She'd sworn off men, sworn off the drama they caused. Damon, who'd professed his love for her, hadn't cared enough to stay faithful. He hadn't loved her in that way soulmates did.

But for some reason, leaving and going home was unthinkable. Instead, she sat on the love seat, kicked off her shoes and wiggled her toes gratefully. She watched as Liam uncorked the wine and accepted the glass he poured her. Trying not to crowd her, he dropped into one of the armchairs. "Cheers," he said, saluting her with the glass.

She returned the gesture, and after the toast, it was as if a dam broke. Deep conversation flowed, moving without awkward pauses or worries. Oh, they circled around their backstories. She sensed his was like hers—some loss or hurt he'd buried deep. But as they revealed other pieces of themselves, she felt as if she'd found a kindred spirit. Both of them seemed to be peering over walls. Afraid to unlock the door to let anyone else in. Both hiding behind something off-limits.

She told him that when she'd decided to move to a new place, she'd been so nervous, but that Clayton's website had convinced her to make the leap. Dating back to the time of Lewis and Clark's famed expedition, the historic town had everything she might need and charm to boot. Beaumont also was home to a local college, and she planned on getting her degree. That was a priority. She'd start in August.

"Even though moving was scary, I realized it was time. I no longer wanted to be ruled by my fears. I've had enough darkness," she told him.

He nodded. "Time for the light. I can agree with that. I probably need some myself."

"As long as it's the right kind of light." While it could have been an option, she hadn't wanted the spotlight of Broadway. Hollywood had been bad enough. The intrusive flashes of the paparazzi and their merciless hounding had worn on her. She'd needed this clean break. She didn't tell him any of that, opting instead to add, "You know the kind of light I mean. That soft glow. The kind that surrounds you and makes you feel good. Like a sunrise." She wanted the light that nurtured and loved. Gave life, not blinded and destroyed.

She'd walked away from the intense spotlight, having her fill of the alpha men who dominated the entertainment industry—including her famous father—powerful men who thought they could do whatever they wanted with her career because she was female and "needed guidance." They'd told her what to wear. Where to go. How to behave. Who to date. No matter where she was, they'd controlled her life right down to the food she ate and the clothes she wore. She hadn't been free to make her own choices. She knew in her gut that Liam wasn't a predator and wouldn't take advantage of her. He lounged in one of the wingback chairs, totally at ease and glad for her company without expecting more. She'd run across those power industry moguls who'd truly preyed on young women, men who needed to be exposed and jailed. Thankfully more and more women were speaking up.

Liam struck her as a quiet alpha, the type of male who had no need to assert or brag, for his power surrounded him with an I'm-comfortable-in-my-skin, all-encompassing aura. True power didn't need to be projected or flaunted. It was inherent and worn as a second, invisible skin. He didn't care what people thought if he'd walked away from the party he didn't want to attend. As he told her about his hikes, she realized she'd never had this type of easy camaraderie. He didn't know who she was, or why she'd thrown stardom away. Though was it really stardom when she played a fictional character trying to have a music career on a TV show about young twentysomethings? Or when she hid her identity behind a pseudonym and a disguise so she could reach number one and win a Grammy? Oh, and she had a CMA award, too, not that Damon had allowed her to speak during their acceptance speech. As for the trophies, she'd left them behind. No need for them in this life.

"Where do you live?" she asked, wanting the focus to shift away from her thoughts. As far as Liam knew, she was Lexi Henderson, bartender at the Chateau. Newbie bartender at that.

"I've been traveling the last few years for work, but my base is usually in Estes Park, Colorado." Something dark, like a sad memory, flickered imperceptibly across his chiseled features before disappearing. "The sky is a blanket of stars for miles. I can see mountains from every window— Twin Sisters to the northeast and Longs Peak to the west. I've climbed them all. But I haven't been back there for two years. Not since I went on the road."

"I can't imagine that." Well, the travel, yes. When not filming, a stadium tour had kept her and Damon on the go. "Sounds like an intense schedule. You must find Beaumont boring."

"Just different. I can see why my family enjoys it. I took a bike out on the Katy Trail yesterday and rode thirty miles. If I'm honest, there's nowhere in the world that's actually boring. There's always something to explore. The key is to get out and do it. Go beyond the tourist traps. I like to see nature. Visit things off the beaten path. I'm not one who follows the herd."

She uncapped the water he'd brought after pouring the wine. "I wish I could be more like that. My big adventure was moving here because I needed a change. I wanted to leave the past, which I'm not going to mention again so don't ask, behind. So far it's working out. I've been here five months and minus being stood up tonight, I've made friends and am starting to feel settled."

"I'm glad."

"Me too. I needed some stability." She reached down and rubbed her toes.

"Here. Let me." He moved then, squatting in front of her. He lifted her right foot. "May I?"

A silly thought of Jane Austen's Marianne and Willoughby flitted through her head, and when Lexi nodded, all sensibilities fled as strong hands massaged her foot and ankle. While never straying to her calf, his fingers worked magic, and she swallowed as millions of sensations rocketed through her. She checked a moan of pleasure. "I'm not sure you know me well enough for this."

His gray gaze caught hers and her heart skipped a beat. "I've done it for hikers I've just met."

"Well, that certainly puts me in my place." She smiled and he laughed, which was an addicting, pleasant, soft, warm musical sound that she wished she could record and listen to forever. Unlike some of her biggest hits that now made her cringe, she would never tire of Liam's voice.

"Climbing can be brutal, and there's no masseuse at fourteen thousand feet and definitely not one at twenty-six thousand. You learn to make do quickly. Tell me if the pressure becomes too much."

"It's perfect." Which was a blatant lie. Even though he didn't intend for the foot rub to be sensual, the kneading of her cramped muscles was seductive. Deeply pleasurable. She'd had massages before to release tension of muscles needed to perform on stage. While relaxing, she'd found them to be clinical. Liam's gentle, deep touch rendered her speechless. And it had been a while since she'd been touched at all. Not only did the pain in her feet ease, but her inhibitions vanished. He set her bare foot on the area rug, and her toes curled into the soft weft. He reached for her other foot. His thumb pressed against the bottom of her arch, and her fingers clutched the armrest. "That feels fantastic. I've never hiked. Unless you count some of the greenways around LA or the path that leads from Santa Monica pier to Venice Beach."

When he shook his head, a long swoop of hair fell over his right eye. He pushed it back. "Those don't count. Anyone can walk a flat, paved trail. Did you go up in the hills?"

"No time. Maybe someday." LA was last on her list of places to revisit.

He returned to her other foot, massaging one more minute before sliding it into one of the slippers the inn provided its guests. Her face flamed—a foot rub shouldn't be so erotic, so decadent. Firm hands slid behind her ankle. The urge to press her thighs and knees together overwhelmed, but she held still so he didn't suspect how much his fingers turned her on. He slid on the other slipper and leaned back. Her feet immediately missed his touch as those fathomless gray orbs sent her a silent message. "Want me to do your calves?"

She already missed his touch. "Is that also part of your hiking therapy?"

"In your case it is." He placed his hand on the back of her lower leg. Her work skirt covered her knees and thighs. She nodded a yes, and he cupped his palm and kneaded her calves until the soreness of a long shift vanished and a strange, anticipatory relaxation began. Never had her core ached from a calf massage, and never had she wanted a massage to go higher, to the apex of her thighs. Her breath grew shorter.

She shifted. "I really should go."

"If that's what you want." Strong yet tender hands fell away, the tantalizing heat and eroticism vanishing. She scrambled to her feet, and despite her height, he had several inches on her. "Your feet are better, right?" he asked.

Her feet felt cradled. Pampered. So did she. "More than. Thank you."

His broad shoulders rolled and stretched. Lexi reached for the water. Sipped until some composure returned. He'd moved to perch on the edge of his chair.

She caught herself before she moved closer to him. "I should order a car."

"As you wish." He rose. "It is getting late."

She found herself hesitating. She didn't want to put her feet back in the tight shoes. But it was getting late. She wanted to go home, didn't she? She'd been the one to push him away. So why did she feel empty? Lost? Rejected?

She tentatively stepped toward him. "I'm sorry, but I'm new to this."

Liam's brow creased. "New to what? I don't understand."

"This." She gestured erratically into the air. She had no idea what to do next. She'd never been seduced. If that was even what was going on. "Whatever we're doing."

"What we're doing is talking and you were thinking of ordering a car. I'm a gentleman and I respect that."

"Oh."

He sensed her hesitation. "Lexi, I'm a straight shooter. You won't offend me. I don't want any confusion between us. What are you thinking? What do you want? Tell me."

She could respect his assertions. She trusted he meant what he said. "I'm new to this chemistry I'm feeling." She tried to control the emotional roller coaster that she'd unwittingly chosen to ride. "I feel like there's some random instant attraction between us. Lust, maybe. Am I misreading your signals?"

"Lust. Perhaps that's a good word for what's going on." He mulled that thought. "As for my signals, I'm not sure myself. But I do feel something."

"Have you ever been in lust?" she asked.

He arched an eyebrow. "Maybe when I was fifteen? That first time you discover the opposite sex. Lust is temporary. Love is different. I had that once. You?"

A harsh, bitter laugh escaped before she could call it back. "Oh, I lust all the time. But acting on it? That's another story. My life has been pretty sheltered. It still is. Now love? That's been a lie. Nothing but pain."

"That I can understand. So back to lust. Is that what you feel? What you want?"

Now might be the time to tell him her lack of sexual experience, but admitting you were a virgin to such a virile man was embarrassing. Admitting why you were still a virgin at age twenty-six was even more humiliating.

He stepped closer but refrained from entering her space. "Because I'll admit I do want you. A great deal. From the first moment I saw you, actually. And I haven't wanted anyone since…"

She waited, held her breath and wondered what secret he'd share. She sensed there was something more he intended to add. After all, he was the one who'd told her he had no interest in women. Someone he'd been in love with must have hurt him a great deal.

"I want you," he said simply, and the way the words rolled off his tongue made her quiver. This man—with the body of a Greek god—desired her. She clung to sanity, to her goals. Long ago she'd let her emotions rule—one of the biggest mistakes of her life.

"I can't fraternize with you," she told him.

"If you want me the way I want you, we'll be doing far more than fraternizing. Much more." The truth hovered in the stillness.

Her throat constricted and she swallowed. Hard. "We shouldn't." She'd meant *can't*. He moved and put the pad of his thumb on her lip and swiped some imaginary droplet. She trembled. Resisted sucking his thumb into her mouth as she'd seen in those romantic movies.

Liam ran his finger along her jaw. "I know it's insane since we just met, but I'd like to kiss you. Your mouth makes me lose focus. I'm imagining the way your lips taste and want to taste to see if I'm right."

"Blunt." Her mouth opened to form a small O.

He didn't apologize. "Very. I call things as I see them. Your hair is like dark silk. May I?" Taking her nod as consent, he reached for one of the natural curls stylists had once bleached blond and daily straightened. He twirled the strand around his forefinger before letting the ringlet pop free and bounce twice. "Tell me it's natural. It has to be natural to be this beautiful."

Her mouth dried and her legs shook. "All me." Changing her hair back had been paramount when she'd called it quits. "My mom always told me my natural hair was best."

He fingered the curl and wound it around again. "She sounds like a wise woman."

"She was." Past tense had become a rote part of Lexi's backstory, and one reason she'd finally found the nerve to flee the toxic environment that had been her life. "She had a fast-acting ovarian cancer. I lost her a year ago."

"I'm sorry. I know how losing someone feels. It's hell."

"It is," Lexi agreed, reading the truth in the serious way his brows knit together. She touched him then—an automatic, empathetic gesture. The lightest touch of her fingertips on his forearm created extreme heat. Dangerous temptation, especially with the way the gray of his eyes darkened to slate. Overwhelmed, her gaze landed on a complicated watch with multiple dials, unlike any she'd seen before.

Go home, that's what she wanted to do, right? She should lift her hand, but her fingers felt heavy. Glued. His aftershave invaded her senses—another powerful aphrodisiac was his intoxicating, woodsy scent. He captured her hand,

and with his other hand, he looped another loose lock behind her ear. Her skin tingled as his fingertip grazed the back of her earlobe. He fingered the back of her silver stud earring—the simple, intimate movement creating a longing in her belly and heat at her core.

This was what passion was about. Sure, she'd acted passionate on screen with Damon, but she'd felt hollow inside when he'd kissed her for real when the cameras hadn't been rolling. They'd been dating, and he'd declared her an ice queen. Tonight she was molten lava. An inferno of desire.

Liam twirled another spiral curl, and even her deep inhale failed to steady the excited nerves clamoring for the pleasure he could bring, should she let herself loose. He lifted her chin. "I can't decide if I like your hair or your eyes best. Or your lips. Everything. May I touch you?"

Her mouth speechless, she nodded instead, and seconds later her brain short-circuited as he moved his hand underneath her hair to caress the nape of her neck. After a brief massage, he slid his fingers down her neck. "Your skin rivals milk. I want to taste it. May I?"

Holy hell. She wanted that too. "I used to have freckles." Until they'd lasered them away and covered the rest with makeup.

His fingers returned to playing with her earlobe. "You're not wearing perfume."

"Not allowed because of guest allergies," she stammered, hypnotized by his seductive and sensual ministrations.

"You don't need perfume. You remind me of…" He paused. Bent and inhaled. "A meadow full of wildflowers. And this…" The pad of his forefinger slid to her shirt placket. Pressed the clear plastic button in the center gap between her breasts. "When this button is closed, your shirt makes the most tantalizing little gap. Pure temptation. Driving me crazy from the moment I sat down at the bar."

She stepped away then, walking shakily to the front window. She gazed at the historic brick building across Main Street. Overwhelming lust. Pure and simple. That's what this uncontrollable desire was, for Liam was unlike any man she'd met before. They were all Hollywood actors or performers of some kind. Liam was real. A simple tweak of her earlobe had created electric tingles that made her want to throw caution to the wind.

She was not reckless. She'd lived the lie her publicist, music label, TV network and fickle public demanded—that Melynda Norfolk, the female half of Damon and Melynda, was as pure as new fallen snow. She'd been one half of a pop duo sensation with a global tour, gold albums and a TV show of twentysomethings whose friendship turned into love. What would Hollywood, or her father, think of her now? Working in a hotel bar? Wanting to lose herself with this man and the pleasure he could give her for one night?

Surely Hollywood no longer cared about her. Once you dropped off the circuit, you were dead and disposable. The label had chosen to move on by promoting Damon Stevener, or Billy Smith, as she'd known him since elementary school, launching Damon's solo career with a ballad of a man scorned and discarded. It had immediately topped the charts.

Melynda Norfolk might have been the sweetheart he'd cheated on, but she'd borne the full frontal of media backlash. She'd heard the criticisms. Had she been a better girlfriend, he never would have wanted to go solo or astray. The internet had labeled the split her fault. She'd been the one to crack under the demands of the industry. Blame the patriarchy for the unfair assumption it was always the woman's fault. That was so far from the truth, but after the death of her mother, the ensuing legal fight to extradite Lexi from her contract had cost a fortune. Finally free, she'd changed her look and fled to Beaumont, taking a job where no one would know her name. She'd always liked the Clayton Hotel chain, so it seemed fitting.

Freedom meant finally being sane. Healthy. Whole. With Damon Stevener's most recent hit at number one for the past three weeks—his second from his solo release—Melynda Norfolk was yesterday's news. Lexi hoped Melynda would stay that way.

Liam stood behind her, his reflection visible in the window glass. "I've made you uncomfortable. I'm sorry. I told you you'd be safe with me. I shouldn't have touched you."

"Yes. No. Yes. Don't stop." She couldn't decide if she was uncomfortable or on fire. Or both. "But both of us need be clear on the rules. This isn't a rom-com movie or novel. This is lust. It's not real. It's a hookup. I don't hook up. I've never hooked up."

"I don't hook up either. But I've learned that I have to live in the moment and not worry about regrets. The here and now is all we have. Nothing else is promised." His mouth hovered a half inch above her skin. "And I don't do casual sex either."

"No?" Her voice was a fairy's whisper.

"Ever." He seemed somewhere else for a millisecond before he dropped a bombshell that stole her breath. "My last relationship ended when she died. I haven't been with anyone since."

Lexi had loved and lost her mother, so she had a sense of

his grief. No wonder he hadn't been interested in anyone. The pain must be too much, too great. Yet he wanted her, at least because he lusted. He filled the silence.

"Also, please know I won't kiss you without your permission. I want you to feel safe, so I'll call you a car right now if you want to leave."

"You won't pressure me?" Part of her wanted him to decide what to do about her lustful thoughts, to take charge and kiss her. That way she'd be released from making the decision to stay or go. After all, the men in her life had always made the big choices for her. If he kissed her, she'd have an excuse to cave in and throw herself on the inviting bed not even ten feet away. Then again, the new version of her was glad he gave her the choice. By doing so, he'd put her in control. Given her agency, which he reinforced when he spoke next.

"If we take advantage of the chemistry zinging between us, it's by mutual agreement. You need to be as into this as I am or it stops," Liam said. "I'm not a playboy like my younger brother. But whatever this is between us is, I can tell you it's natural. My motto is that anything created by Mother Nature is worth exploring. Living life is the best high there is, and frankly she owes me. So I'm willing to break my no physical contact rule for one night."

Lexi could barely speak. "Mother Nature?"

"Fate. Destiny. I like you and I want you. For me, it's as elemental as that. But it's up to you."

Lexi wavered. What would it be like to allow herself sexual pleasure? Do what she wanted for one night, instead of what people expected? Tonight they could enjoy each other. She could experience desire, find out what the fuss was all about. She could live life on her terms.

"No one can know," she whispered. One night of passion, a way to bury the past, to prove that she was worthy exactly the way she was, especially as Liam wanted her for her—not because she was Melynda.

And she craved him. He was chocolate cake and she'd denied herself sweets for far too long. Damn the consequences or the calories; she wanted to indulge. "No one," she said with emphasis, her voice growing stronger. "You see me again, you don't know me. I'm not losing my job over this."

He met her gaze through the window reflection. "Agreed. Tonight is for us. Only us. Nothing goes outside these walls."

"Then yes. Please kiss me."

But he didn't turn her around. Instead his lips lowered to her skin, and Lexi trembled as his lips slid down her neck. His exhale made the little hairs along her arms stand on end, and a delighted shiver raced down her spine when his fingers traced circles on the top of her shoulder. He slid her shirt collar over, his forefinger tracing her collarbone. His mouth blazed a trail. "You taste delicious, like honey fresh from the hive."

She liked the way his kiss made her hot and ready. But she wanted his lips on hers.

"Just so you know, I haven't been with anyone in two years. I have a clean health history," he told her.

Two years? Was that when his beloved had died? As his mouth nipped above her collarbone, she chose not to ask and tilted her neck, provided better access, and threw sanity out the window along with questions.

"Your skin is like satin," he said against her neck.

Her skin was on fire. If he moved his fingers a few inches lower, he could slide his finger under her shirt and... her breasts grew heavy. Raw need pooled.

He drew her back against him. "I want to touch you. May I?"

The fact he kept asking mattered. She made the choices now. He rested his chin on her shoulder, saw her wide-eyed reflection in the window, for there was nothing that she wanted more. "Please."

He cupped her breasts. Ran a thumb over the white oxford shirt material, making her nipples peak into hard, needy nubs. His arousal pressed her backside. "All you have to do is say no at any time and I will stop. I won't do anything to make you uncomfortable."

"I'm comfortable. More than comfortable." Heat flowed and created immense pleasure. His touch was wonderful. Exquisite. No wonder sex was all anyone on the set had ever talked about, including her fellow actors once they'd reached their late teens and early twenties. Under Liam's tutelage, she was starting to understand why sex was such a big deal, and why Damon had refused to wait until their marriage and had instead slept with anyone who threw herself at him. The studio had spent a lot of money keeping that secret quiet, until Damon's actions had blown up in their faces. Then they'd targeted and blamed her.

"Do you like that?" Liam tweaked her nipple—the action heightening the throbbing between her legs. The elemental level on which she and Liam connected was foreign yet instinctively familiar, as old as time itself.

He slid his fingers under her shirt, and then under her bra. His lips slid down her neck, planting a line of skin-tingling kisses. He unbuttoned her shirt, sliding the white cloth from her shoulders and dropping it to the floor. Mirrored by the glass, she shamelessly wore an askew bra and skirt. His breath hissed as he spun her around so he could peer into her eyes directly. "You are perfect."

The words she'd never heard anyone else say pierced her soul, making her crave him more. His hand lifted her chin as he finally bestowed a mind-blowing kiss on her lips, one Lexi quickly couldn't live without. His lips plundered, drawing her bottom lip between his. Their mouths fused and his tongue slid inside, where it mated with hers in a dance preordained before time. Like a raging river, the kiss swept her away. Drove her to new heights and ran ramshackle over any rational thought besides one fact: she had to have him.

Tonight they could enjoy each other. One night and then back into anonymity. Just Lexi, bartender. Liam, adventurer. Two strangers who'd never meet again.

Her bra fell to the floor, and the intensity of their kiss sucked the air from her lungs. Who knew foreplay could be a destination in itself? The few times she and Damon had fooled around hadn't raised her temperature beyond tepid tap water. Damon's touch had left her staring at the ceiling and him headed for the door after her emphatically telling Damon, "No. I don't want to do this."

With Liam, her body was so hot she could boil water. When Liam plundered her mouth, he sent her spiraling. Touching Liam was all she wanted to do. When she did, she floated. Felt alive. Soared, and she'd seen enough movies to know the best still waited. She whimpered as fingers slicked into parts of her body that until now had known only her touch. He reclaimed her lips with a tantalizing and possessive kiss that declared she was his—at least for tonight.

Tonight she wanted to be worshipped and loved not because she was some stupid music star/actress, but because if she and Liam didn't come together they would regret it forever. If she didn't let herself experience what Liam could offer, she would hate herself for passing on this moment. Time to woman up and go on a grand adventure, to cross the final threshold. There was no reason to wait any longer. "I want you."

Gorgeous gray eyes searched her face. Strong warrior arms encircled her. "If you're sure."

"One hundred percent." She'd never been more certain of anything, not even her move to Beaumont.

He lifted her, wrapped her legs and arms around him, and carried her to the bed. He set her on the edge. "I will stop if you say no," he reminded her.

She grew bold. "Why aren't you naked? I want you naked."

"Happy to oblige." He shed his polo, revealing an Incan sun tattoo on a taut, right pectoral muscle. The man was athletic and fit, with lean muscles and six-pack abs that she ran her hands over. He unbuttoned his jeans and slid them down, revealing he'd gone commando. "I'm naked like you wanted."

"Yes, you are." With newfound self-assurance, Lexi took him in hand. He jerked in response, giving her a jolt of feminine power. She savored the soft skin covering his hardness. Firm fingers removed her hand and tumbled her back on the bed. "You can touch me later. I need to be inside you."

"Yes." She wanted that too. He found and rolled on a condom and instinctively she arched toward him, his ensuing welcome, yet foreign, invasion stretching her full. Lexi's body trembled at the small stab of pain, her nerve endings on high alert as she adjusted, the momentary discomfort ceding to the delicious sensations, as if something she'd been missing had clicked into place and completed her. No pleasure compared, not even eating chocolate cake without counting the calories, something she was finally able to do after therapy for the eating disorder she now knew had been a desperate attempt for some control over her life.

She clung to his arms, his muscles corded and strong. This was her decision, and come what may, she planned to enjoy every moment.

"You like that?" he asked, his hair falling over his face.

"Yes," was all she could manage as she discovered new sweet spots with each subsequent thrust. "Oh yes."

"Kiss me." As her lips found his, their coupling became an entity in itself. He eased them to a seated position, pulling her into his lap and deepening their connection. She shattered as they came together on Mother Nature's wildest ride, one that made her see stars and grip his arms, hanging on for dear life as she shot for the heavens.

He gathered her to him—her forehead dropping onto his shoulder—and he ran his hands over her spine as they slowly floated down, heart rates trying to regain some form of normalcy. He kissed her forehead and her lips. "That was good. More than good. Beyond."

Shyness struck. Where had this wanton creature been hiding? She'd never expected to be this sensual. Given her tepid response to Damon, she'd never envisioned she'd be a woman who'd enjoy a man like this. She should have put her own needs first long ago.

"You okay?" Liam's hands massaged her back.

"Blissfully tired." The truth. She kept to herself the fact that she'd lost her virginity to a man she'd known fewer than three hours. She'd thrown herself into the chemistry—the lust—and now that she had, she had no idea what came next, except for at some point she needed to go home, enduring her first awkward walk of shame. Those on the set had bragged about wearing the same clothes home the next day as if the walk of shame was some sort of a rite of passage.

Not that Lexi felt any shame for what they'd done. She had zero guilt.

In September, she'd upended her life. Tonight she'd put the nail in the coffin of Melynda Norfolk. Lexi Henderson had grabbed the brass ring because of a raw, primal, elemental connection. Liam had exposed a side she'd locked away during the singing and acting career that had consumed her youth. With one kiss, Liam had erased her tendency to be the perfect daughter, the perfect platonic and chaste girlfriend, and the perfect employee who followed the rules. She'd lusted, loved—and the sex had been perfect. Everything she'd dreamed it might be.

Except for the permanence. Couldn't have everything. She'd learned that lesson the hard way.

Tonight she would unwind, let go of her ambitions and inhibitions and simply enjoy herself—how long had it been since she'd relaxed? Didn't she deserve it after stepping off the career treadmill? She'd started running there before she could understand the implications. Tonight was another step on a journey to being her true self.

Besides, come sunrise, Liam would be a blissful memory living rent-free in her head, something she could recall and relive whenever she wanted.

"You seem far away," Liam said to Lexi. "I'm going to move you. Be right back." Liam severed their bodies' connection and disappeared into the bathroom. Cold air dropped over her skin, and when he returned, he was wearing a pair of black-and-red-plaid boxers. He held out one of the inn's white fluffy robes. He tucked the soft cloth around her, his mouth placing a quick kiss on the top of her right breast before he belted her tight. "I'd like you to stay." Using the robe's belt, he tugged her toward him. "Spend the night with me. We'll sort out the morning when it comes."

Already she wanted him again, as if one hit of the drug named Liam would never be enough. "I'll stay." She had plenty of time before she had to report for work tomorrow. Besides, most likely her roommate's boyfriend was over.

Liam's hand began to undo the belt, and she reached for his boxers. "You've bewitched me. I can't get enough."

"Then you must have bedeviled me." Tonight she planned to make up for all those years she'd denied herself a life, for what had turned out to be one big, fat lie and a betrayal by the people who claimed to care about her. Tonight Liam promised escape and lessons in lovemaking. He laughed as she pulled him onto the bed. Lexi lost herself in his kiss. Reality could wait.

Chapter Three

Aside from standing atop a summit, Liam's favorite time on a mountain was daybreak. A pale white sliver of light formed along the horizon, and then that crack widened and separated the darkened sky from the earth. Beams of sunlight burst through the fabric of the universe, bathing the world in vibrant pinks, oranges and yellows. High up on whatever peak he was climbing, he'd inhale a deep, nourishing breath and all would seem right with the world.

Until Everest. That loud bang—like two freight locomotives colliding—was the first indication that hell was about to break loose. The noise was permanently seared into his brain, and in the split second it took to register that no coal trains existed anywhere near Everest Camp I, the snow beneath his feet had started to shake, throwing him to the ground. Around him, the mountain groaned. Glacier ice cracked as seismic waves reverberated. When the deep rumble echoed and roared, he'd realized the avalanche was far below his position and powering down the slope. Down where Anya waited at base camp, having chosen not to climb until the next day. He'd been helpless to do anything. The rest was a nightmare he never could forget.

Except for the fact that last night was the first night in

two years he'd slept through without waking. As he blinked away sleep, he found himself somewhat disoriented. Last night his body hadn't had the nightly reoccurrence of the fear and terror that had pierced his soul when he'd learned the avalanche had destroyed base came. His body clock was clearly off. Here in Beaumont, it was just shy of nine, and he never slept in. In Portland, where buildings made of tall steel hid the sky and where he'd lived since the accident, his typical early-morning routine started with a long run. His feet would pound over downtown sidewalks before the city flickered fully to life. But despite his achieving a runner's high, nothing compared to mastering the mountain. Standing on a summit and reaching for the heavens while on the top of the world was the most accomplished a man could feel.

But Liam didn't climb anymore. Even though Anya had shared his passion for the mountains and understood the risks—they'd summited many mountains together—he'd gone ahead. He hadn't protected her. He'd been powerless against Mother Nature's wrath and destruction, and she'd died because of his failure.

He rubbed the corner of his eye as his vision adjusted to the dim light—the bedroom of the Blanchard Inn slowly coming into distinct focus as sunlight edged around the heavy blackout curtains. In proof that last night had happened, the wineglasses and water bottles remained over by the love seat. His clothes were on the floor. He pulled himself into a seated position, the sheet slipping to his waist. He knew Lexi was gone, as she'd slipped out before first light with the skill of a cat burglar. He'd sensed her exit, despite his having slept like a rock. He'd had his first deep, dreamless sleep in two years, and all because he'd had sex with Lexi. Mind-blowing sex. A total loss of control he'd repeated more than once.

He grabbed the bottle of water he'd left overnight on the bedside table and drank the room temperature contents in one long swallow. Was this how his brother Michael felt the next morning? Michael was the family's love-them-and-leave-them playboy who never wanted to spend the whole night and left before sunup. Liam was the one with the long-term girlfriend he'd met in high school. He hadn't added any notches to his bedpost, unlike his brothers, and that fact gave him a certain superiority over his siblings. No longer.

As his phone started to ring with an annoying, rapid, trilling staccato, he scrambled to grab and silence the device. Seeing the caller ID, he swiped and put the phone to his ear. "What?"

"Hello to you, too, crabby. It's almost nine. Where are you?" Eva demanded.

Liam rubbed a hand over a jaw covered with harsh, prickly stubble. "At the inn. In bed. I was asleep until you so rudely woke me up. Why?"

"Dad wants us all to meet in the owners' suite at the Chateau at noon. Didn't you get the memo?"

"What memo?" Liam hadn't seen any email or text message. Then again, last night he hadn't checked his phone once.

"Oh, stop worrying." Eva giggled, and Liam realized she was messing around with him. Typical Eva. "You're testy this morning."

Probably because Lexi had snuck out and now he was being summoned. Liam blew out a harsh breath. "There isn't a memo."

"Not in writing. Dad decided last night. You know, after you disappeared. Maybe if you'd have stuck around you would have known what happened."

"I'd put in my time." He had no regrets about leaving. Doing so had allowed him to the visit the wine bar, where he'd discovered Lexi.

"Well, you missed all the action. Edmund and Lana kissed and made up. All's good there."

"That's great. I'm happy for them." Liam actually cared, but not right at this moment. He'd stood on the summit of some of the world's highest peaks, and last night the sex had equaled—maybe exceeded—that rush. A rush he'd denied himself for two years. Now in the bright light of day the implications of what he'd done crept in. Lexi had left, avoiding that morning after conversation. He found himself wanting one anyway.

"You don't sound happy," Eva pointed out.

Liam fudged for an appropriate reply. "Maybe because I was sleeping? There's a reason I stayed off-site. That way family doesn't bother me this early."

He scratched a chin that Lexi had planted a multitude of kisses over before... Liam shifted and pushed the memory aside. Even Anya hadn't brought him to the same sexual heights, and he'd loved her. Told her those very words before zipping their tent closed that fateful morning. Last night's sex had been earth-shattering—Mother Nature's compensation—like a spring waterfall washing away the past. For one night, he'd rejoined the living. Become whole. Redeemed. Ready to move on. He really needed a shower, a shave and to get the hell out of town.

"Look, no one should be complaining. I did my part. I

showed up and posed for required photos. I'm on an after-noon plane," he said.

"You're on the same plane as the rest of us. The corpo-rate jet," Eva reminded him. "Good try, though."

He could picture her rolling her eyes as she did when-ever he annoyed her. She softened her tone. "Seriously, are you hangry? Do you need some food?"

What he needed was another round with the beautiful woman from last night, the one who'd made him forget the real world, a world that was fast approaching with the force of river rapids. "Did Dad say why he wants us?"

"Would it be so crazy to assume that he and Mom sim-ply want to spend time with their children?" Eva asked, adding that annoying little tsking noise of hers.

Liam scoffed. "Definitely crazy. Dad is one hundred percent business at least ninety-nine-point-nine percent of the time. That's where Edmund gets it. He's Dad 2.0." Liam highly doubted today's luncheon could be one of the rare occasions that wasn't about business. "You know our father has an agenda. When doesn't he?"

"I guess we'll find out what it is. Just be on time for lunch. Although, from the way you sound, be sure you get something first. You're a bear when you're hungry."

"There's food downstairs. It's a B&B. You know, bed and breakfast?" And if their father had summoned them for a luncheon, that meant business casual attire. No jeans or long sleeve polos. Dress shirt and slacks. His father was a stickler. Another reason Liam hated the office. "Don't worry. I'll be there," he told his sister, disconnecting be-fore Eva could add anything else.

Liam loved his younger sister, but she was an opinion-ated chatterbox who had definite ideas about how Liam should be living his life. She'd been taking such liberties since she could speak, probably because of her role as the beloved baby in the family. She'd always been Daddy's little girl. As for her siblings, not only had Eva held her own with three rambunctious older brothers in fighting for their parents' attention, but she'd often bullied her way past their "but you're a girl" protectionisms.

Eva was a force of nature in her own right, and her determination and business acumen made her perfect as Clayton Holding's VP of Corporate Communications. She'd been the one to help their older brother Edmund when he'd filmed a boss-goes-undercover show. Last night she'd told the family that, while Clayton Holdings had seen a positive spike in consumer opinion and brand loyalty, their biggest competitor's show had ranked higher. Edmund had participated at Margot Van Horn's insistence; she'd declared that whoever had the highest ratings would win the right to buy her hotels. He'd lost.

Liam couldn't imagine going undercover as his older brother had, or performing the menial tasks he'd done so poorly on national television. Edmund had looked like a fish out of water or a deer in the headlights, or whatever the cliché was. His brother had been uncomfortable as hell, and it had shown in the footage. But their father had loved the show.

Liam thought the whole idea of reality television pointless. He might have been born into a famous corporate family with a name as common as Hilton or Marriott, but he didn't live the celebrity lifestyle, nor did he want to. He found the flagrant manifestations of wealth and narcissism abhorrent. Liam liked to know the truth about people—or at least where they stood—no matter how harsh.

Had he known the truth about Anya, they never—ever— would have been on Mount Everest that day. He couldn't forgive himself for his failure to protect her, and he certainly couldn't forgive her for keeping the secret that had sealed both of their fates.

He showered, dressed and made his way downstairs to where the innkeeper, Mrs. Bien, had arranged a delicious buffet. He filled his plate with sausage and eggs, a flaky croissant and a medley of assorted fruit. Not usually one to eat tons of refined sugar, Liam grabbed a homemade chocolate doughnut anyway. Last night's activities had him craving something sweet. Several couples ate at the huge dining room table, but besides giving him a welcome smile, they kept to themselves. Liam put his plate at the head of the table on the opposite end and went back for coffee and orange juice. He ate in relative peace and complimented Mrs. Bien on her hospitality. At eleven thirty, he checked out and took a rideshare to the Chateau.

Unlike the six-story Beaumont Grand Hotel, which had four penthouses dominating the top floor, the shorter Chateau contained seven suites on its highest floor. With a layout mimicking an apartment, Room 34 contained a living room, dining room, full kitchen, powder room, and two bedrooms with en suite baths, and a den/office. A corner unit, it was twelve hundred square feet and overlooked both the hotel's wooded area and its series of terraced French gardens. Besides Liam's cousin Jack, his wife, Sierra, and Jack's parents who all lived in Beaumont, Liam was the only family member not staying at the Chateau.

"Hey." Liam planted a kiss on his mother's cheek. Most of the family was already in the suite, including Liam's dad and his dad's brother, Liam's uncle Jonathan. Liam's dad and his brother had built Clayton Holdings into a juggernaut, and they stood off to the side in deep discussion. Liam's younger brother, Michael, was there, lounging on a couch and texting. Eva spoke with Jack and his mother. The only family member missing was Edmund, but he rushed in exactly at noon. "Sorry I'm late," he said. He appeared tired yet content. Someone else had had a fantastic, sleepless night.

"How's Lana?" Their mom asked the important question first.

"Great. Everything's great." Edmund's wide grin made Liam happy for his brother.

As if on cue, a knock sounded on the suite door, and wait staff brought in chafing dishes. Minutes later, the family was seated around the dining room table. Their father was at one end with his brother at the opposite. Liam found himself somewhere in the middle. After enough interval for everyone to eat something, Liam's dad set his fork down.

"Last night's gala and this morning's reviews were exactly what I'd hoped for when we envisioned this project years ago. We knew we had skeptics who thought Jonathan and I were crazy to bring a bit of the West Coast to the Midwest, but the gala proved them wrong. Both the Chateau and the Grand are booked solid. We have a hit on our hands."

Everyone clapped. "The wineries are also doing well," Liam's dad continued. "Which finally means it's time to make some big decisions."

Liam tensed. Here it came, the moment that Edmund took over as CEO. His brother had been working toward this goal his entire life. Liam was happy for him, truly.

"As everyone knows, my brother has already moved back here." Liam's dad nodded toward his brother.

"And today I'm announcing that I'm officially stepping down and officially retiring," Uncle Jonathan said. "It's time, so I'm giving in and getting out."

Liam joined the others in clapping and saying congrats. When Liam's aunt added, "Finally. I want to play with those grandbabies," everyone laughed and applauded more. Jack gave his mom a kiss on her cheek. "And we love you playing with them," he said.

Liam's father waited until the congrats died down. "Just in case anyone's wondering, I am not retiring." He added a chuckle before turning serious. "However, since Jack's too busy running his own projects, and since last night we learned that we will be acquiring Van Horn Hotels after all, it's time to do some upper-level restructuring. For the time being, we've decided to divide our winery and hotel operations. Michael, you'll be spearheading incorporating Van Horn Hotels into the Clayton Hotels portfolio and brand. Margot suggested it herself. Congrats, son, we're naming you the new VP of Clayton Hotels."

For a moment, Michael looked shocked. Then he grinned. "Cool! I won't let you down."

"I know you won't," their dad said.

As everyone began to congratulate Michael, Liam shook his head. Everyone knew that Michael didn't work. He was a playboy. Did Liam have to be the one to say it? "Okay this is crazy."

"I know you think so." Michael glared at his brother. "But I can do it. I've just been waiting for my chance."

Liam snorted. "Sure you were. That's why you never went into the office."

"What? Just because you sold a successful start-up, do

you think you're the only one besides Edmund who knows what he's doing?"

Their dad gave a cough, interrupting and refocusing the brothers' attention. Liam folded his arms across his chest. Van Horn had been Edmund's pet project for years. "What's Edmund doing?" Liam asked. He couldn't help himself.

Edmund Junior smiled at his namesake. "Edmund will be traveling. Lana will be joining us at Clayton Holdings, and the two of them will be spearheading our global expansion initiatives."

"Lana and I are going to see the world," Edmund said. "It's her dream and I'm going with her."

"But you were going to be CEO." Liam frowned at his older brother. Edmund III, the heir, was giving up the throne? Now was Edmund's chance to shine, to grab the brass ring.

"Someday," Edmund said. "Right now my relationship with Lana is far more important. I love her."

Liam stared at his older brother. Had some sort of alien taken over Edmund's body? Edmund lived for the work, the power it gave him. He didn't do love.

Liam's dad chuckled, trying to diffuse the tension growing between his sons. "Let me reassure everyone that I'm not ready to give away the CEO title yet. I am, however, ready to make some major changes and start winding down some of my sixty-hour work week."

"Finally," Liam's mom Laverna muttered. Her sister-in-law patted her hand in support.

"To do that, we're moving the corporate headquarters of Clayton Holdings from Portland to Beaumont. With our expansion into the valley, we've already begun, and I expect the transition to take around a year before the entire Clayton Holdings operation is in the Midwest."

"That makes no sense." Liam wished he had something stronger than water in front of him. He also wished he could keep his mouth shut. Normally he never said much at family meetings. He'd lay low—get in and get out. During the past two years, everyone also gave him a wide berth. Now it was like he was watching a movie where he knew a jump scare was coming, a fact made worse by the fact that when he hadn't been sleeping like a rock last night, he'd been making love to a beautiful woman. It meant he was out of sorts and off his game, and a tension headache was starting to take hold. "Clayton Holdings is based in Portland. Van Horn Hotels is on the West Coast."

"Which is why Michael will stay in Portland until we have the Van Horn Hotels under our corporate umbrella. The hotel division of Clayton Holdings will stay in Portland for now. Hence the year timetable. We've decided to move the winery division first. We can oversee all our wineries from here, including those on the West Coast. We built a private airstrip just for this purpose. From Beaumont we can be on the East Coast in two hours and the West Coast in four. It's the ideal location."

Liam rubbed his temples. "I still don't understand why this is happening."

"It's happening because our company has always been about family," his dad said simply. "My brother and his son are here. Once they return from traveling, Edmund and Lana will live here. Since your mother and I have decided we want to live here too, it's logical that our company should be here."

"Okay, fine. Whatever." Liam tried to blow it off. After all, none of this impacted him. He lived in Colorado. Sort of. He wasn't part of the family company. But his father was giving him the same big smile that he'd given Michael.

"Oh no," Liam said, trying to stop the train about to wreck his life. "Dad, don't do this."

But his father was too far gone and too excited. "Liam, since Edmund will be traveling globally, and since Michael will be working in Portland, Jonathan and I have decided you'll be relocating to Beaumont as our new vice president of Winery Operations. Congrats, son."

Oh, hell no. Liam bit back the words as around him family members clapped and offered congrats. Liam didn't want any of this. He'd shown up to attend a gala, not get sucked into working for the family company. He glanced at the delicious food, which suddenly appeared unappetizing as his stomach rolled.

If Liam's dad knew how upset Liam was, he never let on. Liam knew that was by design. His father hadn't built a successful empire by chance. "So to summarize, Michael will oversee hotels from Portland. Liam will move the winery division over the next few months, and after that, we'll relocate the hotel division. When Edmund is ready to return, we'll adjust again. But I expect within three years we'll all be living in Beaumont."

"Beaumont's a backwater," Liam protested. "You and Mom will be bored."

"Hey, don't insult my town," Jack growled. Liam's cousin shot Liam a dirty look. "Beaumont's a great place. You might actually like it here if you gave it a chance. It has a lot going for it."

"I agree," Jack's dad said. "You'll like living in Beaumont once it grows on you. We hated moving away and are so happy we're back."

Liam had liked Lexi, the woman from last night. He'd liked the wine bar. The inn was lovely. But he didn't belong here. His heart was in the mountains, in Colorado. Although was it really home when he hadn't been back since Anya passed? "What about my charity initiatives?" he asked. "I'm not giving those up. Those have always been my focus, especially after I sold my company."

"You can still do them," his father said. "The Clayton Holdings Foundation is already extremely invested in this community. We'll put the foundation under your jurisdiction. You'll have complete control."

As long as Liam worked for the family company. The carrot had been dangled; the shot fired across the bow. If Michael was the prodigal son, Liam was the heir spare who'd carved his own path. That freedom was clearly over. His father had played the trump card. Worse, his mother appeared hopeful and excited. He hated disappointing her.

As if daring Liam to protest, Eva arched an eyebrow. His sister wanted him back to the land of the living. She wanted him to stop wallowing and take his rightful place. Edmund's expression remained neutral, but Liam knew his older brother waited on tenterhooks. Edmund had fallen in love with Lana, and Edmund deserved this chance at happiness. If Liam refused, his brother wouldn't be able to travel with his beloved.

Liam had had his one big love, and when Anya died, she'd taken their dreams with her. His whole family had given Liam the space he'd needed to grieve, and while he might never heal, he did need to step up and do the right thing by them. Especially for Edmund, who'd managed to get the Clayton Holdings jet to Nepal in the aftermath of a natural disaster. Edmund had taken charge, putting all the resources of Clayton Holdings to use in cutting through red tape, allowing Liam to quickly bring Anya's remains home to America and her family. Edmund had also kept his grief-stricken brother somewhat sane and from doing anything stupid. He owed his brother big time for that.

"Fine. One year," Liam heard himself say. "I'll do it for one year. Then we'll reassess, not when Edmund decides he's done seeing the world. Until then, you let me direct the charity funds the way I want them."

"I'll accept those terms," his dad said. He glanced around. "I think this calls for champagne. I had some iced."

"I'll get it." Liam's mom rose and went into the kitchen. With the help of her sister-in-law, they began handing out flutes filled with bubbly.

"Stop looking like a sourpuss," Eva whispered as she passed Liam a glass. "You know I'm going to be going back and forth between Portland and Beaumont nonstop. You'll see me tons."

"I don't like being trapped," Liam told her. "They got me hook, line and sinker."

Eva gave him a wry smile. "It's what our family does best. And you know it was time to return to the company. Surely there will be something in Beaumont that will make things feel better for you."

Liam thought about Lexi, the woman he'd met last night who he'd cradled in his arms. "Maybe."

Although she was now officially off-limits.

He was her new boss.

Chapter Four

By 11:00 a.m., Lexi was on her second cup of coffee, sipping from a red I Decorate with Cats mug that had black cats and white paw prints all over. While the words *crazy cat lady* didn't apply to Lexi, they did to her roommate-slash-landlord Dawn. The mug was typical of the ones in the house—nothing matching, all funky and fun, and always animal themed. When Lexi first moved in, Dawn had told her that most of the mugs were Christmas gifts from her veterinary clients.

This morning Lexi was simply grateful the mug held caffeine. She couldn't believe what she'd done last night, or the fact she'd snuck out while Liam was sleeping. Once his breathing became deep and regular, she'd eased out from underneath the muscular arm that had been such a pleasant weight when wrapped around her waist. She hadn't wanted to leave, but clueless as to proper morning-after etiquette, she'd gone home. Besides, she had a staff meeting at 3:00 p.m., and she'd wanted to get some sleep.

When the Uber driver dropped her off, she'd discovered she was too wired for any shut-eye, her brain processing the night's activities. Even though she'd known their evening was simply a hookup, she'd overheard enough talk from her former assistants to deduce she'd had really, really good sex. Fantastic sex. Her body being pleasantly sore was another indication that Liam had been an extraordinary lover. She doubted if she'd ever see him again. If she did, she'd play it cool. Pretend she didn't know him. Not think about how she'd watched him sleep or counted every inhale and exhale, and how she'd resisted the urge to touch his glorious hair or run a finger along the stubble shadowing his jaw. No wonder people succumbed to passion, and oh, it had been that. The night had proven one thing—she was far from the frigid bitch Damon had called her. She could torch that particular demon and bury it forever. He'd been wrong about this—about everything. She was normal. Someday she would find a nice, average guy. Maybe fall in love and settle down.

"How was last night's gala?" Dawn padded into the kitchen. Besides being Beaumont's favorite vet, Dr. Dawn Dulle was also an avid animal rescuer. Currently she was fostering ten-week-old cats that followed her everywhere. Proving the point, two of the orange striped kittens bounced into the room and skittered across the linoleum floor.

Lexi set the mug on the counter. "From what I saw of it, fabulous. I spent most of my night in the bar with nary a customer." *Except one.*

"Well, I'm off to work, and then I have a date later with Dulany. Will you be home after your shift? Can you check on the kitties? Lisa's popping by around five."

Dawn's practice was open seven days a week, eight to eight. Along with the other vets in her practice, she worked the occasional weekend. "Of course. I should be home around one o'clock. If I'm not cut earlier."

"That'll work. We're going to a concert and then an after-party. I'll text you."

As one of the kittens started batting her bare toes, Lexi scooped it up and it immediately began purring. "You are so cute," Lexi cooed as she scratched its ears and under the colored collar that told Dawn what kitten it was. The purring noise got louder.

"He is a menace. He or one of his siblings found the toilet paper in the half bath and it's in shreds," Dawn said. "That's a roll we won't get back. I got it cleaned up, but I didn't have time to change it. So be forewarned."

"I'll get it changed." Lexi held the kitten next to her face, turned it around so it faced Dawn, and pouted. "How can you blame a face like this?"

"Easily. He went to town on the TP." As Dawn reached for the kitten, its sibling tried to climb up Lexi's leg. The moment Dawn freed Lexi's hands, Lexi swooped down to catch a kitten trying to free-climb her jeans. "Ow, that hurt," she gently scolded. "We don't climb pants."

The kitten simply blinked and mewed. Dawn retrieved the second kitten and held the two small, wiggling bodies against her chest. "Let's get these locked up in the foster palace for the day. You'll check on them later if I'm not here, right?"

"Yes, don't worry. I'll even scoop the litter boxes." Lexi made a shooing motion.

"You're a saint," Dawn called over her shoulder. "I knew there was a reason I rented my spare room to you. By the way, I put your flats in the laundry room. I was cleaning so I moved them. Sorry if you couldn't find them. I noticed they were still there last night."

"It's all good." She'd gotten a great foot rub and more be-cause she'd worn the wrong shoes. "I'll grab them in a bit."

Dawn left to put the kittens away. One bedroom—the foster palace—was dedicated to the animals temporarily living with Dawn in the three-bedroom house she owned. The house also had two other bedrooms, both with private baths, a living room, family room, kitchen, half bath and full, finished basement. Lexi rented one of the bedrooms and found it the perfect arrangement. On days Dawn wasn't working, she was volunteering at the local animal shelter. Hence, the fostering. Dawn and Lexi got along well, but with about a decade between them, they really weren't in each other's lives much.

Once Dawn left, Lexi managed to catch an hour nap. She took a shower, dressed in her work uniform, and after fighting with starting her car for a few moments, made it to the Chateau with five minutes to spare. She used the em-ployee entrance, found a seat in the empty bar near her other coworkers and listened while Alvin debriefed his team on the night before. The gala had gone off without any prob-lems or issues, but there was always room for improvement. Overall, though, Alvin's fiftysomething face kept smil-ing, which meant her immediate supervisor was extremely happy. "The Claytons were pleased with our performance and execution," he told them, his bald, black head bobbing. "When they're happy, I'm happy. And that bodes well for our year-end bonuses."

Then he added a tidbit of gossip. "They've been meeting in the suite upstairs since noon. If you haven't heard the news, Edmund III made it official with Lana last night. He kissed her and danced with her. It was lovely."

"That's great," someone said.

"It means he's surely in a great mood," another coworker chimed in.

"No wonder the Claytons are so happy. Edmund's finally settled. You remember how he went viral with that video with his ex?" someone asked.

"And his appearance as an undercover boss did not make him look very competent. He was so awkward," yet another person said.

Lexi tuned out the animated conversation. She knew some of the story about Edmund's going undercover. She'd watched the episode. Heard he'd fallen hard for someone who'd been in charge of supervising the interior decorating. But Lexi tried not to pay much attention to gossip, especially having been the subject of malicious rumors herself. This, however, sounded joyous.

"That's all I know," Alvin said, taking the conversation back in hand. "When I know more, I'll tell you. But I don't expect any major changes in how we do things. The Chateau is fully booked and we treat all guests like royalty."

The meeting ended, and most of the servers and bartenders headed to the main restaurant or over to the Grand. Lexi followed Alvin into Esprit's back room. The bar opened at four, so they had about fifteen minutes to prep before she unlocked the doors for the evening. The two of them quickly peeled oranges, sliced lemons and quartered limes. "Tonight should be more exciting than your shift yesterday," he said. "I'm sorry to say it picked up after you left."

"The irony doesn't escape me." Lexi liked working with Alvin. He treated his employees fairly, almost like he was a second dad, and a far better one than her real father.

"Hopefully your night wasn't a total waste." Alvin

rubbed a spot on the back of his hand before getting back to business. "You're young. Surely you had plans."

"They sort of changed, but it was a good night." Lexi felt a flush spread. Alvin's watch beeped.

"Well, that's us." He gave the place a quick once-over. "Let's get this joint hopping, shall we?"

Liam wanted a drink. After the longest family meeting ever—one that had stretched from lunch almost to dinner—he felt like he'd run a gauntlet. Not even being oxygen deprived at twenty thousand feet had given him this much of a raging headache. But then, his family tended to drive him crazy, which was one reason he'd always avoided working for Clayton Holdings. The business journals would have a field day speculating about his joining the family firm, but Eva, the company's PR genius, already had a plan. She'd accompany Liam back to Beaumont when he returned to take over in what was to be the first phase of the company's relocation.

While Liam's uncle and aunt had lived in Beaumont for several years before they'd moved to Portland when Jack was in high school, Liam's branch of the family had always lived in Oregon. Growing up, Liam had fallen in love with the Pacific Ocean. He'd climbed Matterhorn Peak. Eagle Cap. South Sister. Finally, Mount Hood. Then he'd turned to the Front Range in Colorado, conquering peaks higher than fourteen thousand feet.

Now he'd be stuck in Missouri, where the tallest peak was Taum Sauk, in the St. Francois Mountains. More of an elongated ridge, Taum Sauk was a whopping 1,770 feet above sea level. Child's play. Worse, tourists could simply drive to the scenic overlook. "Liam, are you good? Do you need anything?" Cheryl asked. She'd been the flight attendant on the family jet the past twenty years. She peered down at him. They were cruising at thirty-nine thousand feet on the way back to Portland and still had several hours to go.

"Painkillers," Liam told her. When Cheryl walked off, Liam faced Eva. She sat next to him, with both of them a distance from the other family members on the flight.

"Your head hurts?" Eva asked. "Are you okay?"

"Doesn't matter if I'm not. I committed to the decision I made. One year then I'm done."

"I'll help you every step of the way. Unlike when Jack had to work out of an old B&B, we've rented two office buildings in Beaumont. I've seen them and you'll have a nice view of the Missouri River."

Liam avoided a snippy "Yippee" and instead accepted the water and acetaminophen tablets the flight attendant brought him. Soon he'd be in Beaumont for one year, faced with seeing the one woman who he couldn't touch again. He had to tell her who he was, but at the same time, this wasn't something he wanted to put in an email.

He spent part of the flight instead renting a historic brick bungalow on Third Street from Zoe Reilly. Zoe was Jack's wife Sierra's sister. When Clayton Holdings had purchased Sierra and Zoe's family winery, it hadn't bought the portion of the family homestead where Zoe and her husband, Nick, now lived with their daughters. That meant Zoe's house on Third Street in downtown Beaumont was available to rent. Nick was also Jack's business partner, and with Jack's help, Liam completed the entire transaction over video call.

Compared to a tent, Liam figured the hundred-plus-year-old house would be a castle. Compared to his home in Colorado, the place was a shoebox. But Liam didn't need much. He'd have a postage-stamp backyard and a carport. In the front, there was a swatch of yard and a small porch. The living-dining room combination wasn't big. Nor was the small kitchen he'd probably never use, especially as one of the selling points for the rental was that he could easily walk to Main Street and visit its many restaurants, shops, including the wine bar where he'd run into Lexi. The primary bedroom fit a California king-size bed, and the bathroom had been updated and remodeled. He had no real use for the second bedroom except as storage, and he'd also have plenty of that in the basement. As for Eva, she'd rented a condo out near the wineries.

Two weeks later, after nonstop onboarding meetings with his father, brothers and sister, Liam returned with Eva to Beaumont. They landed in Chesterfield and picked up the keys that had been left for them at the counter of the small private aviation company. "You're going to have a great year," Eva told him before she drove off in her SUV.

Liam loaded his bags into the Subaru Outback he'd leased. He had a Range Rover in Colorado, but since he was in Beaumont, he'd chosen a crossover that still would allow him to explore the wilds of Missouri and handle any gear. He'd learned there were some great trout streams within an hour or so where he could fish, and that had at least cheered him up.

He drove out to Beaumont and thought of the workday ahead. He and Eva had chosen to return on a Thursday night. That way, after a full Friday of meetings with the employees who already worked at the new Midwest head-quarters, everyone would have the weekend to regroup and relax. Eva texted him that she'd reached the condo, and Liam sent back that he'd found everything to his specifications at his rental. The house was a few blocks away from the office building where he'd take up residence tomorrow. Tonight, though, he was free to do whatever, so already feeling caged in, he walked to La Vita è Vino Dolce. Soon he had a flatbread and a glass of Norton in front of him.

Then he felt someone to his left, and sensed her before he turned. "Fancy seeing you here," Lexi said.

Liam's heart jumped. "I'm back."

"I can see that." She appeared surprised and slightly nervous.

"How are things?" he asked. He indicated the seat to his left. "Join me. We'll catch up."

"Oh, I can't." She pointed toward a table where several women laughed. "That's my roommate and some of my coworkers. It's girls night, sorry. But it's good to see you."

"Same." He drank her in—those high cheekbones he'd kissed, the arched brows he'd traced with his fingers and the smooth creamy neck he'd planted kisses all over. He wanted nothing more than to press his lips to hers and see if she tasted as sweet as their perfect night. See if she was as real as she'd been in his dreams. "Are you working tomorrow?"

Her face flushed, and her chin dipped once before she met his gaze again. "Actually, I am. Have a good night."

Liam watched her walk over to the table, her gait strong and confident. He willed her to glance back at him but she didn't. She never turned his way once, either. She sent him no side glances. She didn't point in his direction and then whisper softly to her friends. No one at their table looked his direction or paid him any attention.

She'd meant what she said, Liam realized. She'd told no one about their night. He didn't know if he liked that fact or not, for it meant she'd dismissed what they'd shared. That hurt, especially when the memories of that evening lived large inside his head and had for the past two weeks. Appetite lost, he had the bartender box the leftovers. Liam settled the bill and drained his glass. As he left, he gave one last glance toward her table. She'd tucked her hair behind her ear, and he noted the tiny stud twinkling there. He made his way toward the exit.

He hated to admit it, but it was probably for the best she'd put their night behind them. As a newly minted VP of Winery Operations for Clayton Holdings, Liam had responsibilities. He had family expectations weighing on his shoulders. He also wanted Edmund to have this well-deserved chance for happiness.

Liam would tell Lexi who he was tomorrow, and then, like her, pretend nothing had ever happened. Only 365 days to go before he could get the heck out of this town.

"Lexi?" Hearing the voice of one of the hotel managers, Lexi glanced up from wiping the bar top. It was almost eight, and they'd already had a good crowd for a Friday night. It was the first week of May, and if things went this well during the summer, not only would she be set financially, she might be ahead on her budget. The only disappointment was that she hadn't seen Liam. After asking last night if she was working, he hadn't visited Esprit.

She knew they'd said one night, and that she'd reinforced it, but when she'd seen him at La Vita è Vino Dolce yesterday evening, it had taken everything she had not to say goodbye to her friends and return to the bar. But then he'd left, and part of her had been relieved not to be tempted while another part had regretted not taking a chance. He wouldn't be welcome tomorrow because a Hollywood film-maker and his wife had rented out the Chateau for their fif-tieth wedding anniversary. They'd booked an entire week for their friends and family, with overflow guests staying at the Grand. Loretta had snuck Lexi a look at the guest list. No one she knew. No one who would recognize her.

Lexi smiled at the assistant manager. Nancy wore a blue pencil skirt, suit jacket, silk shirt, designer heels and an air of curiosity mixed with expectation. "How can I help you?"

"I need you to come with me. Alvin can cover. I was told this shouldn't take long and then you'll be right back."

"Raney and I got this. Go." Alvin gave Lexi a shrug. Nancy outranked him, so if she wanted Lexi, off Lexi went.

Lexi smoothed the pointed bottom of her black vest and followed Nancy back behind the bar and into the staff por-tion of the hotel. Like when directors used to call her aside, she tried not to panic as they left the bar area. "Did I do something wrong?"

Like sleep with a hotel guest? That had been weeks ago, and Liam hadn't been staying at the hotel.

"I have no idea what this is about, and I don't like to speculate." Nancy pushed through another set of swinging doors and wound past one of the Chateau kitchens before leading Lexi through a set of heavy wooden doors. Why was she here in the managers' offices? To keep the Chateau intimate, things like personnel hiring and training, order-ing and receiving, and even excess housekeeping storage, were handled at the larger Beaumont Grand. A service path led between the two hotels.

Lexi's nerves frayed and she made fists and relaxed them to calm nerves. "No one gave you a reason?"

"It's not my place to ask. Mr. Clayton requested your presence, so that's what I'm doing."

Well, that told her, didn't it? Lexi tried not to worry. As part of her recovery, once she'd walked away last September, she'd made the deliberate choice to stay off social media and gossip sites. Seeing her name over and over and the nasty things written about her had contributed to her eating disorder, so once she'd put Melynda behind her, she'd done a cold turkey with consuming media. She doubted Edmund knew her true identity.

Minus a glance at his back during the grand opening, Lexi had never seen Edmund Clayton in person, much less met him. Edmund was the one who'd built the Chateau. When he'd joined the family company, he'd transformed the hotels from above average to exceptional. Alvin had kept the staff informed, telling them that Michael Clayton was now running the hotels in Edmund's place. William Clayton had taken over the wineries.

Nancy led Lexi into a conference room that sat six people maximum. The tiny window looked over the French gardens. "Sit down. I'll see if I can find where he went." Behind her, the heavy door closed with a firm click. Lexi took a deep breath. She'd been in trickier spots before. One was when she'd faced her father, told him she was quitting, and that her lawyers would be in touch.

The door opened, but she didn't turn around from watching the sunset. She had no idea why she was here. She was too far beneath Edmund Clayton III's notice for him to want to meet with her.

"I do like it when you stare out a window." That deep, husky voice she knew intimately sent chills up her spine and desire weakening her knees. "Makes the view far more interesting than it's ever been."

She whirled and there he was. He'd chopped his wavy blond hair—could he have gotten more handsome? His short-sleeved knit polo—in light pink, the color confident men wore with impunity—clung to the hard muscles beneath. Firm, strong arms, dusted with golden hairs, crossed over his chest. Dark blue dress pants molded to every sculpted curve she'd kissed. Gray eyes gave her a head-to-toe appraisal that stripped away her clothing. His gaze lingered. His smile made butterflies take flight "Hi, Lexi. I figured we should talk."

She hated how comfortable he was. Almost as if he owned the place… Her face drained of color, and she placed a steadying hand on the polished wood table. Liam. As in *William* Clayton, brother to Edmund. The heir spare as some of her coworkers called him. The recluse. No wonder why he hadn't wanted to be at the grand opening party and had wandered into her bar. Her face flamed. She hadn't just fraternized with a guest. She'd slept with one of the owners of Clayton Holdings.

"Miss Henderson." Nancy poked her head through the doorway. "Oh good. You found Mr. Clayton."

"Yes." Her mouth dried into coarse sandpaper, and she wished the floor would swallow her whole. "I found him."

"I've got it from here, Nancy." Liam gave the assistant manager a half smile. "Thanks for your help. I'll remember how invaluable your assistance has been and mention it to Michael."

Once the door shut, Liam shoved his hands into the front pockets of his dress pants, stretching the fabric. Lexi's knees gave, and she dropped into a soft, overstuffed leather chair, her stomach sick and churning. How could she not have made the connection? Why hadn't she studied up on the Clayton family? "You're Liam Clayton."

Interpreting her train of thought, Liam interjected, "Not once did I lie. Omitted some truth, but not one word from that night we shared was a lie."

That fact shouldn't matter, but it did. "You knew I worked here. You still should have told me. Like maybe when you saw me last night."

He tilted his head. "I asked you to sit with me. You were with your friends. And the fact is that I rather enjoyed meeting you. For once a woman wasn't after me because of my name. Unless you knew who I was and were acting dumb."

"I'm not that good of an actress." Which was why she'd sucked in that short-lived, reality-style TV show she and Damon had made for that teen cable network. She couldn't look adoringly into Damon's eyes and pretend to be his girlfriend. How could she want to be his future wife when he was cheating on her? Lexi dropped her face into her fingertips and set her elbows on the table. She rubbed her temples.

Liam moved like a panther, prowling closer. The hair on her arms tingled. Goose bumps prickled. A finger crooked under her chin and she lifted her gaze to his. Her voice quavered but the words held firm. "I never would have slept with you if I'd known who you were."

"Where's the fun in that? It was good sex. I haven't stopped thinking about it. But in one of those ironic twists of fate, that next morning my brother Edmund decided to take a new role in the company and my dad passed the reins of the winery division to me. So, if it helps your sensibilities, at the time we met, I was unemployed. Now that the whole corporate office is relocating to Beaumont, I'm here at least a year. I told my dad I'd give him that."

Her stomach rolled with the implications. She felt queasy, somewhat sick. "I don't hook up. I don't fraternize with hotel guests. This is so awkward. I let myself break my rules for one night."

"I broke mine too." He rested a hip against the table. "And I'm not a guest. I wasn't that night either."

"No, you're the boss. That makes what I did worse."

"I wasn't the boss then." He pointed out, using his foot to swing her chair around. "I was a man who wanted you very much."

"Except we weren't supposed to see each other again." She sucked in much-needed air as desire for him flared. He was too close. Too virile. She rose and Liam wrapped his arms around her waist. As if a switch had flipped, nerve endings hummed. Heat built. Her face flushed and her lips parted. "I need this job. No fraternization. That's why I said no one can know."

Especially no one in LA, like her father. The last thing she needed was for the ghost of Melynda Norfolk to follow Lexi to Beaumont. The internet gossip sites and supermarket tabloids would have a field day: "Former pop star a fallen woman and bartender!" The paparazzi strongly featured in her nightmares. They'd chronicled her life and held her up to scrutiny, labeling her talentless. Too fat. Too homely. Too brazen. Too boring. Too pitchy. Too everything.

"And I've kept your secret and will continue to do so. But there's something here." Liam touched the side of her face. "You and me, we have something rare."

Which scared her beyond reason. Liam made her want dangerous things. He had the power to upset her perfectly outlined plan for her life. She wasn't looking for a partner. She still had to find out who she was first, to accomplish her goals. To get a degree. To be healthy. She couldn't let someone get too close, for if they did, she might slip back into old patterns where she let the men in her life dominate her choices and make decisions for her.

"I'm sorry. We can't," she told Liam. With worries and fears creating endless cacophony in her head, her chest heaved and she fought for breath. He let her go and stepped back. She worked for air. Her heart pounded, sweat formed and her hands shook. She hadn't had a panic attack in almost six months, and her fight or flight instinct screamed, "Run!" She wanted to go home and hide under a pillow until the noise in her head stopped. The best night of her life had turned into a nightmare.

"Hey, are you okay? You've paled." Concern laced Liam's voice.

"I'm fine." It was shaky, but a working voice. And no, she wasn't fine, but she couldn't tell him that.

"Hey, you have nothing to worry about. Your job is safe. The office is in town. I'm not going to be on-site much, as Michael's in charge of the hotels. You just told me no, that we can't pick up where we left off, and I'll respect your decision. If our paths cross, it'll be like last night. A quick hello."

"Thank you." She wished things could be different. She touched his face and his mouth parted as she ran her thumb over his cheek, memorizing the texture of his jaw. His kisses had taken her to heights never imagined. If she leaned closer, she could kiss him again. She wanted that kiss. More sparks. Tingles. Heat. It was as if he were the air essential for life.

He shifted to put some space between them. Lexi knew she should walk away, but her feet wouldn't move. Instead, she reached out her hand as if to shake his. His fingers laced through hers, and heat fused them together. Like that night weeks ago, a simple touch created a flare that made her sensibilities fly right out the window like the birds flitting about in the garden. "Thank you."

"Goodbye, Lexi. You need to go." His voice had dropped, lowered, as if he held himself in check.

She didn't release his hand. "Why do I feel like this?"

His hair swooped into his face and he pushed it back. "I've been asking myself the same question and have no answer. Whatever the reason, it goes beyond an understanding of natural laws. I don't know why touching you is so incredible, but I want more."

Lexi hated this. She placed her other hand on his cheek. "I should go."

Instead she stepped closer. Tilted her head. Lifted her mouth. He stood like a statute as she planted a kiss on his lips. Then, he groaned and devoured her. He hoisted her up, set her on the edge of the mahogany tabletop. She wrapped her legs around his waist and planted kisses down his neck. Her body was made for this, for his touch. His mouth moved to the spot behind her left ear and she trembled. She clung to his forearms. Her train of thought derailed as he nipped her earlobe. She succumbed to Liam, the irresistible Pied Piper. Her body hummed, sang beneath his fingers. "We shouldn't do this," he said. "You were right. I can't let you change your mind. You'll regret it."

Lexi was beyond caring. The moment she walked away, this—them—was over. Her body was a fire only he could quench, and she'd learned six months ago to grab what she wanted and damn the consequences. She deserved some happiness. Pleasure. If only for this moment.

But he pulled away before things got too far out of control. "Not here. Not like this."

She crashed to earth, the euphoria ending as she set her clothes to rights. "Sorry. I guess I got carried away. It won't happen again, and don't worry, I won't say anything."

"I'm not a dirty little secret. I'm not ashamed of what we did." Liam appeared offended.

She'd deal later with clamor of feelings crowding her head. She'd just lost control and been compulsive, something she considered her worst flaw. Once she'd thought bingeing and purging or starving herself had been exercising control, but really those actions had represented her lack of it, her desire for her own agency. Had he not stopped, she would have had sex with him on the conference room table, something she would have regretted once she came down from the orgasmic high. These past six months she'd learned to control her impulses and develop healthy habits, or at least until she'd met him. He was danger personified, like an adrenaline rush she didn't need but couldn't resist.

Somehow she'd learn to keep her distance from Liam Clayton and her overwhelming attraction to him. "Thank you for respecting me."

"I will always respect you."

But he might not if he knew who she really was, or the life she'd left behind. She couldn't tell him. He wouldn't understand how hard she'd fought to escape the prison of being Melynda Norfolk. "I wish things could be different." For that was the truth. Had she not been on a life do-over. Had he not been a Clayton.

Liam reached for her hand, and his touch created heat

and zing before she jerked her fingers away. "Me too. You're an awesome person, Lexi."

His compliment warmed, but she knew he thought her awesome only because he didn't truly know her. He knew the version who'd had sex with him. Few had liked the real her, preferring perfect Damon instead. She'd been the one labeled the problem. The troubled one. The one who'd needed therapy to heal from her self-inflicted wounds, who still battled her impulses.

Trying not to look at Liam, she managed to put one foot in front of the other and left the conference room. What had her mother said? *Stay on the path, Lexi. That's how you get places in this world. Always honor yourself and be true to who you are...*

She missed her mom. What would she have thought of Liam? What advice would her mom give her in regards to the fact that with Liam, Lexi had caved to the passion and let her body rule her head. Would her mom say it was normal? Or that Lexi had erred?

She'd never know. The only truth was that Lexi had let herself be sucked into a pleasure vortex, a Category 5 force that had spiraled her far upward to bliss, only to crash her down with equal, if not greater, strength. He was her boss. She should have predicted this cruel twist of fate. Her life had always been a series of highs and lows.

She'd heard rumors of William Clayton. He was Edmund's brother, the reclusive one. She'd seen it for herself in the way *Liam* stayed at the inn instead of his own hotel. On the walk back to Esprit, she Googled him on her phone, quickly learning he was the heir spare who had traveled the world, until two years ago he'd survived the quake on Everest and his girlfriend had not. The one he'd mentioned.

The love he'd lost. The article she read said the incident had damaged his soul. Made him bitter. Damaged. Emotionally bankrupt.

She could see those traits, even though she didn't "know" that William Clayton any more than Liam knew Lexi as Melynda. The Liam she'd fallen for had made her feel magical, if only for a night. After a quick restroom stop to ensure her appearance revealed nothing of what had happened, Lexi returned to her spot behind the bar and logged into the computer. "Hey, I'm back."

Alvin arched a quizzical brow. "You okay?"

"Fine. It was nothing," she told him as she reviewed orders. "Some missing paperwork I'd forgotten to fill out. No big deal."

"Good." Alvin unknowingly accepted her lie and went to check on his customers. She had her own customers to serve, and ice rattled in the silver container as Lexi shook a lemon drop martini. If her father could see the actress she'd finally become, he'd have been so proud. Lexi poured the pale yellow liquid into a glass and smiled at the woman who'd ordered it. Lexi could forget Liam, would forget him. She'd already put one life behind her. Surely she could do the same with the handsome, enigmatic, magical and perfect Liam Clayton.

Chapter Five

Six weeks later, she was late. Worse, her ballet flats didn't fit, and she had to leave for her Saturday night shift. Lexi cursed as her stomach rolled and threatened eruption. She sipped some clear soda and washed down another antacid.

Hopefully she hadn't caught the same stomach bug that had stricken many of the other Chateau employees. It was almost July, so why were people still getting sick? Didn't germs go away once summer arrived? Lexi didn't want to be ill. She needed tonight's pay and tips because her enrollment deposit was due. And Alvin had already texted her to make sure she'd be there. She'd taken her temperature with her housemate's digital thermometer—perfectly normal. Her roommate didn't show symptoms.

As for the water retention and swelling in her feet, that was easily attributed to the irregularity of her monthly cycles. Back when Lexi had been performing as Melynda, her doctor had prescribed diuretics to prevent bloating. Couldn't have any puffiness.

Before, when she'd been pencil thin, Lexi could go six-to-eight weeks without a period, and then have one that lasted at the most twenty-four hours. Once she'd started eating healthier, some of the drastic irregularity of her cycles had gone away, but not all.

Still, the thought nagged that there was a chance she might be pregnant. Liam had used condoms, and while there was always a chance of any contraception failing, he hadn't mentioned there being an issue. He would have told her if the condom had torn, right? Of course he would. Lexi had also had some light spotting, so maybe that had been her cycle for this month. Nothing to be anxious about. If she didn't feel better by Monday, she'd break down and buy a pregnancy test, but surely it would be negative. She already felt better, and she was keeping food down.

The wedding and reception of a local St. Louis Fortune 500 CEO's daughter would be entirely outdoors, with the wedding in the French garden and the reception on the terrace. Lexi crossed her fingers for excellent tips and slid into her car. The drive took twenty minutes. She eased up on the gas pedal and navigated a tight curve on Winery Road. The scenic, two-lane highway connected each of the six Clayton-owned wineries, the eighteen-hole golf course, and the Grand and Chateau hotels.

She lowered the visor against the midafternoon sun and felt relief as she parked in the employee lot. She clocked in on time, tossed her things into her locker and smoothed a few wrinkles in her clothing. In addition to her standard uniform of a long-sleeved white dress shirt, black dress pants, and matching vest, Lexi also wore a blue-and-green-striped tie.

Lexi grabbed the end of one of the rolling racks stacked with glassware and moved it outside before returning for two hangers worth of linens. She spread the black tablecloths over the two long tables already in place. Alvin had rolled out the coolers, for which Lexi was grateful. Weighted with iced beer and wine, the coolers were heavy. She polished the glasses to remove water spots, and set them into rows on the tablecloth, creating patterns of wineglasses, whiskey glasses and champagne flutes. She'd learned that having the glassware to her left and right helped to speed things along. She saw Alvin speaking with a woman who she assumed was the wedding planner since all Lexi could see was the back of her head.

"What did the wedding planner have to say?" Lexi asked when Alvin joined her behind the bar.

"That's not the wedding planner. She's over there." Alvin pointed to a fortysomething wearing a headset and carrying an iPad. "That was Eva Clayton. Eva went to college with the bride and is in the wedding party. I'm surprised she was out here instead of getting ready, but she wanted to make sure that we had the right champagne. I told her we did, that the shipment came in this morning and I put it on ice."

"That makes sense. She wants things perfect for her friend." Lexi craned her neck. Eva had disappeared. Having only caught Eva in passing a few times, Lexi wished she'd gotten a better look at Liam's sister, but all she'd seen was the back of her dark, French-cut bob. She pushed away any worry. Just because Eva was here did not mean Liam was. Now weeks after he'd admitted who he was, Lexi felt far more confident in the fact he'd kept his word. No one gave her odd looks and she hadn't seen him. She'd finally stopped looking over her shoulder, because Liam either avoided the Grand and Chateau, or if he visited, he didn't seek her out. She'd also avoided the wine bar, eliminating any chance of another encounter. On the plus side, that act of staying home had saved her money.

Work had settled into a wonderful normality, and she'd passed her review with flying colors. But at night, when she was in bed with only one of Dawn's cats for company, the relief she'd felt at not seeing him often warred with the desire to touch him again. The time they'd spent together had been perfect. She could still picture his handsome face and remember how his lips had felt against hers, and how they'd moved with delicious ecstasy over her body. But as her time as Melynda had proved, the fantasy often hid the reality. To her fans, everything had looked perfect. How little they knew.

To divert herself from going down that rabbit hole, she asked "How's Melody?" The inquiry about his wife started Alvin talking about the vacation they were planning, which segued into another topic. Two hours later, Lexi watched as a crowd of people dressed in designer clothing crossed the terrace and headed toward the garden for the ceremony. What would it be like to find someone and fall in love? She was twenty-six and had had one relationship, and that hadn't even been real. Her one night stand had stayed just that. Lexi sipped some club soda to settle her stomach. Once her shift ended, she was going home to bed.

Liam wasn't a fan of weddings, especially since his sister saw them as the perfect occasion for matchmaking. He ran a finger underneath the starched collar of his white dress shirt, luckily not sweating too much as he watched his sister's college roommate say her vows. Eva stood behind her friend. Eva's happy smile showed more proof she was a hopeless romantic.

Well, that and Eva refused to let her ex see how hurt she'd been when he'd called things off. He was somewhere in the crowd of guests, which was why Liam was Eva's plus-one. She'd told Liam he'd make a good buffer. He had suggested she take Michael, but Liam's younger brother had business in Portland this weekend and had flown home yesterday. Although home was a misnomer. More and more Clayton Holdings employees relocated weekly, and the transition of the home office was moving at a faster pace than expected. That should make their dad happy.

Liam gave his sister credit. No matter how many times some guy disappointed her, Eva kept going and kept smiling. Maybe that was because she was twenty-five to his jaded thirty-two. He'd had a lot more time for disappointment. Or maybe it was because she hadn't lost the love of her life like he had. He shifted, trying not to manspread his right leg into the space of the woman who'd been inching closer to him during the ceremony. She'd introduced herself at the start, but while Liam could remember her bloodred fingernails, he couldn't remember her name. Unlike when meeting Lexi, when this woman had shaken his hand, he'd felt nothing. Then again, maybe sparks only flew in April.

"Isn't this so lovely?" the woman gushed, her hand lightly brushing his dark blue jacket sleeve. "They are such a perfect couple."

Raised to be polite, Liam attempted a half-hearted smile to show his agreement.

The crowd clapped, and Liam followed suit. He joined the guests in rising automatically as the bride and groom made their way back down the aisle. Thank God this part was over and he could go get a drink. Maybe even disappear to Michael's penthouse at the Grand during the social hour, which was that time gap between ceremony and dinner reception where guests stood around, drank too much and ate pricey shrimp appetizers while they waited for the wedding party to take photos. Being a Clayton, he could easily commandeer one of the staff golf carts and come back later, with Eva none the wiser.

He nixed that idea. She'd know. Somehow his sister always did. Since it was 6:00 p.m., a cocktail was in order. If he had to be at this social hour, his antisocial self might as well make the best of it. He joined the four-deep queue and used his phone to answer email. Jamestown Winery's bottle recycling program had been so successful that he'd expanded it to all their Clayton Holdings wineries across the country, and one of the managers had a question. "Whiskey," he said absently when he reached the front of the line. His attention was still on reading email.

"We don't have Old Forester. Will Jameson be okay?"

His head jerked up so fast he fumbled his phone. He managed to catch the device before it hit the table and then bounced who knew where. Her. In front of him.

"Hi. Um. Yes. Fine. Thank you." He should have been better prepared to see Lexi, but he wasn't. Instead, he stood like a gawky teenager watching his first crush, that one girl who Liam had forgotten once he'd met Anya.

Lexi lifted a pair of tongs and dropped a square cube into the glass. He swore the little clink reverberated, but perhaps that was his heart missing a beat. "I like Jameson," he managed to say once the shock absorbed. Did she appear paler? Tired? Her curly dark hair was pulled away from her face, giving her an even more innocent appearance than the night he'd met her. He had the immediate urge to spirit her away to somewhere safe. He shoved the phone into his front pants pocket. "How are you?"

Buffed clear fingernails poured two fingers into the glass. "Good. Thank you for asking, Mr. Clayton."

"That's good. Glad to hear it." Could a conversation be more awkward? He willed her to look at him, but she kept her head bent, concentrating on the task at hand. She slid the glass forward, almost as if afraid she'd drop it if she passed it to him. "Enjoy the reception."

"Liam!" A male voice caught Liam's attention, and he stepped aside to let those behind him in line get their turn. He let the whiskey burn down his throat as he noted that Lexi greeted the next person with far more enthusiasm. That was the thing about one-night stands. Seeing the people later, pretending that what had happened hadn't meant a thing when it had meant everything...there was no greater discomfort of knowing a secret worth shouting about but having it instead forever silenced.

"Hey, man, can't believe I'd run into you here of all places!" Scott Cleveland, one of his former hiking buddies, approached. The two had met in Colorado and summitted much of the Front Range together.

"Me either. Shouldn't you be on a mountain or something?" Liam clinked his glass to Scott's. Scott was Liam's age, but was a bright red ginger with a wind-worn, friendly face covered by a beard and mustache.

"The bride is Julia's second cousin. Didn't I tell you Julia's from St. Louis?"

"Maybe. Small world," Liam said, before sending more fire down his throat. "At least I'll know someone here besides Eva. I'm her plus-one. Her ex is here. Alone."

"And you're supposed to ensure she doesn't do anything stupid, right? That sounds like the makings of a movie!" Scott laughed. His wife, Julia, approached and slid her arms around her husband's waist. Scott, who stood six inches taller, bent to give her a quick kiss. Liam couldn't help but laugh. How many times had he teased Scott about the PDA?

"It's so good to see you, Liam," Julia said. "Aren't you nice in helping your sister. I do believe you hate these things."

"I do. And how do you know it's not me who's the one who'd do something stupid?" Liam teased. He'd always liked Scott and Julia. He arched his brows. "Maybe my sister is saving me."

Julia's smile lit her face when she laughed, but it didn't impact Liam the way Lexi's did. "Because you dot every *i* and cross every *t*. If you make a list, you check it twice. That's why I always trusted Scott would be fine whenever he hiked with you."

Liam shrugged. "Sadly not much hiking to do around here. I do get out and ride on the Katy Trail, though."

Freeing herself from her hubby, Julia gave Liam a gentle smack on his forearm. "Listen to you grouse. There's plenty to do. Just without the altitude. I grew up here, remember?"

"And I'm moving here," Liam announced, as if that justified his criticism.

"Really?" This came from Scott.

Liam rattled the ice against the side of the glass. "Dad wants to relocate the company, so you're looking at the new VP of the wine division. The entire headquarters will be located here in the next ten months. The Claytons are moving to Beaumont."

"Say it with more enthusiasm," Scott said, sarcasm evident. "Even you?"

Liam sighed. "Not permanently. I told my dad I'd give it a year. Edmund's off traveling with Lana, his girlfriend, well, fiancée. At some point, he'll tire of that and come back. Well, not of Lana. He's found the one. He's never been so happy, and I'm glad. He deserves it."

Scott studied Liam in a way that made Liam shift his weight. "So a year…" Scott trailed off, leaving the statement more of a question.

Liam's fingers tensed on the glass. "I owed my brother that. He deserves to be happy."

"As do you," Julia pointed out. "It's been two years. We miss having you as our neighbor. You deserve good things in your life, too, Liam."

He fought the urge to turn and look at Lexi. Instead he twisted his lips. "So people keep telling me. But hey, it's a wedding, so enough about me and this depressing talk. Tell me about you. What's been going on? How's Karly?"

"Going to get a little brother or sister in about five months." Julia patted her stomach and Liam saw the small bump.

"Congrats!" he said. "That's great. Karly must be thrilled."

"Thanks, man." Scott couldn't contain his excitement. "Karly is over the moon. She's three and a human tornado. She's demanded a sister so she can have a playmate. We've told her she gets whatever the stork brings. Can you believe it? Two kids. Gonna be busy."

"I bet. And you did not tell her babies come from storks."

"Oh, he's joking. Karly knows moms bring babies into the world," Julia said.

Liam brushed aside the twinge of jealousy and fought battles with the guilt and sadness that threatened. When Julia had been pregnant with Karly, Anya had once joked about how they'd have their kids around the same time and that their children would grow up together and be best friends and playmates. Another dream that had died on

Everest. Liam lifted his glass and realized it was empty, but
he made no move to refill it. Instead, he instead caught up
with Scott and Julia and let them talk. Before he knew it,
Eva joined them. "Look at you actually being social," she
said to Liam before greeting his friends. "Hey, Scott and
Julia. How are you? So great to see you."

"I hear you're avoiding an ex," Julia said. "Who is he?"

"I am. I'll point him out, and you can help me commis-
erate. He looks so good tonight it's sinful. Liam, brother
dear, will you go get me a glass of white wine? I need some
fortitude." Eva nudged Liam with her elbow.

"Oh, and I want some ginger ale if you don't mind,"
Julia added.

"Looks like we're on drink duty." Scott lightly clamped
his hand on Liam's shoulder and pointed him toward the
bar. "Shall we?"

He was coming back. Of course, Liam and whoever the
red-haired gentleman he stood with couldn't have chosen
Alvin's line. No, Liam had to put himself in her direct line
of sight, edging ever closer as the line moved forward.
Lexi wiped suddenly sweaty hands on her pants so that
she didn't drop the next glass. The evening temperature
was a palatable low eighties, but suddenly her underarms
felt as if she stood in full sun instead of under a protective awning. She'd never seen him interact with someone
who was clearly a friend. The man in front of her shoved a
ten-dollar bill into the tip jar before lifting the two glasses
of wine she'd poured. Lexi's mouth dried as Liam stepped
closer. She took a quick sip of water before handing the
next person a glass of champagne. As the woman stepped
away, Lexi swiped her hand again, tilted her head and tried

to appear professionally disinterested. "Hello again, Mr. Clayton. Same as last time?"

"Yes. And a ginger ale, glass of white wine, and..."

"Whatever he's having," Liam's friend said.

"That's Jameson," Lexi said.

"This is Lexi," Liam told his friend as Lexi began to pour the whiskey. "She's one of our most valuable employees."

Upon hearing that, Lexi gripped the tongs wrong and the square cube went skittering across the linen, onto the ground, and bounced into a flower bed. How embarrassing. Her face flamed.

"I can see that." The man's eye twinkled, indicating he was teasing. "She's dropping things because you're making her nervous." To Lexi he said, "He's not really the big bad wolf, you know. Don't let him get to you."

Lexi noted Liam's friend was as tall as Liam. They had a similar lean and fit stance. She saw a wedding ring, though, while Liam had none.

"You're the one scaring her," Liam accused. "Lexi, this is Scott. Don't let him give you any grief. We used to hike all the time in Colorado."

"My wife and his girlfriend were also friends. Make sure he gives you a raise. You deserve it working for this bloke."

"He's in charge of the wineries," Lexi said, adding a friendly smile. Scott seemed nice.

"Well, you are serving Clayton wines. Liam, be a good gent and drop a good tip into the jar." Scott grinned and grabbed the ginger ale, the glass of wine, and one of the whiskey glasses. "Next round's on me. I'll bring this to Eva and Julia."

Liam opened his wallet and peeled out a hundred. He

held it out. "Put that in your pocket, not the jar. Don't argue with the boss."

Lexi narrowed her gaze, but he'd already turned and walked away. She fumed. Yes, she wanted tips. Worked for them. But after what had happened between them, she wasn't going to take money from Liam. He never would have tipped Alvin that much, so to tip her like that because of what had happened between them was insulting. She'd find him later and insist he take it back. She was not a charity case or a woman who was paid for her favors. The two women approaching the bar caught her attention.

"Did you hear that before the dancing starts we're getting a mini concert? It's a surprise for the bride. Her new husband flew in her favorite performer," one woman said. She glanced at Lexi. "Two white wines, please."

"Do we know who it is?" her friend asked.

Lexi passed over two glasses of wine but didn't hear the answer as to who was singing because they'd already stepped away.

"Hey, Lexi." One of the servers approached. She carried a set of hand chimes resting on top of a wooden base. "I'm going to call everyone for dinner now. Just wanted to be sure you're ready."

Lexi nodded. "We're good."

The server randomly hit each of the seven circular bars with a wooden mallet, the tinkling noise notifying the wedding guests that it was time to find their seats. Lexi knew that each table would have both wine and champagne, but there was still a slight crush at the bar as she and Alvin served guests who wanted to bring something else to their place setting.

"I've got this," Alvin told her once the last guest left. "Time for your break. You appear flushed."

Lexi wiped her brow. "Maybe a little. It's hotter out here than I thought."

"Wait until the dog days of summer. Doesn't help that our uniform is always long sleeves buttoned to our wrists. At least we're not in the direct sun. And if it's anything like the Grand, we'll mostly be inside. Gets too hot by mid-July, and no one wants to be out here."

"I'm new to Missouri," Lexi admitted.

"Our heat and humidity is its own version of hell. Trust me, everyone wants air-conditioning. You included." Alvin pointed. "Now go and find some."

Lexi slid through the employee door and into the kitchen. She used the bathroom, washed her hands and splashed water on her face. The nerves making her feel lightheaded had to be from seeing Liam, especially since his money burned a hole in her pocket. She finger combed her hair and left the room. She slid past the runners bringing out loaded trays of food, carrying the salads to the servers who had specific, assigned tables. Safely out of the way and out of sight of any guests, she leaned against a wall and enjoyed the coolness falling from the vents above her head. The two-course meal service lasted approximately forty minutes, although it could last about an hour when including grace and after-dinner speeches. Lexi would rest for a moment and then go give Alvin his break. She closed her eyes, not enough to fall asleep but enough to find her center.

"Melynda?"

Her eyes opened with a snap. She knew that voice. Before she could think to deny her stage name, she said, "Damon?"

Her five-eight ex stood in front of her, his expression

of surprise evident in the blue eyes she'd once looked into every day. "What are you doing here? What the hell are you wearing?"

Shocked to her core, Lexi's mouth tried to form words but nothing came out. Dressed in tight jeans, tennis shoes and a Beatles T-shirt, Damon looked as good as he always did. His dark hair curled at his nape and swooped back from his forehead. A gold stud glittered in his left ear. The full lips that millions of girls swooned over parted as he peered at her.

With flight winning over fight, Lexi turned and beat a hasty, undignified retreat to the kitchen. She heard Damon's "Hey, wait" as she pushed through the swinging door but she didn't pause. "You okay, Lexi?" someone asked.

"Great." Lexi cut through the room and exited out the side door. Skirting around some large planters, she made her way to the safety of the outdoor bar.

"You okay?" Alvin studied her. "You look like you saw a ghost."

No, just her former bandmate, boyfriend and business colleague. The last person she'd expected to see.

"That's silly. I'm fine." The lie slid out easily, for what else could she say? There was no way Damon-slash-Billy would get his own drinks. He had people for that. The terrifying unknown was if her father was also at the Chateau. "So you know how you were thinking of training Erik to be a bartender?" Erik was a new hire.

"Yeah, why?"

"Most likely he's going to be the first one cut and sent home tonight, right? I'm feeling a bit under the weather. Is it okay if I go instead?"

Alvin frowned. He folded his arms and peered at her like

a child who'd announced they had a temperature. "Are you sure about that? You needed the tips, I thought."

"Yeah, I don't mind. Just let me know. Go take your break."

"Okay, if you're certain." As Alvin walked off, some relief filled Lexi. At least if Damon did approach her, or if her father were here, she'd be alone. The last thing she wanted was any kind of dramatic scene, such as the one her father had made when she'd told him she was quitting. She edged as far back as she could from the front of the bar. Occasionally a server would come to replenish a cocktail, but otherwise she was left to her own devices. Normally during the dinner lull, Alvin might check his phone or play an online game, but Lexi simply watched the area where guests ate filet mignon and salmon at round dinner tables decorated with tea lights and flower centerpieces.

"Here you are."

Lexi jumped. Liam stood off to the side. Her heart gave a tiny leap. "Hello, Mr. Clayton. Another Jameson?"

Liam stepped behind the bar. "No. I just wanted to talk to you. Figured this was a good time to do it. How've you been?"

"Fine." One word was all she could manage. Oh, why wasn't Alvin back?

Liam tilted his head and studied her thoughtfully. "You didn't look fine earlier and you look worse now."

"There's a stomach bug going around. You know, the one that's sidelining everyone? I'm hoping I haven't caught it. But since you're here, you should take your money back. I don't want it."

"No, you provided a service and I gave you a tip."

"Provided a service?" Lexi tried not to screech the words.

Liam protested by holding up his hands. "You know I don't mean it like that."

"Well, that's how it comes across. You wouldn't have put that much in Alvin's jar. I won't have you patronizing me or trying to compensate me for…" Lexi's face flamed. Had it gotten even hotter now that the breeze had died down? She was overheating and flustered, and not simply from agitation, panic and stress.

Liam peeled off another hundred and shoved it in Alvin's jar. "There. Better? Trust me, patronizing you is the last thing I want to be doing. I have nothing but respect for you. Can we talk later? Please."

Lexi reached for water and took a long sip. "I asked to be cut early. Potential stomach thing. I probably shouldn't be around guests." He didn't appear convinced, but a woman approached.

"Liam, what are you doing?" A frown etched a face similar to Liam's. Her gaze sharpened on Lexi. "He's not bothering you is he?"

"Lexi, this is my sister, Eva. You may have seen each other around."

Lexi couldn't throw Liam under the proverbial bus. She would disrupt family harmony, and Eva was part of the wedding party. "Nice to meet you, Ms. Clayton. And of course not. Your brother was looking to see what Clayton vintages we were serving." Lexi gave what she hoped was a convincing smile. She really was getting good at lying, wasn't she?

Eva's head swiveled from Lexi to Liam. "Right. Okay. If you say so." Then again, it was clear she didn't believe Lexi's explanation, so maybe Lexi wasn't as great a liar as she thought.

"She thinks I'm trying to duck out," Liam explained. He grinned at Lexi, and she felt heat spread. "She knows I have the tendency to do that."

"Aren't you?" Eva demanded. "You hate social stuff. He left the gala early too."

Lexi knew how that had worked out. Liam cut a hand through the air. "I'm behind the bar looking at wine. I'm headed to the table now."

Eva rolled her eyes. "Uh-huh. You forget that I know you. If I hadn't come after you, you'd be halfway to the Grand by now. Anyway, the concert's about to start. You know, Damon Stevener?"

"No clue. Don't care." Liam looked at Lexi. "Do you know who he is?"

Lexi lifted teeth she'd dug into her bottom lip and hoped she appeared the right combination of nonchalant disinterest and excited enthusiasm. "He's pretty famous. A bunch of number one pop hits. People like his music."

"Whatever." Liam shrugged. "I'm sure he'll be great. How much did it cost to bring him in? Wouldn't that money have been better spent on a charitable donation?"

Liam's focus on charity impressed Lexi. Eva gave a harrumph.

"Come on. Lexi doesn't want to know about your opinions on saving the world." Eva gestured, and Liam gave Lexi a half smile as he followed his sister.

Lexi turned to the back table and began straightening things. Her relief was short-lived when she heard Damon's voice behind her. "You're a bartender here."

She whirled around. "Yes. Some of us work for a living."

Damon frowned. His eyes were hidden by designer sunglasses so she couldn't read the rest of his expression. He'd also changed into a suit. "What the hell? You were on the top of the world. This is not the place for you."

"But it's where I am and I'm happy here," Lexi argued. "It's a fresh start."

"Which is ridiculous. I've been looking all over for you. You dropped off the face of the earth."

She wouldn't go back. "You don't need me. Your career is skyrocketing."

Damon gave her his trademark smile, the one Lexi knew firsthand was saccharine. "Come on. Forgive me. I miss you. I got this great new duet lined up, and it's perfect for us."

"And you couldn't record it with someone else? Taylor? Olivia? Miley?"

He lowered his sunglasses and peered over the top. "I want you."

Once those words may have held more sway. Lexi shook her head. "No. I walked away. I can't go back to that place. It wasn't healthy."

"That's because of your dad. You don't need him. You're a performer. You could get up there with me, on that stage tonight, and sing 'One Night' and be flawless."

She could, but that wasn't the point. "That's not really a wedding song."

"You know what I mean. You shouldn't be shlepping drinks. You should be singing."

Lexi lost it then. "What else was I supposed to be doing? I didn't have any work skills besides performing. You and my dad made me a pariah. Buying out my contract wiped out my bank account. This job will allow me to go to school, which was always my goal. You don't need me. Move on."

"You are a star." He pushed his glasses on top of his

head and they held his hair back. Once she had thought herself in love with him. How naive and dumb she'd been.

Damon walked around the bar and studied her. "Wait, no one here knows who you are, do they? That's classic. No wonder no one can find you. You've gone undercover."

Lexi took a step back. "Melynda's gone, Damon. She was a fool with no backbone. I'm Lexi. I like it that way. You can't tell anyone. No one here recognizes me."

"But I recognized you." He paused. "And sorry, I didn't realize what happened to you was this bad, especially with your dad."

"I had an eating disorder, Damon. I was going to die if I kept up that lifestyle. I'm not perfect, but he demanded I be."

Damon frowned. "I knew he was an ass. Between you and me, I'm ready for new management. Working on that while I'm here and he's not."

Thank God, Lexi thought. Her dad wasn't in Beaumont. "I'd be fine never seeing my father again." The words were out before Lexi could stop them. She realized her mistake when she saw the gleam in his eye.

"Then sing the song with me, and I won't tell your father I saw you. I won't tell him I found you. I'll even come here and record the duet in Beaumont. Or St. Louis as I doubt there's a quality studio in this town. Say yes. It will be our secret and in turn I'll keep yours. You can fade away. But first I want a song with you on my next album. We'll call it closure. That's more than fair, don't you think? One last time to bury the hatchet and show everyone we can still be friends? It'll go a long way, don't you say? Get the press off your back? You'd truly be free, and with enough money so you didn't have to do this."

Before Lexi could figure out an answer, the wedding planner came scurrying across the terrace.

"Damon." The planner fanned herself as she arrived. Clearly impressed by his stardom and winded from the exertion of speed walking across the terrace, she touched her headset twice. How many times had Lexi seen the fawning? "Sorry to bother you, but you're on in a few minutes. The band's waiting."

Damon grabbed a bottle of chilled water from the back table. "I was getting a drink." He winked at Lexi. "We'll chat later."

The wedding planner gave Lexi an odd look but turned and ushered him along.

Alvin arrived at that moment and joined Lexi in watching the two of them walk off. "Was that Damon Stevener?"

"Yeah. He was just getting a bottle of water." Lexi put her hands on her hips and took deep breaths.

Alvin swung around. "Everyone in the kitchen was beside themselves that he was here, but I didn't think his good looks would get to you, too."

She picked up a paper and fanned herself. "I'm just hot and not feeling well. Believe me, he's not that impressive up close."

Alvin's brows shot up in his "are you crazy" expression. "Sure, if you say so. My daughters love him. I'm going to sneak over there and film the concert for them. Can you manage by yourself? I figure everyone will be watching the show."

As long as Damon was on stage, Lexi was safe. "I got this. Go. If not, you'll miss the start."

"Thanks." Alvin gave her another once-over. "While I'm gone, drink some more water. You look parched. You'll need your strength because Missy said I can't let anyone leave."

Missy was the Chateau's event coordinator who liaised with the wedding planner. It was Missy's job to ensure that nothing went wrong. "I need to go home," Lexi protested weakly.

"I'll cut you as soon as I can. None of the servers can leave because they'll be setting up the dessert bar, the smoothie station and later serving pizza. Erik can't come over yet. I'm sorry. It's going to be a long night for everyone. But hey, lots of tips, right? The jars are overflowing."

"That's a bright side," Lexi mumbled as Alvin took off. Soon the crowd began to roar, indicating Damon had joined the wedding band. The light breeze carried his greeting to the bride, and as his vocals began to carry across the terrace, Lexi absentmindedly rubbed a water spot on the white linen. What was she to do? Would Damon keep her secret? She didn't want to leave town.

She liked Beaumont. She had a great job, a wonderful roommate and college classes starting in August. She didn't want to run away and start over. Even avoiding Liam hadn't been as problematic as what faced her now—trusting Damon to keep her location and new life secret. Which he'd promised he would—as long as she recorded one more Damon and Melynda song.

The trouble was Damon had little to recommend him as trustworthy. He'd cheated on her, lied to her about it and failed to show her any respect. On the other side of the terrace, around a slight bend, Damon began one of his latest hits. Lexi couldn't see him or the crowd, but she heard them screaming and singing along. She picked at the linen. Once hearing that thunderous applause had been a constant soundtrack of her life. Admittedly her ego missed the adulation. But it had come at a terrible price.

"I see you're alone again." Liam reappeared.

Her hand flew to the knot of the green-and-black-striped tie that was part of the uniform. "You're back. Another Jameson?" She reached for a glass but paused when he shook his head.

"I'm good." He grabbed a water instead. "Figured we'd talk while the concert was going on. You didn't seem too excited about it, and frankly, it's not really my kind of music. I'm much more into alternative. But I guess it's what the bride wanted. She's dead center in front of him. Her hubby's earned a lot of brownie points with this surprise. Do you know anything about the guy?"

"He's pretty popular. Was once part of a duo. Huge scandal when they broke up about six months ago." Lexi tested the waters and found herself rewarded when Liam gave a broad-shouldered shrug.

"And? Not sure I'm following or care. I don't pay attention to celebrity stuff unless it affects my family. You heard about Edmund and his ex?"

Lexi dipped her chin. "That their breakup went viral, but now he has found true love. Alvin's into celebrity stuff. He keeps us up-to-date. We're all very happy for Edmund."

"As am I. He deserves it." Liam uncapped the water and took a drink. "That should be what really matters, right? Love? The rest is distraction. Noise. The key is to remove both noise and distraction. It's like that moment you're standing on top of a snowcapped mountain with your lungs filled with air. It's the purest one can be, when you're one with nature and the universe and alive with endless possibilities. Love is a million of those moments. But then they end. You can't get them back and the memories, well, they aren't enough."

"I'm sorry about your girlfriend. She sounds lovely."

"She was. Sorry. I'm melancholy tonight. Eva's right. I'd like to get out of here. But I can't."

Lexi stared, spellbound. What would it be like to be loved by a man like Liam? To be his sole focus? For one night, she'd been in his arms. But a night didn't make a life, and they came from two different worlds. It was unrealistic to think things could work. Enough that she'd remember the night they shared until it eventually faded like an old photograph.

"Anyway, ignore me. Eva would say I'm wallowing."

"You went through a tragedy. I think you can wallow all you'd like." Made sense now, why he'd sought her out that night and let his lust rule.

But before she could broach that subject, Liam gestured. "Customers coming."

About six or seven elderly guests had left the pop concert. They began to approach the bar. As Lexi made ready, Liam shed his jacket and moved next to her. "What are you doing?" Lexi asked.

He grinned. "Helping out. I can't leave, so I'm letting Alvin enjoy the concert. I saw him over there, filming and dancing."

"He's trying to get some video for his daughters. You don't really have to do this. You're the boss. An owner."

"Which means that ultimately the buck stops with me." Liam rolled up his sleeves and sent her a grin that made butterflies dance. It amazed her how he'd stepped in. "Besides, I haven't done this since college. It'll be fun."

Chapter Six

"Chardonnay, please." A gorgeous brunette in a low-cut floral dress stood in front of Liam. She eyed him speculatively, a hint of a smile on her face as Liam grabbed the bottle and poured. While she might be beautiful, Liam felt no flicker of interest as he passed over a glass of white wine with a cheery "Here you go." The woman appeared to be around his brother Michael's age, and upon seeing that Liam wasn't going to engage in a little flirtation, she walked away without a thank you or a tip. Liam arched an eyebrow at Lexi, who shrugged.

"No tipping comes with the territory," Lexi said as she poured the night's signature drink, a blackberry whiskey lemonade. She handed three glasses to a man patiently waiting. In return, he shoved a five into her tip jar.

"Maybe you should smile more at the single women," Lexi told Liam. "Use some of that charm you have in spades. That'll get the dollars going."

The only person Liam wished he could get going with was Lexi. Liam poured another drink. "I'm not certain if you're complimenting me or insulting me."

"That's the mystery, then, isn't it?" Lexi rewarded him with a secretive smile that made Liam think she might be flirting with him. However, Liam never took anything for granted, especially without proof. And with Lexi, that proof had to be undeniable and crystal clear.

Lexi had already told him she didn't want to pursue anything with him, and he had to respect that. Still, the last thing he wanted to be doing was flirting with another woman in front of the one he really wanted. Liam served the next person in line, and when the elderly man moved off, the sudden crowd that had swarmed them had dispersed as quickly as it had arrived. Across the way, pop music still blared, the bass thumping across the distance.

"How many songs is he doing?" Lexi asked.

Liam frowned. Did she sound irritated? Or put out? Lexi didn't seem happy about the concert. Maybe it was because it cut into her tips? While Liam wasn't into bubblegum pop music, the guy singing wasn't terrible. He was actually pretty good. Liam had heard far worse.

"I don't know how long. How many songs is a full set? Do you want me to text Eva and ask?" He reached into his pocket for his phone and unlocked his screen and began typing. "She'll know."

"No. That's okay. I just wondered." Lexi lifted a glass of water and sipped.

"Well, too late." Liam's phone pinged. "Eva says he's singing for about forty-five minutes." His phone pinged again, and he held the text message out so that she could read what Eva had sent. Damon Stevener is the bride's favorite performer so the groom went all in to make her happy.

"How nice," Lexi said.

Liam smoothed the frown that tried to form. She'd sounded bitter, and the disgust crossing her face—an expression that had appeared almost like a fast trick of the light—hadn't fooled him. The fact Damon Stevener was performing at the Chateau bothered her for some reason. "What's nice? Because you don't seem like you're pleased. Are you referring to the groom's grand gesture or the musician? Damon sounds okay and most women would find the gesture pretty romantic."

Lexi gave a small shrug, as if trying to downplay her earlier reaction. "I just agree with your earlier assessment. The money could have done a load of good elsewhere. And you're right in that he's just okay. Nothing exceptional. Just the latest pop star."

Liam sensed there was far more to the story. Lexi didn't have a good poker face. "You don't like him?"

"I didn't say that. Pop stars are a dime a dozen. Only as good as their latest hit."

"And that's all your disgruntlement is? Besides the waste of money? Because you sound cynical."

"Maybe I am." Grabbing a used glass, Lexi turned. The motion gave him a view of her profile as she set the glass in the washing rack. "It doesn't matter. I'm gossiping and I don't like gossip."

"Yeah, it can be vicious. But you sound like you know about music."

"It was something that interested me for a while. And it's always on social media. You know those reels that pop up in your Instagram feed? Mine used to be all celebrities, those two brothers who play pro football, and cute cat videos before I stopped caring about social media. I probably should just delete my account. I rarely get on anyway. When I do, all I watch is kitten videos."

"Do you have a pet?" He'd never been home long enough

to have one. He and Anya had always been traveling some-where.

Lexi leaned against the back table. "I did, but my cat Wiggy died at eighteen just a few years back."

"I'm sorry." He genuinely was.

She shrugged off the loss. "It's okay. It seemed to start a bit of a bad luck streak, but hopefully I'm on the upside. And I love animals. That was one reason I didn't have any issues renting a room from a veterinarian. She's always fostering something. Currently we have a litter of kittens that are running amok. And that's in addition to her two cats who are also adorable. There was a rabbit, but that only stayed for a month."

"That's quite the menagerie. Would you say cats are better than dogs?" He liked talking to her and wanted to prolong the conversation.

"They are much easier to take care of," Lexi replied.

She finally turned toward him, smiling as he chuckled. "True. And what a totally politically neutral answer. But that's it? No more to say? You won't offend me if you go on a dogs versus cats diatribe."

Lexi arched a brow. "My mother didn't raise a fool." For a moment she smiled, and then her face clouded, as if talking about her mother had brought up a bad memory. Liam wanted to press, but more than anything, he wanted to see her smile again. They hadn't talked since that day in the conference room, and he wanted to know what made her tick. His desire for her hadn't abated. Put the gorgeous brunette in a floral dress versus Lexi in her Chateau uni-form of a vest, long sleeve white shirt and black pants and Liam would choose Lexi every time. "So what do you think about pineapple on pizza?"

A dubious M formed between her eyebrows before her face twisted into disbelief at his question. "What a wild question to ask. Heck no. Gross. No anchovies either. And where did that question come from?"

"I figured we'd play the twenty-question game or something. Get to know each other. That's allowed, isn't it?" Before she protested, he added, "We sort of missed that part, and if it's okay with you, I'd like to at least be friends. Like you are with Alvin." He sipped some of his own water, trying to wet a throat parched by desire.

She remained skeptical. "Alvin and I don't have our history."

He poured more water into his glass. "You know what I mean. We went from zero to sixty in two-point-nine seconds."

She could arch her brow like that daily and he wouldn't mind. "That seems oddly specific."

He couldn't help but grin. "It's how fast my brother Michael's Corvette goes. I drove it once out on a track and he yelled the entire way. It's his baby. I'm surprised he hasn't already brought the Vette to Beaumont. Or bought a second one to use here."

"And weren't you just saying that the concert seemed overkill and a waste of money?" Lexi loosened her arms. "A vehicle moves you from point A to point B. I've never seen the point in having something that expensive."

"Well, if Michael wasn't such a big donor to my foundation, and if he didn't do carbon offsets, I'd give him tons of grief. And for the record, I do not own a sports car."

"I don't know you well enough to know if you'd be the type. But you did stay at the inn instead of here the night of the gala, so you'd probably find that type of car impractical."

"Exactly. That's why I have a Subaru. See, you already know me. And I'd like to get to know you better. We have to work together, and you're one of the few people I know in town who doesn't want something from me. I'd like us to be friends. I thought that maybe we should slow things down this round. Perhaps it won't be so awkward between us if we do?"

"It's already awkward," Lexi admitted. She shifted her weight, the solid black tennis shoes moving slightly.

"It doesn't have to be," Liam said.

Lexi shook her head, which loosened a strand of hair. She shoved it behind her left ear. "It always will be, at least on my end. I think of that night a lot. Dream about it, actually. Not sure why I'm telling you this, because it gives you a sort of power over me, but it's the truth. That night I acted totally out of character. Broke my rules. I wasn't supposed to see you again. Then here you are, like a curse of fate. And I want more. But I can't risk it."

"What if I tell you I feel the same? That I still want you?"

She blinked several times. "I'd say we might have an HR problem as much as we wish otherwise." Then she spoke with even more care, as if each word mattered. Liam knew whatever she said next, she mattered to him. Her smile turned wistful. "Fate is unfair, you know? But I'm used to denying myself. It's better this way." She paused and tilted her head. Listened. "Sounds like he's wrapping up. This is usually his encore song."

Still trying to process what she'd said about denying herself, Liam zeroed in on the fact she knew Damon's encore number. "So you've heard him in concert? Thought you didn't know much about him."

Her eyes widened, and she inclined her head, acknowledging the fact she'd left that out. But she offered nothing further in explanation as a twentysomething couple approached the bar.

"See, we beat the line," the guy told his date. Liam noted the man's date didn't look too thrilled to have been dragged away. Her lips puckered, and she kept looking back over her shoulder toward the concert.

Liam watched as Lexi served both of them before the couple began making their way back to the show. If the show was ending, that meant Alvin would return soon, and when he did, Liam would have no real reason to stay, even if he did want to linger and hang out with Lexi. He'd meant what he said. He wanted to get to know her, learn what made her tick in areas outside the bedroom.

"Do you think we can talk more when your shift is over?" he asked as another couple walked off after grabbing a drink. "We could go get something to eat. Have a purely platonic friend date. I'd like that very much. Please say yes." He held his breath as he waited for her answer. It never came for the crowd began cheering wildly, meaning the show was over. Already Liam could see Alvin rushing back.

"Mr. Clayton." Alvin gasped, slightly out of breath from the speed walk. Alvin slid behind the bar. "I'm sorry, sir, I…"

"It's fine," Liam reassured him. "Lexi had everything under control. She did a great job."

"But, sir, you shouldn't be working." Alvin began rearranging glasses.

"No worries. I volunteered. I'm back here because I wanted to see things from this side of the table. I poured a few drinks and asked Lexi to give me some feedback. This

helped me get a good perspective of how things are working, which is fantastic. You're a good supervisor, Alvin, so
relax. In fact, here comes a crowd, so let me get out of your
way so you and Lexi can do what you do best."

Liam stepped out from behind the bar, but he didn't
move far. He stood on the periphery, his gaze watching
Lexi. She had a natural way about her as she chatted with
wedding guests. She knew how to charm when needed.
How to offer a light smile, or a serious one when required.
With the wedding band on a break, a DJ played music and
a flash of white alerted Liam to the approaching wedding
party. The bride had her arm linked through her groom's,
but as she walked, she spoke with the man on her right.

This must be Damon What's-his-name, the famous
singer, Liam realized. Damon wore a bright blue suit and
an open neck white shirt. When they reached the bar, the
guy made a beeline for Lexi's side of the bar. Liam started
forward, but paused as Eva approached. "Are you wanting to meet him? I can introduce you." Eva fanned herself
with her hand. "I danced the entire time. He's even cuter
up close, you know? My ex was so jealous. Liam, are you
listening to me?"

"What? No. Sorry. What were you saying?" Liam turned
to his sister.

She shot him an exaggerated eye roll. "I asked if you
wanted to meet him."

What Liam wanted was for the guy to get away from
Lexi. Was Damon flirting with her? He seemed overly
friendly. He'd leaned forward, which made Lexi step back.
She appeared uncomfortable. Her shoulders had stiffened.
Her movements had become jerky. No one in the wedding
party noticed, but Liam did. The smile she gave didn't reach

her eyes, and she avoided eye contact if possible. Liam knew he didn't have the right to be possessive or jealous, but he did have a right to make an employee feel safe. He turned to his sister. "Sure. Why not? Introduce me to the man of the hour."

"You'll also get to meet my friends." Eva led him over to the group clustered around Lexi's end of the bar. Blocked, the other guests queued in front of Alvin. Eva slid into the group, dragging Liam behind her. "Liam, this is the new Mr. and Mrs. Johnson. Alec and Clarissa, meet my plus-one, my brother Liam."

"Hey man, great to meet you. Great place you have here." Alec pushed his glasses back onto his nose before shaking Liam's hand. "We've had the best time."

"I'm glad," Liam said noncommittally, his full attention on Lexi. He caught her gaze, and she gave him a shaky smile before serving someone who'd stepped into the gap.

The bride turned and immediately drew Liam into a hug. "Liam! It's been too long! So good to see you! Did you meet Damon?" The bride placed her hand on the singer's arm. When he turned and extended his arm, Liam shook the shorter man's hand with more force and for a second longer than necessary.

"Nice to meet you," Damon said, shaking his fingers once Liam had freed them. "Nice grip you got there."

"Comes from climbing mountains." Liam watched as Lexi switched sides with Alvin.

Damon appeared impressed. "Really? You free solo?"

Now that Lexi had moved away, Liam met the man's gaze. "Not as much as I did when I was younger."

"Liam's summited some of the world's highest peaks, but he's too modest to brag about it," Eva told Damon. She looped her arm through the singer's. "Now that you've got your drink, we're all going back to the dance floor. You are partying with us, tonight, right? Because I want to see what moves you have, and I do happen to know that you have a room here."

His sister was the ultimate flirt, but she wasn't a one-night-stand type, so Liam wasn't worried about Eva. She'd handle herself and Damon with no issues. What Liam worried about was how often Damon's gaze strayed to Lexi as the group left. Every one of Liam's radars chimed that something was wrong, and he'd long ago learned to always trust his gut. Out on the mountain, a hiker knew it was imperative to read Mother Nature's signals. Being in tune to those of his traveling companions also mattered. He'd been in several situations where hikers thought they were fine, only to have a pulse oximeter show that they had AMS, or acute mountain sickness. The symptoms started so mild that many hikers dismissed them, a dangerous mistake.

So yes, he might be acting overprotective, but he couldn't let this situation slide until he knew exactly what was going on. Which meant he waited until another lull, which came once the wedding band began playing again. "More water?" Lexi asked as he approached.

Liam failed to keep the hint of jealousy from his tone. "What is going on between you and Damon?" Lexi's eyes widened. He'd shocked her. "Sorry that seemed harsh."

"I don't know what you mean."

She tried to cover with a shake of her head, but Liam pressed forward. He'd ignored the signs with Anya. He'd vowed not to do it again.

"It's obvious you know him, and I don't mean in that you went to a concert way. I may be antisocial, but I'm a people watcher. I'm an expert at reading body language. He made you uncomfortable when he approached, and you became even more upset when he flirted, which is why you and Alvin switched places. Spill. I can handle whatever truth you throw at me."

Lexi's face blanched. "I grew up in the same neighborhood as he did, that's all. I knew him when he was just Billy. Back when we were both children with big dreams and stars in our eyes. Then he became a big star and we—"

The wedding planner raced up and interrupted them. Her chest heaved from the exertion. "Can someone bring two bottles of champagne and one bottle of red wine to the wedding party?" As quickly as she'd arrived, the planner disappeared.

"I got it," Lexi told Alvin, who was in the middle of mixing a cocktail.

"I can do it," Liam offered. Damon was with the wedding party, and Liam didn't like the idea of her having to face him again.

Lexi shook her head and scowled. "No, Mr. Clayton, I will do it. It's my job."

Well, that told him. Liam gestured his surrender and watched Lexi grab two bottles of champagne from the ice. Once balanced, she fisted a bottle of red wine. Because they were waiting for clean glassware, Alvin popped some plastic cups onto the top of the wine, and when Lexi brushed by Liam, she accidentally bumped him.

"Let me take one of those bottles," he offered.

To his chagrin, she cold-shouldered him and walked faster. He lengthened his stride to keep pace. They reached the dance floor, and realizing he was chasing her like a rejected, bad boyfriend, Liam held back as Lexi jostled her way through the undulating, gyrating crowd.

The wedding band singer was in the middle of the dance floor, wireless mic clutched in his hand. Everyone around him belted out the lyrics into the mic. Her path blocked, Lexi froze. Trapped on the dance floor amid the revelers, she was unable to reach the head table, and she was becoming surrounded by more and more of the ever-growing crowd. Liam's gut instinct blared another red alert, and he thought to hell with the optics and began to push his way through. He got close enough to read the words on Damon's lips. "Hey Lexi, sing," Damon called.

Following Damon's directive, the wedding band's singer moved closer to Lexi, Damon fast on his heels. "You know the words," Damon called.

She did? Liam absorbed that but didn't slow, instead shoving someone out of the way. Did no one else see that Lexi's face had paled? Or that her body trembled as if she stood on a tilting platform? She appeared as fearful as a rabbit trapped by a pack of wolves. The champagne bottles sweated water droplets, which meant the open necks covered with condensation had to be slippery in her hand. The plastic cups shook, dancing on the top of the red wine. People sang along and jumped up and down, oblivious to Lexi's growing discomfort.

"Come on, Lexi. You know you want to," Damon cajoled. Liam was close enough to hear the words above the din. Like that moment on Everest when the ground began to groan and shake, the world shrunk to a pinpoint. Everyone around her blurred, but he could see her clearly. Lexi shook her head, the ponytail she wore swishing from side to side like an erratic metronome or an agitated racehorse.

Liam knew what came next. Uncaring how he appeared, he pushed someone dancing badly out of the way, ignoring the person's indignant "Hey! What the heck, man!"

Mere seconds became extreme slow motion as Lexi lost her grip on the three bottles she attempted to balance. Liam shoved his way through the revelers, reaching Lexi as the bottles fell. Champagne and wine flew from open necks as the bottles crashed to the terrace. Glass fractured, skittering under stiletto heels and leather dress shoes. Champagne and wine splattered outward and upward, changing the crowd's singing into dismayed shrieks as the red and white liquids hit not only the bride's dress, but also her mother's and anyone else in the impact zone.

People rushed away, creating more chaos. Lexi's mouth formed a wide O, and her hand moved upward to her throat. She stared at the mess at her feet, and then her shocked, panicked gaze caught Liam's. "Lexi!" He sidestepped someone rushing away and moved forward.

"Liam?" Eva called, but Liam ignored his sister as he darted forward. He had to be in time, for Lexi's eyes had rolled back in her head and she began to crumple. Ignoring the glass crunching under his dress shoes and determined to protect her from it, Liam threw out his arms and managed to catch her before she hit the ground. He pressed Lexi's stiff figure to his chest, holding her aloft as her feet slightly dangled. Wide eyes stared at him. Her mouth tried to work but no letters formed.

"Is she okay?" Damon appeared, with Eva behind him.

"Liam, what's going on?" Eva asked.

"Call 911," Liam told his sister. "Lexi, are you okay?"

"I'm fi…" Lexi managed to say, but the words faded and faltered as she fainted.

As her body went lax, Liam moved his arms to cradle Lexi and he lifted her high. "Move," Liam shouted as he rushed her past his confused sister and other wedding guests. Already the efficient Chateau servers had arrived to clean the terrace, and the crowd circled back, ready to move on from the momentary drama. The band started a new tune, and as he went by, Liam knocked a phone out of some guy's hand. No one needed to film this. Knowing a fast way into the hotel, he carried Lexi down a service path and out of sight. But before the door closed behind them, he paused and turned to the singer—Damon, Liam remembered his name—who trailed behind. "Look, I don't know who you are, but I got this. Go back to the party."

"But I…" the man began.

Liam shot him a cutting glance. "Don't care. My hotel and you're not welcome in this part of it." Liam swiped through and found a service elevator. He had a key to Eva's suite, and once inside, he set Lexi on the couch and elevated her legs onto a pillow. He loosened the knot and removed the green-and-blue tie from her neck before undoing the top two buttons of a damp white shirt that was now covered with red wine and champagne splotches.

Eva entered the suite a minute or two later. She was thankfully alone because Liam didn't want to deal with Damon again. "Paramedics are three minutes out."

"Great. Let's get her out of those wet clothes. She's close enough to your size that she should fit in one of your T-shirts and some yoga pants. Get them and also a cool damp cloth." He didn't want to leave Lexi or lift his fingers from her wrist.

Eva checked her phone. "Gate says the paramedics arrived. Valet is watching for them. How's she doing?"

"I don't know. But her pulse is starting to come down. I think she had a panic attack." Liam checked her pulse again, which was still erratic but stronger. Her chest rose and fell with air. Anya, when rescuers had found her, hadn't shown any signs of life. He'd taken comfort in the fact they said she'd died instantly. He'd been unable to help Anya, but he wouldn't fail Lexi. He began to strip off the uniform, starting with the wet tennis shoes. "She needs shoes too!" he called.

Eva brought back a stack of clothes and a pair of flats. She hovered as Liam stripped Lexi to her bra and underwear. He worked Lexi's limp arms into the sweatshirt and had Eva help him with the pants.

"Liam, who is she to you?" his sister demanded as she slid a pair of designer flats onto Lexi's feet. Liam noted the shoes were a little tight, but they'd have to do. Lexi groaned once, but didn't stir.

"She's…" The paramedics' arrival kept him from telling Eva that Lexi was a woman who'd touched him in ways he'd thought long dead. That she was more beautiful than any other woman at the party. That he'd found himself jealous, worried and angry at the scene on the dance floor, and all at the same time.

"Liam…" Eva's words traveled on a sigh.

He stood to follow the stretcher. "We'll talk later. Gotta go. Just do me a favor. Make sure none of this debacle reaches social media. That's the last thing I need."

"Liam!" But determined to accompany the ambulance, he was already out the door.

Eva stared at the closed door. What had her brother gotten himself into? Clearly something. As for social media, they'd established a media blackout and blocked the Wi-Fi during the wedding. But that had lifted during the concert and reception. Eva would see what she could do, but Liam had to be realistic. If someone had recorded Liam's gallant gesture, most likely it would make social media. Eva could do damage control, but she couldn't make his actions totally disappear any more than she'd been able to stop Veronica from livestreaming her breakup with Edmund.

Thankfully Veronica was gone and Edmund and Lana were somewhere in Australia. Or was it New Zealand? Did it matter as long as they were happy? Eva unzipped her dress, which had taken a direct hit of red wine. She changed into her after-party outfit early and then began to make her way to the bridal suite. Her phone pinged, and she read the message from the valet, who let her know that Liam had retrieved his car and was headed to Beaumont General.

Eva knocked and then used her master key to enter Clarissa's suite.

"How is the girl? Your employee, right?" her friend asked. Clarissa still stood in a soaked wedding gown, her bare feet poking out from underneath. She clutched a bottle of water. "People told me she fainted."

"She did," Eva confirmed. "She's on her way to the hospital now. Liam thinks she had a panic attack and she'll be fine."

"Please keep me posted."

"Of course I will. Here let me help you with that," Eva told Clarissa, wondering where the other bridesmaids were. Had they also decided to change? Probably. Eva began unbuttoning the back of the wedding gown. Soon she had Clarissa in her second bridal gown, the one Clarissa should have already changed into as the dress had been designed specifically for dancing at the reception. "The real question is, how's your mom? I'm surprised she wasn't already in here."

"Oh, she's probably still trying to get wine off her. She's wet and angry, but she'll get over it. She'd better anyway." Clarissa surveyed herself in the floor-length mirror. She giggled. "I shouldn't laugh, but did you see my mom's face? That'll be a story in itself for the future. I thought she'd pass out."

"She did look apoplectic."

"That's an understatement. You know, there's always drama at weddings, but I certainly didn't expect this. Maybe some hookups, but not some server passing out. Your brother seemed pretty intent as he carried her away."

"Liam's always been the rescuer. Small animals. People. That's why he runs all those charities and our family's foundation." Eva wasn't going to speculate until she heard from her brother.

"Well, other VPs wouldn't be so caring. He's a good one, your brother. I hope he finds the right person. So tragic what happened with Anya."

"I know. Terrible. But enough on that. Can you believe Alec had Damon Stevener come play just for you? You got a good one too."

"I did, didn't I?" Clarissa smiled dreamily.

Eva plucked the stained wedding dress from a nearby chair and hung it up. "We will, of course, pay for all the cleaning and damages to the dresses. You look gorgeous. Are you ready to go back down?"

"I am. And as for the dry cleaning I don't really care, but you know my mom will appreciate that gesture. I guess we should go check on her. Thankfully nothing got in anyone's hair, at least I don't think so. Speaking of Damon?" Clarissa waggled her eyebrows.

"Oh, no," Eva said. In fact, thinking back on it, she had noticed the singer had been really into the server. "Damon seems nice, but I'm just having fun and flirting in an attempt to make my ex jealous, that's all. Besides, he kept pressuring that poor girl to sing. That didn't seem nice."

"I wonder why he did that? Good thing Liam was there," Clarissa said. "Your brother is the best."

"Yeah, good thing." Eva followed Clarissa from the suite, her brain trying to link the events. Why had Liam been there? Why had he been around Lexi? And why had Damon been pressuring Lexi to sing? If there was one thing Eva knew how to sniff out, it was a backstory. There was a narrative here, and she planned to get to the bottom of it. She withdrew her phone and pulled up a search engine. She'd do whatever it took.

Chapter Seven

Something was beeping. That meant she needed to get up. Wait. The *beep-beep-beep* wasn't from Lexi's alarm clock. Instead, as an annoyingly long *b-e-e-p* sounded, the noise became Lexi's first indication something wasn't right. Why did her left arm hurt? Why couldn't she open her eyes? The lids seemed crusted together. Same for her lips, as if someone had glued her mouth shut. The machine beeped faster.

"Hey, there you are. It's okay. Shh. Drink this." Even in the dark haze, Lexi recognized Liam's voice. But why was he here in her bedroom? She managed to pry her lips open and felt a flexible straw slide inside. She sucked and soon cool water slid over her tongue as she took a much-needed sip. "Uh."

Lexi felt the straw slipping away. Liam's voice came through the blackness again. "You gave me quite the scare. Damn it. Where's that call button?"

"I'm fine." Lexi's words came out on a soft gasp, as if she'd used all the air in her lungs to expel them.

I'm fine. That's what she'd been trying to say after she'd fallen. She remembered Damon shoving a microphone in her face. Wait, was Damon here, too? Had he spilled her secret that she was Melynda? He had been trying to make her sing. The vise on her arm tightened again. "I'm fine." Even though she wasn't, the words sounded stronger. That was good, right?

"You're far from fine, and the doctor said you can't be agitated. Take another sip. Come on, do it. Let me take care of you and do what I say. The doctor says you're dehydrated, so drink."

The straw slipped inside her lips again, the water soothing a throat as dry as the Sahara. She scrunched her face, wrinkled her nose and forced her eyes open, only to blink rapid-fire as overhead fluorescent lights assaulted still-blurry vision. She screwed her eyes closed again, then opened her lids more slowly, the movement bringing into focus a sterile room filled with medical machines. The pain in her arm was an IV needle wrapped with a clear bandage to keep the line in place. The squeezing came from the blood pressure cuff. She had sticky monitors on her chest, wire connectors dangling under the blue cotton gown. This wasn't the Chateau, or her bedroom, but a hospital. Liam was the only one in the room.

"It's okay. Calm. Shh. No panicking," Liam soothed.

He ran a hand on her forehead, and Lexi worked to control her heart rate. She'd been in hospitals before, twice after passing out from a lack of nutrition. Usually after an IV cocktail, her father would hush it all up and she'd go home. "What happened? Were things really this bad that I had to come here?"

"You were out about five minutes before you came to the first time, so yes." Liam leaned toward her and gave her another sip of water. He'd lost the suit coat from the wedding reception, and the top buttons of his dress shirt were undone. His gaze reflected fear and relief. "The paramedics brought you to Beaumont General. It was closest, and it's also one of the best in the region. I followed the ambulance. I wasn't letting you be here alone when you came to."

"Okay." That sounded like a nice thing to do, but her cynical nature reared its head, reminding her that she was a Clayton employee. And she'd... Oh no. The horror returned and Lexi closed her eyes. Let the blackness come as the memory returned like watching a movie stuck on a loop. Damon had been shoving a microphone in her face and she'd lost her grip on the bottles and... "I ruined the wedding. Embarrassed everyone. People were having fun and I dropped the wine."

"Shh. None of that is important. Take another drink." Liam brought the bent straw to her lips and she sucked in another sip. "Now it's my turn to tell you everything is fine. You gave us quite a scare and your health is what really matters. The party went on after we left. Eva texted me. The bride put on her reception gown, the wedding party dressed in their after-party clothes and they went right back to celebrating. No harm. No foul."

That didn't make it better, and as the rest of the night flooded back, Lexi squeezed her eyes shut again. "I remember some of the ride here. We were in a suite when paramedics came."

"Right. I caught you and took you to Eva's room. Eva and I changed you into what you're wearing. You woke up briefly when the paramedics got to the suite. Once we arrived and the doctors checked you over, you fell asleep. The doctor said that was okay since the CT didn't show a concussion. Do you remember the CT scan?"

"Yes. No. Maybe." Having her eyes closed against the embarrassing memory allowed Lexi to hear the concern infused into Liam's baritone, his tone having a musical symmetry of soothing and persuasive power. The man was a dangerous mix. A machine beeped a fast staccato as another memory flooded back. When she'd dropped the wine bottles, the liquor had splashed... Lexi's eyes flew open. "The bride's dress!"

"Don't worry about it. Clarissa is pretty laid-back. She had another dress she should have been wearing so she changed into that. You gave her a story to tell, that's all. Nothing to stress over."

Humiliation flooded Lexi. How many times had she been told she'd been too clumsy? Too awkward? Forced to practice the dance steps or her lines for hours? At least her humiliation hadn't been public. Her eyes flew open. "It'll be all over the internet! I can't believe that happened. I ruined the wedding."

Liam gripped her hand. "No, you didn't. And I scooped you up so quickly I doubt anyone had time to get their phones out. Besides, if things hit the socials, Eva will put a damage control plan into place. What happened? Do you remember why you fainted?"

Lexi had panicked because of Damon and his insistence that she sing. "Not really."

"I think you had a panic attack."

Liam had mad observation skills, Lexi realized. Time to get him off this train of thought. "Thank you for getting me out of there. You carried me?"

"I did." A knock sounded and the heavy door to the hospital room pushed open. Liam gave Lexi's hand a squeeze. "Here's the doctor."

"Hey there, Lexi," the doctor greeted as he and an emergency room nurse entered. The doctor came over to Lexi's bed on the side Liam wasn't. "I'm Dr. McMenamy. How are you feeling now?"

Lexi tried to return his smile but winced instead. "Better. I made quite a mess of things when I fainted."

Dr. McMenamy nodded sagely. "Fainting's never good, but messes can be cleaned up. What concerns me is why you fainted, so we've been running some additional tests while you took a nap. We took the blood when we put in your IV. Have you been getting enough sleep lately?"

"Enough." Not necessarily a lie.

"What about food? Have you been eating?"

Surely he couldn't know her medical history. Lexi tried to nod her head but found it took too much energy. She settled for saying, "Yes. I don't know what happened."

The nurse busied herself with checking Lexi's vitals, and Lexi shifted to give her better access. The blood pressure cuff squeezed again, and the nurse rubbed the silver ends of a thermometer over Lexi's forehead.

"Tell me, how have you been feeling lately? Before you fainted," the doctor said.

Lexi couldn't get a read on him, so the panicky feeling returned. "I've had some stomach sickness. But there's been this virus going through the Chateau employees, so I figured I'd caught that."

"Those viruses can be potent, but I don't believe that's your issue, which is a good thing. The virus can knock you down for a while. Then again..."

Fear raced through Lexi's veins as Dr. McMenamy paused. Oh no. Please no, Lexi thought. The doctor was getting ready to drop a bombshell. He knew her secrets.

"I'm pleased to see that your vitals are checking out in the normal range. Mr. Clayton thought you'd had a panic attack, and the symptoms described indicated that clearly could have happened. However..." Dr. McMenamy paused yet again, this time to glance at Liam and then back at Lexi. "Would you like to speak privately? Or is it okay that Mr. Clayton's here? Because he can leave. No one's allowed to access your medical diagnosis but you. No employers or boyfriends."

On cue, Liam stood.

"He's not my..." But Lexi couldn't get the word *boyfriend* out. If the doctor said what she thought he was going to say next, then Liam deserved to hear. "Go ahead. He can stay. Tell me what's wrong with me."

"Your pregnancy test came back positive. I'm hoping this is happy news."

Since the floor wouldn't swallow her whole, Lexi closed her eyes briefly. And there it was. The truth she would have found out for herself on Monday once she'd been to the store and purchased a test. A truth she'd been avoiding, maybe because some deep, needy part of her didn't want to know. Perhaps she'd wanted to make sure her pregnancy was already too far along for her to have any other option but to carry it to term. Lexi supported a woman's right to choose, and when the thought had first crossed her mind that she might be having Liam's baby, she knew she'd choose to have the child. The child would give her someone to love and nurture, even if having a baby upended her college and career plans. Her subconscious, like her health, was constantly messed up. What would her therapist say about her need to be loved? Lexi wouldn't know—she'd stopped seeing him since she'd moved to Beaumont.

"Thank you for letting me know," Lexi told the doctor. "Of course it's welcome news."

As the doctor relaxed, Lexi felt Liam stiffen. "You're pregnant? How far along?"

"I'm about ten weeks," Lexi said before the doctor could speak. She dared not meet Liam's gaze. "But I didn't think I was pregnant since my cycles have always been irregular. I was going to take a test Monday to confirm."

The doctor took that information in stride. "Being pregnant is probably the biggest reason you fainted. Being in that crush of people, and given the outside temperature, you became overheated and overwhelmed. Your body couldn't handle the strain. To help, I'll be starting you on prenatal vitamins, iron supplements, and before you leave, I'm going to recommend a good ob-gyn and make sure you're on her schedule. What I'd like to do next is order a sonogram. I expect you want to take a look, right?" The doctor put a gentle pressure on Lexi's arm as she struggled to sit up. "Just lie back and relax. We'll see how big it's gotten. Make sure everything is as it should be. Then we'll chat again about our next steps."

"You're pregnant," Liam said as the medical team left the room.

"Looks like it."

A fresh-faced transport technician entering the room saved Lexi from having to say any more. "They're ready for you, Miss Henderson." The man unlocked the wheels on her bed and pushed her from the room. Thankfully Liam didn't ask to accompany her to radiology. She wouldn't have known how to handle that.

"Hello, Lexi." A midthirties female sonographer beamed a warm smile that made Lexi instantly more comfortable. The sonographer undid some buttons on Lexi's hospital gown and squirted some warm gel on her stomach. "Let's take a look, shall we?"

A wand rubbed over Lexi's stomach, the light pressure not uncomfortable. On the monitor, the dark screen changed and Lexi saw a big black bubble appeared. "That's your uterus," the sonographer said. In the middle of that bubble, some white shapes formed. "Huh," the woman said.

"What's wrong?" Lexi craned her neck so she could see better, not that she could really understand what she saw.

"Nothing's wrong. Everything actually looks great. Give me a minute," the sonographer said. "Yep. Confirmed. Okay, take a look. You've got a great view of your fetuses."

Had Lexi heard the sonographer correctly? She craned her head, this time starting to make out the shapes. "Did you add an *s*? Like, as in plural?"

The woman smiled as she typed on the keyboard with her left hand, using her free hand to move the ultrasound wand again. "Yes. Two. Here's the first one, and here's the second. You're having twins."

Twins. Not one baby, but two. Lexi's eyes widened and her lips quivered as she looked at the images. "Twins."

"Yes. Twins." The sonographer pointed. "You can see here they are sharing one placenta but there are two sacs. That's a good thing. It's known as monochorionic-diamniotic or mono-di. I have a feeling the doctor is going to tell you that this explains why you're a lot weaker than you should be, why your morning sickness hasn't yet abated and why you fainted."

Lexi inhaled a breath and tried to absorb the implications. "Two babies."

"Yes. Identical twins," the sonographer confirmed. She

gave Lexi a friendly smile. "The fertilized egg split between day four to eight. Congratulations are in order, I hope?"

"Surprising as I didn't even think I was pregnant," Lexi said. Tears began to form as shock mixed with joy. "Well, this is going to be a big change. Twins."

The sonographer gave her a facial tissue and Lexi dabbed her eyes. "The radiologist will review, as will your ob-gyn, but I'm not seeing anything to cause worry with this multiple pregnancy. Everything appears perfectly normal."

But Lexi knew that any pregnancy by nature was high risk, with multiples even more so. Liam waited in the ER exam room, and immediately concerned, he rose. "You've been crying. What's wrong?"

She and Liam were the only two in the room, and Lexi felt the tears flow again as she handed him the printout the sonographer had given her. "We're having twins."

His jaw dropped. "Twins?"

"I'm sorry. You didn't ask for this. I promise you I can handle it." She'd sing Damon's song. Do another album with her ex if needed. She dabbed her eyes with the tissue. She would get through this. "We had a one-night stand. You don't have to be involved. This isn't your problem."

"What type of man do you think I am? I'm going to be very involved. I don't shirk my responsibilities They're mine."

The way Liam said the statement came across as an assertion of possession and not as if he needed clarification. She also heard the awe in his voice. Part of her leaped with joy, but part of her felt the panic returning as the implications set in.

"You shouldn't have to deal with this if you don't want

to," Lexi protested. "Children are lifelong commitments. Especially as I didn't mean for this to happen."

"Neither of us meant for this to happen, but it has." Liam paced slightly and dragged his hands through his hair. "That means we're in this together. They're mine, Lexi, and I want to be their dad. Even if that means a lifetime. You and I, we're in this together. I will be involved."

The extreme relief she felt that he wouldn't abandon her should have soothed, but instead Lexi felt more panic. The machine began to beep faster as her heart rate increased. "You don't have to do anything. I'm not trying to trap you. I can afford it. I just have to move things around." And call Damon. He wanted her to sing? She'd demand her terms.

Liam's next words shocked her. "I won't lose anyone else. Not you. Not my children."

The force of Liam's declaration made Lexi's eyes widen and her tears dry. Liam meant his girlfriend, the one who'd died. Guilt plagued her. She couldn't take his children away, not when he'd already lost the woman he'd loved. Liam gentled his tone. "We'll talk more tomorrow. For tonight, let's get you home once the doctor gives the okay. You're pregnant, you fainted, and you need your rest. I'm sure sleeping in your own bed will feel fantastic."

The doctor returned to face Lexi and Liam. "I've reviewed the sonogram. Obviously carrying multiples changes things. The first thing you need is to visit with the ob-gyn next week. They'll have the final say, but it's common practice to deliver twins by C-section no later than thirty-seven weeks. Your doctor will monitor you frequently, most likely every two weeks instead of monthly. Sex is fine. The number one thing I want you to do, though, to ensure a healthy pregnancy, is avoid stress. No stress. None. Got it? No more panic attacks that make you faint. Also, while you aren't confined to bed, you might be later. Avoid heavy lifting. Your ob-gyn will give you other instructions. And again, let me repeat it, no stress."

No stress? That was going to be impossible, Lexi thought. She was having Liam's babies. Panic clawed and she fought it back. She would be forever tied to him. But really, would that be so bad? He'd rescued her. He'd carried her to the suite. Come with her to the hospital. He wasn't Damon, who thought only of himself. He was Liam, who thought of others and who'd made love to her with a ferocity and tenderness that had made that night one of the best of her life. And now she'd always remember it. Her hand naturally found her flat stomach.

"We'll take care of making sure she's stress-free," Liam was telling the doctor. "And she'll be at that appointment this week."

Lifting her head, Lexi wanted to tell the two men that she was right here, and that she would be in charge of the decision-making. During her entire career as Melynda, she'd had no agency, no choices. But as she rubbed her stomach, the words didn't seem to matter. She was too tired and overwhelmed to protest. She'd fight the point with Liam later, when she had more energy and after she got control of the anxiety that ran through her veins like the contents of the IV drip. Besides, the doctor seemed pleased with Liam's answer.

"It's been nice meeting you, Lexi," Dr. McMenamy said. "I'll send in the nurse to get you unhooked and have them get your discharge papers so you can go home."

"I'll take you," Liam said. "My car is here. I'll go get it."

He followed the doctor out and Lexi leaned back and shut

her eyes. What was that line? Something about tomorrow being another day? Even though Lexi knew nothing would ever be the same again, she was going home. The sooner she was safe in her bedroom, the sooner she could figure out what to do next. "Don't worry," she whispered to her babies. "We got this."

It was a quarter past midnight when Liam finally returned to his house on Third Street. He'd driven Lexi home and found himself frustrated when she'd shut the front door in his face with a "My roommate is sleeping. We'll talk tomorrow."

He hadn't planned on staying, but he had wanted to make sure she'd gotten safely to bed. He unlocked his front door and stepped inside to discover his sister waiting for him. Eva flipped off the 70-inch television, took one look at him and demanded, "What the hell is going on?"

He ran a hand through sticky hair. "Lexi is pregnant with twins. And before you say it, yes, they're mine."

Eva was across the room in a shot and drawing him into her arms. He nestled his head into her shoulder for a second until she said, "Oh, Liam. What did you do?"

He released her and dropped onto the couch. Kicked his feet onto the coffee table. "I had sex with her obviously. The night of the gala. A one-night stand where she was Lexi, I was Liam, and I wasn't her boss. First time since Anya. She's the first one who tempted me, and we had this connection. Obviously the condoms didn't work as she's ten weeks along. I'm going over to her house tomorrow morning to talk and figure things out. I saw the sonogram, Eva. Twins." He planted his feet on the ground and put his head in his hands. "I can't believe this."

Eva gave a shake of her head as she sat next to him. "Nothing's infallible. Accidents happen."

"You don't think I know that?" Liam shot back, thinking of Anya.

Eva winced. "Sorry. Wrong choice of words. Bad choice. I stuck my foot in that. But whatever the reason, you're going to be a dad, Liam. You've always wanted kids. Heck, I figured Michael would be the one to have an oops, not you."

"Well, it's me. Twice now."

Eva winced again. "Fate's clearly giving you some sort of karmic do-over. You're going to be involved, aren't you?"

"I told her as much."

"Good. And you know Mom is going to freak. She's always wanted grandchildren, even if not like this. You know she's flying in tomorrow, right?" Eva patted his arm. "Liam?"

"Well, don't tell her. Not until I know what I'm doing. I'm freaking out. Do not make it worse. It's not your place to say anything."

"Okay, I won't tell her," Eva promised. "But you must."

Liam gripped his knees. "Let me figure things out first. It's like, what the hell, Fate? You take away the woman I love and my unborn child and give me two children in return with a woman I don't even know and who wants nothing to do with me. What is the universe thinking?"

"That you'll be a good dad and deserve another chance," Eva soothed. "It's the twenty-first century. We'll find Lexi a good job in Clayton Holdings. Then the two of you can figure out a way to co-parent. Co-parenting happens all the time and people make a success of it. It will be fine, Liam. You'll see."

There was that ugly word again. *Fine.* What did *fine* really mean when so much could go wrong? Liam knew that firsthand, with Anya, and with Lexi's fainting. He was in Beaumont because of a twist of fate. He knew Eva was trying to say the right things, so he focused on the future, as the past was nothing he could change. "I will protect her and ensure she's cared for. She fainted tonight. Had a panic attack. Something about that singer guy freaked her out. She said she knew him in elementary school or something."

"Well, Damon is on a private plane out of here sometime tomorrow, so he'll be long gone. The last of the wedding guests and the wedding party leave Monday. As for the reception, the terrace got cleaned, the band finished its set, and the bride and groom partied until the end and have a great story to tell. Clayton Hotels, of course, will be taking care of any dresses and suits that need cleaning. As I told Clarissa, no harm, no foul. The bride changed into another outfit. She had three. Clarissa's cool. I checked on her myself."

"Three dresses? That's overdoing it." Criticizing Clarissa's clothing choices was easier than processing the fact Lexi was pregnant with his twins.

"In hindsight, having so many outfits was rather good foresight. I had two outfits and now am in this." Eva had changed into jeans and a T-shirt, and she rubbed her hands on her thighs. "So you're going to be a dad. Does this mean I get to be a godmother?"

"I have no idea about that. But I'm for sure going to be a dad and you'll be an aunt." As long as nothing went wrong, which he'd ensure. "I do want this. The minute I heard, I wanted those twins more than anything." It didn't matter that he hadn't wanted to conceive them, hadn't even worried about the risk of conception since he'd taken precautions.

As soon as he'd heard the doctor say the words that Lexi was pregnant, Liam knew he'd be 100 percent involved in their lives. If this was Fate's way of giving him a second chance, he'd take the offering and run.

"What's the plan? What will you do next? Do you need a lawyer?"

"Lexi had a panic attack. I'll hold off on the legal stuff for now. The doctor said no stress. If the thought of a lawyer stresses me out, what will it do to her?"

Eva nodded. "True. Probably not a good idea to call the lawyers. So what will you do?"

"I don't know. Talk to her, clearly. She's off tomorrow. Doctor's orders. She's to take it easy." He'd make certain of it.

"I'm sure Alvin will have someone cover for her. The wedding party is attending the Sunday brunch, and that's it for events at the Chateau. Esprit should be rather quiet."

"I'm giving Lexi until eleven to contact me before I show up on her doorstep." Not that Liam expected Lexi to blow him off. Despite her leaving the bed they'd shared the morning after, she didn't seem like the type. She'd been as shocked as he was to discover she was pregnant and carrying twins. He glanced around the living room. While the house was perfect as a yearlong rental for one person, he'd need something else once the babies arrived.

"I know that look," Eva said. "What are you thinking?"

"Just how much there is to do. How everything's about to change. How I'm going to need to start making lists." Liam was known for his extensive lists and for planning for every contingency.

"Are you ready for this?" Eva asked. "Really?"

Liam didn't have a choice. "Even if I'm not, I'm all in, Eva. All in."

* * *

Lexi awoke to something warm and fuzzy sleeping on her chest. When she opened her eyes, Dawn's adult cat Sampson opened one eye and stared at her. "Hey buddy," Lexi said, reaching to scratch Sampson's scruff. I need you to move."

Sampson was eleven pounds, and he clung to the blanket as she moved him over to the other side so she could scoot off the mattress. She didn't bother straightening the comforter. As soon as she used the bathroom, she was climbing right back underneath.

The moment Lexi had pulled the covers back to her chin, Dawn knocked and cracked the door. "Hey, I don't want to intrude, but how are you feeling? You didn't seem well the other day, and you came home pretty late. I checked the kittens. They were fine."

"You can open the door," Lexi said. "I was at the ER. Don't worry. You can't catch this."

Dawn stuck her head around the door frame. "You poor thing. Are you okay? It's around nine. You're usually awake by now. Can I get you anything? I've got some fresh doughnuts in the kitchen."

The thought of doughnuts made Lexi's stomach churn. "Thanks, but no. Turns out I'm pregnant."

"What?" Dawn pushed the door open fully.

"Came as a surprise to me, too," Lexi said. Seeing he wasn't going to be petted, Sampson jumped off the bed, rubbed against Dawn's pant leg and trundled out.

"Dare I ask?" Dawn's curiosity was clear.

Lexi rolled her neck to work out a kink. "Feel free. Since the dad-to-be was there when I fainted, it's not like word won't get around. It's Liam Clayton. He carried me through the hotel." Lexi explained the parts she remembered and added the parts Liam had told her. "I haven't checked social media to see if I'm on any of the sites because of him." Hopefully not. If so, she hoped no one recognized her as Melynda.

"Well, this sounds complicated." Dawn reached down and scooped up a kitten. "The Claytons are a pretty big deal. They transformed this whole area without destroying the small town feel or charm. It's been great for business. Including mine. Jack and Sierra Clayton are some of my best clients and big supporters of the no-kill shelter."

"Liam and I plan to talk later today. He moved into town somewhere. Don't worry, I won't bring him here. And I will find another place to live before the little ones come."

Dawn's smile was a reassuring burst of sunshine. "No rush. I get up around-the-clock when I'm bottle-feeding kittens. I don't think having twin newborns will faze me. Besides, it'll be good practice for when I have my own someday." With a now sleeping kitten pressed against her chest, Dawn checked her Apple watch. "Oh, gotta run. If you need anything, text. Seriously. If nothing else, Door-Dash."

"I will. Promise." Lexi watched as Dawn closed the bedroom door behind her. Telling her roommate had gone better than she'd expected. But then that's who Dawn was and why Lexi had won the roommate lottery. Dawn was always taking in strays. Lexi simply was the human kind.

Maybe things wouldn't be so bad after all. Her phone pinged, and she read the text from Liam: How about I pick you up for lunch in three hours?

She liked Liam's message, sent back a thumbs-up and set her phone alarm for an hour and a half. Closing her eyes, Lexi went back to sleep.

* * *

Three things woke Lexi from a deep sleep, and none of them were the cat currently kneading the blanket next to her. Rising from the bed, she pulled the robe tighter around her middle and made her way into the living area. The pounding on the front door and insistent ringing of the doorbell joined the shrilling of her phone. All three made her wince and her head throb.

"Lexi? Are you in there? Are you okay?" Liam shouted.

Lexi checked that the alarm was off, looked through the peephole and opened the door. "Hey. Sorry. Guess I overslept."

"Are you feeling okay? It's twelve thirty, and I've been knocking and ringing for ten minutes. Well, more like two. But you had me worried. Have you eaten? Why do I even ask? I know you haven't."

Lexi stepped back so he could enter. "I've been asleep, so no, I didn't eat and that's the reason. Come in. Give me twenty minutes. Food actually sounds good. You're not allergic to cats, are you?" She shut the door and scooped up a kitten. "I told you my roommate's a vet. She's always fostering. This little guy's one of those. Back into the foster palace for you."

Liam peered at the kitten in her hand. "Who's this orange bit of fluff?"

"That's Roger. See the blue collar? That's how we tell them apart." When Liam reached for the kitten, Lexi passed him over.

"He's wiggly." Liam cradled Roger to his chest, put a finger under his chin and the kitten began to purr. "Seems like a friendly little guy."

"You like cats?"

"Never had one. Never had time for a pet and I travel too much. Not fair to keep boarding one. Eva has a Yorkshire terrier named Princess. She's a purse dog. Yaps constantly but is otherwise sweet. Eva takes her almost everywhere."

"One of the pluses of living here is that I can get my fill by loving on Dawn's cats." Lexi reached down and plucked another kitten before it tried to climb her bathrobe. She reached for Roger and held them both. "Have a seat. I'll be right back. Dawn's resident cats probably won't come visit."

She put the kittens in the foster palace, did a quick head count to ensure the kittens were accounted for and closed the door to the bedroom. After a quick shower and blow-dry, she dressed. When she returned to the living room, she found Liam sitting with a black-and-white cat in his lap. "Don't you two look comfy."

"Yeah, he came out pretty much as soon as you disappeared." Liam scratched the cat's ears. "He's got good taste, I'd say." Liam moved the cat to the floor and rose. "What, no comeback telling me the cat's wrong? Ah, there's a small smile. Are you ready for lunch? It's a beautiful day outside, so I've arranged for a table at Jamestown."

"A winery?" Lexi couldn't help but chuckle. Liam could be endearing when he wanted to be. "I can't drink wine."

"We're going for the food. Jamestown has some of the best around. It's worth going just to eat."

Outside the day was pleasant, with little humidity. Liam opened the passenger door and made sure her seat belt was fastened before rounding to the other side. "We're late for brunch, but the winery's restaurant has a full menu. We also have two flavors of grape juice, if you want that. We've discovered that a huge growth area is in mocktails, non-alcoholic seltzers and juices."

Lexi leaned back against the leather seat of the Subaru. "I've never been to Jamestown."

"Which is why I chose it. You're in for a treat. The view is phenomenal. Like the Chateau is the crown jewel of our hotels, Jamestown represents the best of our Missouri wineries. Sierra, that's my cousin Jack's wife, her family used to own it before they sold it to us."

"And now you oversee it."

Liam nodded, but Lexi noted he kept his entire focus on the winding, twisty road. "As part of my many roles, I suppose I do. My office is downtown, right on the edge of the historic district. But let's not talk about my work or yours today."

"I'm obviously not at mine," Lexi said.

"You don't have to work, you know. I will support you." His fingers tightened on the wheel as he slowed to take a hairpin turn.

"You're not going to start in on some old-fashioned notion that we should get married, are you? Because that will make for an awkward lunch." Lexi nervously picked at her sundress, her actions more from the marriage topic than the way Liam was driving.

Liam shook his head. "No, no proposal. I won't insult you by trying to enforce some Dark Ages ideal. But I will be caveman enough to say I don't like the idea of you working. There's no reason for you to do so. I'm rich, Lexi. I can well afford keeping you in any style you wish."

"That sounds even worse. I'm not taking any more money from you. It's bad enough I still have the hundred dollars you made me put in my pocket. And women have been working for years. There's no stigma in being a single mother."

"You say that only because you haven't met my mother yet. She's flying into town sometime this morning, so I'll do my best to run interference. And I'm not saying you can't work. Just that I don't like you working behind a bar. You fainted. You have to take care of yourself. I can find you a job at Clayton Holdings. And don't give me grief about nepotism. It's a family company, and you're carrying my twins."

"I'll think about it, and I promise I'll slow down when needed." As for money, singing Damon's song should set her up nicely, at least for a while. Especially if she played her negotiating cards correctly. "I don't want someone to be running my life, including you. Been there, done that, so I'm doing this on my terms."

Liam shot a quick glance her direction. "Who said anything about running your life? There are days I can hardly run my own. I'm in a VP job I wasn't ever planning on doing and in a town I wasn't planning on living in. But here I am, so I'm going to make the best of it, like when I climb a mountain. Do you know when you climb, you shouldn't look at the summit? That's always too far away and far too big for you to reach, especially when the climb can take eight hours to get to the top. Instead you concentrate on what you can control, which are the steps immediately in front of you. One foot in front of the other, over and over. After you do that, suddenly you're on the top of the world, and you've made it. Hopefully, if you and I can follow that philosophy and take things one step at a time, then we can be successful co-parents and raise our children with the least amount of friction. We each love them and want what's best for them, so we should be able to work things out."

That sounded fair and plausible, but also more akin to a dream than reality. However, Lexi didn't need to answer as they'd reached Jamestown. The main parking lot was full and the shuttle running, but Liam drove past the overflow parking, waved at the attendant and moved into a staff space closer to one of the side outbuildings.

"You're right. The view is incredible," Lexi said as she stepped out of the car. A grassy meadow stretched as far as the eye could see until it met the rolling hills beyond.

"You should see the stars out here at night. They're incredible. Follow me." He led her down a path toward the front doors. "We'll go in this way so you get the full experience. So Sierra's dad built this, and when we came into the area with our plan for the region, this was the final piece of the puzzle. It's actually a rather funny story. Turns out Jack and Sierra knew each other in high school and met again when Jack came to buy the place. Given their history, she saw Jack as a pompous interloper, but now it's all happily-ever-after. As for Sierra's dad, we're still using his recipes, especially when it comes to making his famous Norton red wine. We're also continuing to bottle his drier, yet semisweet white wine made with a French-American Vignoles grape."

"You know a lot about wine."

As Liam shrugged, the short-sleeved polo shirt inched out of the shorts he wore. "Not really, but I know more than I did the night of the gala. I'm a fast study."

They'd reached the front doors, and Lexi let Liam reach for the handle. "Marvin James, Sierra's dad, modeled this place on Yosemite's Tenaya Lodge. You'll see what I mean when we step inside what he affectionately called the Great Room."

A blast of air-conditioning hit Lexi as they entered. "Oh my. This is lovely."

The Great Room was a huge, open expanse with two-story-high ceilings, dark wooden trusses and rustic chandeliers. Having an Old West, pioneer/prospector feel, the tasting room was a huge expanse built so the length of the gigantic room was double the width. To her right, on the far wall, was a massive eight-foot-wide, floor-to-ceiling stone fireplace. Straight ahead and directly across the room from where she stood was a wall of two-story-high windows. Sliding doors allowed access to the outside areas, and the glass wall provided sweeping views of rolling hills. Liam stopped at the long wooden bar running along the entire left side, where a server recognized him and quickly provided him with two bottles of water.

"We're at table 65," Liam said. "Follow me." They bypassed the indoor tables and went outside onto the huge deck where a trio played classic rock music. "It's this way."

Their square, four-top table was down a dogleg bend around the corner of the building. This area was a far more secluded area than the main deck. Lexi settled onto one of the chairs. To avoid blocking her view, Liam sat to her right. "They're even sitting out in the field," Lexi said. "You must do a great business."

"We make most of our profit during the spring and summer, and also during October for Oktoberfest. During the winter, to keep people coming in, we hold monthly wine dinners that bring customers back for a multicourse experience. We also have a wine club."

"I never knew running a winery was this involved."

"Honestly, I didn't either," Liam admitted. "But since I've gotten here, I've learned that this area surrounding the Missouri River reminded early-nineteenth-century Germans of the beloved Rhine Valley. Once they settled, they started planting grapes. Did you know that before Prohibition, the state of Missouri produced almost as much wine as California?"

"I did not," Lexi said. "Learn something new every day."

Liam had grown animated. "Yeah, now Missouri's wine industry consists mostly of mom-and-pop wineries. My parents wanted to move here, and so did my uncle, so we decided to invest. Clayton Holdings owns six wineries in this area."

"What's your favorite wine?" Lexi watched as a server wove through guest tables and headed in their direction.

"From Jamestown? I really like the Chambourcin. It's a purple-skinned, French-American hybrid grape. We make our red wine by fermenting it in steel to give it a light body. The finish has hints of tart cherry, dried cranberry and fresh herbs. We're actually exporting it from here and selling it in our West Coast hotels and wineries."

"I'll have to try it someday." Lexi smiled at the server who'd arrived beside the table. The server set down a bottle of sparkling grape juice that rested inside a bucket filled with ice, two wineglasses, an appetizer of toasted ravioli and two menus.

"Thank you," Lexi told the server before facing Liam. "And thank you. I didn't know I was craving these, but it turns out I am." Lexi lifted one of the crispy squares. Toasted ravioli, she'd discovered, was a St. Louis thing. Whoever had first thought to toss ravioli in Italian bread-crumbs and then deep fry the pieces until golden was a pure genius. She dipped the morsel in marinara sauce while Liam poured the dark-purple-colored juice into their glasses.

He passed one to Lexi and lifted his glass in a toast. "Cheers."

"Cheers," Lexi said, appreciating how Liam was sharing the nonalcoholic beverage with her. It was a thoughtful gesture of solidarity that spoke volumes about his character. She took a sip, and the sweet grape juice bubbled against her tongue. "This is good. Tastes somewhat like that kind I had as a kid but not as sweet."

Grape juice had been her favorite until her trainer had declared that grape juice had far too many carbs to drink. He'd said she could dilute it and have exactly four ounces, but the flavor hadn't been the same.

"Like the supermarket brand everyone knows, Clayton's grape juice is also made with Concord and Niagara grapes. We just put our own spin on them. This bottle comes from the Yakima Valley in Washington State where we grow both of those grapes. And I see your impressed expression. Don't give me too much credit. I just learned all this. I'm becoming a fount of wine formation."

She lifted another ravioli square. "Good pun. I see what you did there."

Liam laughed as well and reached for the menu. "My sense of humor is often terrible. Glad you appreciate it. What to order? Everything's good. One of my onboarding tasks was to visit each of our wineries and sample the food. It was a dirty job, but someone had to do it. Luckily the Katy Trail and I are good friends. I run or bike almost every day."

"I bet." The Katy Trail was a rail-to-trail state park that went through most of the state. People walked, ran, and biked the trail, which in Beaumont wove past many of the wineries. Lexi studied the menu and settled on a southwest chicken salad. When the server returned to take their order, she didn't ask for the kitchen to remove the "unnecessary carbs" croutons. When their food arrived, she stared long-ingly at the Parmesan chicken panini and fries Liam had ordered. He noticed.

"Would you like some?" he asked.

One of the first things Lexi had done when she'd es-caped her old life was to binge on french fries and junk food. She'd felt sick afterward and not because she'd forced herself to be. "Just one," she said.

"I can see you salivating from here. I've had this before and it's delicious. Take some." He held half of his sandwich out and set it on her plate. Then he added a handful of fries.

Using her fork, she pushed some of her salad onto his plate. "How about we go halfsies? That way you can say you've eaten some veggies."

His cheeky grin was fast growing on her. "Works for me."

With their food shared and sorted, they settled into easy conversation, staying on safe topics as they ate. Lexi kept waiting for them to run out of things to talk about, and found it amazing they never did. She appreciated that Liam kept clear of discussing the twins. They had seven months or so to sort that out.

Instead, as if by unspoken agreement, they used the af-ternoon to get to know one another in ways they'd skipped the first night when they'd fallen into bed. As they talked, Lexi found herself relaxing. The musical trio played upbeat early eighties and nineties rock classics, and from where they were, they could hear the music but it wasn't too loud. The view from their table was phenomenal, and the June weather was perfect.

She and Liam sat in the shade, and a light breeze kept things cool while the ice in the bucket kept the grape juice cold. Not that she'd had more than one glass. Unlike with wine, she wasn't going to get a buzz, much less a sparkling grape sugar rush. But the fact that Liam had ordered grape juice proved another thing about him—he noticed things and tried to make the situation between them feel as normal as possible.

She was also impressed that he'd listened when she'd spoken to him, and he'd been genuine in his responses. He'd also respected her boundaries. For instance, once after he'd talked about his childhood, he'd asked about hers, and when she'd deflected, he'd moved on. Instead of pressing, he'd told her the story about how, when he was twelve, he'd wanted to play paintball with his older brother. Edmund, of course, had said no.

"I was so angry he wouldn't let me tag along that I went into his room and took some of his paintballs. Then I went outside and started throwing them. They hit the neighbors' garage door and *splat*—" Liam made an explosion motion with his hands. "Needless to say, I didn't say a word about what I did, and since the paintballs were Edmund's he got blamed. I still haven't confessed. Maybe I will at his wedding."

"Don't worry. I won't tell him." She made a show of locking her lips.

Liam wagged a finger. "You best not. I'm giving you blackmail over me, so I'm trusting you."

She'd laughed at that story, but realized the significance of the secret he'd shared with her. As an only child, she didn't understand sibling dynamics, but she enjoyed listening to him. Many of Liam's stories had centered on Eva, who, as the youngest and only sister, had easily held her own with three rambunctious older brothers.

"You should know that I did tell Eva about your being

pregnant," Liam said. He fingered the stem of a long-empty wineglass. "She was waiting for me when I got back to my house. She wanted to know what was going on. She might have been hell on earth as an annoying little sister, but she's one of my biggest supporters and friends now that we're grown. She's great at running social media. If we need her, she's in our corner. She texted me that most people at the wedding were more interested in Damon than our drama."

"I don't post on social media." Someone else had managed Melynda's sites, and Lexi didn't have any of the apps on her phone for the accounts under her real name. Those she rarely checked. "I find it toxic."

"I don't see the point. From what I've seen, everyone curates their perfect life. Either that or social media is a cesspool of watching everyone else's misery. It's like cheering for the lions to eat the poor souls in the Colosseum," Liam said.

"That's a good point," Lexi agreed.

Liam shifted and stretched out his legs. "For about two weeks, after the accident on Everest, there were a lot of poor Liam posts. The local media reported on Anya's death, and then the national media picked up the story, and then afterward came the hordes wanting to see if they could get a picture of my grief. They sent a chopper out to cover her funeral."

"I'm sorry. They're so invasive." Lexi knew that firsthand.

He shuddered. "I don't understand why. I'm not a celebrity. Just because my family's hotel business might rival the Hiltons' or Marriotts' doesn't mean that me or my siblings want the attention like some of the Hiltons did when they were part of those reality shows. Edmund wouldn't have gone undercover if it hadn't been for a business deal.

As for me, after Anya's death, all I wanted was to be left alone. And then you came along."

"And then I came along," Lexi said. She gazed out over the grassy meadow. Groups of people filled tables, laughing and drinking and enjoying the sunshine. How carefree they appeared from a distance. If they were looking at her and Liam, she and Liam most likely looked the same. How far from the truth.

"I need to tell you something," Liam said. "I still want you."

Lexi stilled. His declaration had come out of the blue. "Oh."

"I know today is about us becoming friends, but I also needed to be honest. You rocked my world, and I'm sorry if I'm coming across crass and blunt, but I needed to be direct and tell you that. I also wanted to say that I won't make any moves. We have to get along. Today's been nice. It bodes well for the future."

"I'm hopeful we can be friends too," Lexi said. "I hated telling you no that day in the conference room, but you're my boss. Or close enough."

"However, before we go any further, I have something else I have to get off my chest. I have to be truthful and tell you that I don't think I'll ever fall in love again. It's not even on my radar to try. Anya and I were soulmates. I don't know what type of relationship you and I will forge as we move forward. Hopefully friends. Maybe lovers— for your body turns mine on like nothing I've ever experienced. Hopefully we'll make great co-parents who do an excellent job raising our children. Maybe we'll be all three. I'd like that. But we can't go into this with any type of false expectations."

"At least you're honest. I can appreciate that. It helps," Lexi said, not knowing why his honesty hurt so much. She should be happy he was so direct and forthright. She and Liam had already discussed how they weren't getting married, something she'd brought up. She didn't want that anyway. The fact he'd reinforced that he didn't want to marry her shouldn't have stung. For some reason it did. Badly.

It was the death of another dream, Lexi decided, but one she would give up, just as she'd given up fame and fortune. Surely she wouldn't be the only woman who'd envisioned her future differently—fall in love, marry, have children and grow old together once said children were launched—only to discover that future wasn't possible.

As for Liam not loving her, Lexi had expected to suffer some heartbreak before finding her soulmate, who of course would become her great love. But some part of her had hoped Liam might be her great love, which was foolish. They'd had a one-night stand. They'd never had a relationship. She was having children with a man who would never love her, so she shouldn't have unrealistic expectations. He might lust, but he would not love. His heart had died on the mountain. At least he wasn't insisting on marriage or cohabitation. She should be grateful he was allowing her to have some independence. She would do Damon's song and meet Liam as a co-parenting equal.

As for the fact that he wanted her still, well, her body wanted him right back. But to have sex without love? She'd done that once with him, and while her body would enjoy nothing more than another go-round, the idea didn't sit well in her soul. Perhaps she was an old-fashioned girl in that respect after all. She wasn't notching her bedposts and bragging about it on the set like many of her stylists.

"Here you are!"

A woman's sharp voice jolted Lexi. Next to her, Liam straightened. "Eva. What are you doing here?"

Liam's sister lifted her oversize designer sunglasses and pushed them atop her head, making the points of her bob wind around the base of her ears. A dog's face poked out from a corner of her oversize designer pooch purse. "I'm looking for you. Did you not see the texts I sent?"

"Put my phone on silent and left it in the car." Liam gestured toward the meadow. "Why do I need it? I'm at a winery enjoying the day. And that doesn't answer the question of why you're here or how you found me."

"I found you because of the Find My function on your phone."

"You can track me?" From the fold of his arms, Lexi could tell Liam wasn't happy about his sister's appearance or the fact she'd enabled a function on his phone. "When did you set that up?"

Eva made an impatient hand flip, which jostled the bag on her arm. Her dog dipped back inside. "That's irrelevant. The point is that he didn't get on the plane and he's here."

"Who's here? What are you talking about?" Liam demanded.

But Lexi already knew. She could tell by the way the crowd first went silent, and then quickly began to point and whisper. Because of the position of their table, her back was to most of the other guests enjoying the afternoon on Jamestown's patio. All around the deck, the whispers rose to excited cries and shouts of "Damon!" Lexi's stomach churned and she dropped her head into her hands. A perfect day, ruined. How could he be here?

Eva's words raced forth as if fire and brimstone would

descend if she didn't get them out fast enough. "The wedding party finished brunch and most of them wanted to come here. Well, the bride and groom—you know, Clarissa and Alec—they did, so what's left of those still in town followed along. They've been touring the wineries. As soon as I found out they were coming here, I came straight over. He's with them, Liam."

Behind her, Lexi could already hear people saying his name: "Damon!"

"Hey, that's Damon Stevener!"

"Damon, over here!"

Her famous ex was supposed to have left. Of course he hadn't. She shouldn't have been surprised he'd changed his mind. Once Damon had discovered she was in Beaumont, she should have expected him to stick around until she agreed to sing. She hadn't given him her answer, and she'd passed out during the wedding throng. Damon was nothing if not persistent. He wanted Lexi, and he'd pester her until he got his way. She didn't want him to find her here.

"Lexi, are you okay?" Liam had bent his head so he could lean into her space and peer up at her.

Jerking her head from her hands, she rose shakily to her feet. "We need to go. Now. Can you settle up and I'll meet you at the car?"

"What is going on? You're going to have to explain it to me." But thankfully Liam had gotten to his feet. "But yes, we can leave."

"Good." Lexi's chest heaved as the panic attack began. "We need to go. Now Liam. Please."

"I'll run interference and settle the bill," Eva said. "They're coming this way."

Hearing that made Lexi turn. While a totally normal

reaction, like a person glancing over their shoulder to see how close behind a pursuer was, it was a costly mistake on Lexi's part. Turning around meant that she was visible. She could be seen in between the gaps made by the approaching wedding party. If she could see the guests beyond the wedding party walking toward her, then those winery guests could also see her. Many held up their phones, recording Damon's approach.

Lexi whirled quickly and her hands became lobster claws as she grabbed Liam's arm. "Get me out of here." Shielding her, Liam moved Lexi in front of him and toward the end of the deck where stairs awaited.

"Alec! Clarissa!" Lexi heard Eva say. "Welcome to Jamestown! I didn't think I'd catch up to you. Damon, great to see you again."

"Hey Eva," Damon said. Lexi could hear how close he was.

"Keep going," Liam whispered in her ear.

"I need to talk to Mel… Lexi…" Damon began to say, but whatever he said next was lost when Eva blocked his way. Whatever Eva said didn't register as Lexi kept her head low and moved in the opposite direction. Liam held her tightly to his side and guided her to the stairs.

"Crap," he said.

Lexi glanced up. "Oh no."

Intent on reaching the side stairs that would take them to the ground, and then to the car, neither Liam or Lexi had counted on the crowd of young people, who after discovering Damon was in their midst, were making their way up the stairs to get access to the singer, phones out and ready.

Liam began to push though the twenty-one- to twenty-six-year-olds, but to do this, Lexi had to lift her chin and turn sideways. When she did, she saw the widening of the eyes. Saw the mouths round into large Os.

Perhaps it had been bound to happen. While her hair was different and she'd put on a few pounds, she was still the same person she always was. The pileup began after the first person recognized her and stopped, causing everyone behind her to halt their forward momentum. The eager fan turned around, and as Lexi glanced behind her, the woman pointed. She was Damon and Melynda's ideal fan, one who'd grown up with them. Her passion was the reason for Damon's recent string of number one hits.

"That's Melynda!" the woman shouted. She began waving her arm. "Melynda!"

Panic rose like bile, and Lexi had to give Liam credit, he plowed through the crowd like a tight end carrying the ball to the end zone. The faces Lexi passed became blurs, but the screams and the excitement grew louder as many in the crowd turned in her direction.

Melynda Norfolk, missing for the past six months, had been found, and in the same place as Damon Stevener.

From nowhere, Jamestown servers appeared and ran interference, giving Liam and Lexi a head start in which to reach the car. She climbed inside, threw on her sunglasses and slumped into the seat as Liam let gravel fly as he raced down the long drive.

"What the hell was that?" Liam demanded as he fishtailed onto the main road and brought the Subaru back under control. On the infotainment screen, the texts from his sister began to ping, waiting to be read.

Lexi eased to a seated position and glanced behind her. No one was following. No cars chased at high speed. Her heart pounded, and she took deep breaths as she worked to calm the adrenaline racing through her. For the moment she was safe. But for how long?

Her father's minions monitored social media. She'd been found. If her father came to Beaumont, what next? What would he do? She might have bought out her professional contract, but family ties were much harder to cut. Despite everything, he was still her father. Soon to be a grandfather.

Panic began to climb. She'd text Damon. Tell him she'd do the song. Tell him to lie and say that wasn't her the fans thought they'd seen. Those people had thought they'd seen her, but he should tell them it was all wishful thinking. They'd believe him. Her hands shakily grabbed her phone and sent the text: Say it wasn't me. I'll do your song. That wasn't me.

Once she sent the text, her fingers fumbled her phone and it fell to the floor.

After she retrieved the device, she arched upwards and straightened. Liam's fingers gripped the steering wheel. For a brief second he turned his head and her gaze connected with his.

"Tell me the truth," he demanded. "Who are you, Lexi? Who's Melynda? And what the hell is going on?"

Chapter Eight

She almost felt as if she were in a confessional booth, not that she'd ever been in one, minus that one time on television.

"I'm Lexi Henderson. That's my real name. Well, Alexis. Lexi for short." She drew in a breath. "But that's not how people know me. For most of my formative years I was Melynda Norfolk, the other half of Damon and Melynda."

"Damon, the singer at the wedding the other night. The guy there today. That guy."

"Yes. That guy. Currently the biggest pop star on the planet with two consecutive number one hits. We were a duo." Lexi twisted her fingers into the material of her sundress, making it stretch. "I bought out my contract and walked away six months ago. He went on to be a solo act and I moved here."

"Where you and I met."

"Yes." She gave him an abbreviated version of her celebrity career, leaving out her battles with anorexia, anxiety and depression. She left out the death of her mother and the fights with her father. "I wanted to be normal. No more stylists. No more having the media trolls dissect my life. I had these big plans to go to college and get my de-

gree. I would be more than a bartender. I'd be someone who
had a career that didn't involve selling my soul for the next
dime. I still plan on college, but that goal may have to wait
as I'm having twins."

"Why?"

She tilted her head. She'd expected Liam to add some sort
of caustic commentary about celebrity culture, but instead
he'd simply asked her why she couldn't go to college. Or had
he? Her brow creased. "I don't understand the question."

"Why can't you go to college and get your degree?" he
repeated.

She had understood him correctly. "Because I work? Because I'm having twins? Because I can't do it all?"

"That's why you have me." He turned on Third Street,
drove down the block, turned onto a side street and then
into an alley. He drove past a series of single and double
garages set inside privacy fences.

"Where are we going?" she asked.

"My rental house. I thought being there might be
quieter and it would be more respectful of your roommate
if I wasn't hanging out in the living room while we finished our conversation."

Liam pressed the remote on a garage door opener and
a few houses down the double door began to open. Once
they pulled in, Lexi discovered that the garage was in name
only. It was actually more of a carport, open on three sides.
The garage door closed behind them, sealing off the alley.
A single sidewalk led to a small patio off the back door.

"This is interesting," she said as she closed the car door.

Liam waited for her at the front of the SUV. "Having
carports like this is pretty common when you have small
yards and alleys. When the cars are parked on the street,

having a carport adds a huge covered patio space to the yard for parties and things."

"I can see how it would be useful."

"Welcome to Zoe's place," Liam said as he unlocked the back door. "She owns Aunty Jayne's Cookies. She's Sierra's sister, that's my cousin Jack's wife, and how I found this. Zoe and her husband live in the family homestead on the other side of Jamestown Winery. When her parents moved out, she and Nick moved in."

"This house is lovely." Lexi meant it. The updated kitchen might be small and compact, but it had the latest appliances and granite countertops. She'd had a huge rental in California with a kitchen that was designed to be used by caterers and personal chefs, not Lexi herself. She didn't even understand how to work half the appliances, not that she was allowed to cook anything anyway. Her nutrition coach had monitored every meal. Lexi wandered into the living room and dining room combination. "I think it's perfect. Especially if you're here for a year."

"I'm actually looking for something bigger, something to buy. Something with at least three bedrooms so the twins won't have to share. Since my parents are moving here and since I'm assuming you'll want to stay in Beaumont, it's probably best if I own something too." He tossed his keys on the coffee table. "The remote for the TV is there. Take a seat and I'll get you something to drink. What would you like? I've got water, soda, iced tea?"

"Water will be fine." Lexi dropped onto a leather couch. Liam was already thinking ahead to where the kids might sleep, whereas she hadn't gotten beyond the last twenty minutes. Her phone pinged with Damon's reply: Done.

Lexi heaved a sigh, leaned forward and rested her head

on her fingertips, something she seemed to be doing a lot of lately. A glass of water came into view. "Take this," Liam said. She sipped the ice water, which cooled her throat. "So what next?" he asked.

She gave him a half smile. "I go to work tomorrow like always. The whole thing will blow over." Especially if Damon kept his word and said that Melynda and Lexi were not the same person.

Liam held his own water. "I meant after that. At some point we're going to have to hammer out parenting details, but we have time for that. First, we need to get you to the ob-gyn and make sure you're healthy. The appointment is Tuesday. I'd like to join you, if you don't mind."

"I don't want to think about any of that right now, not when I'm still trying to calm down after being outed as Melynda. It'll send me into another panic attack. Those are not good for the babies."

"No, they're not," Liam agreed. "You have to take care of yourself."

She closed her eyes for a brief moment. "It still hasn't sunk in that I'm having twins. We're going to be parents, Liam."

"I know. I'm excited. You're giving me a huge gift. I always wanted to be a dad. I hope I make a good one." He reached to gently push some of her hair aside. "Turn around. You're tense. Let me give you a massage."

"I know where those lead," Lexi said, but she allowed him access to her back. He started at her neck, his magical fingers soothing and stretching. He worked his way to her shoulders, easing the knots and tension that had built from the day. He ran his thumb along her spine, moving the muscles so that they released. "You could do this for a living," Lexi whispered. She shifted as heat began to press against her core.

"All you have to do is ask and you shall receive," Liam said. "You're the mother of my children, Lexi. You matter to me."

She turned around. His face was so close to hers and his lips slightly parted. If she reached, she could touch his eyebrows. Stroke her finger down his cheek. She could kiss him.

The sound of her phone pinging had Lexi jumping. She knocked her knee against the coffee table and cursed. Liam, who had better and faster reflexes, caught her as she toppled. "Steady there. I got you."

Lexi stepped out of his magnetic proximity, reached for her phone and swiped. Was it really only three o'clock? "It's Alvin. One of my coworkers came down with the stomach thing. He needs me to come in just for a short shift until Toby can get there. Can you take me to my house?"

Liam crossed his arms and frowned. "Why is he calling you in? You're supposed to be off today. Doctor's orders."

Lexi nibbled a lower lip that had moments ago wanted to kiss Liam. "Please don't get him in trouble. I feel fine, especially after this afternoon. It's a few hours, tops. Mostly just the bar prep. Not even a full shift. We were already short-staffed, and Alvin said he's called everyone else. He knows I could use the money."

As Liam continued to frown, Lexi thought fast. "If you want, you can sit in Esprit and watch me work and make sure I'm not overdoing it. Does that sound fair? But I need to change and get in there."

"Sure," Liam said. She could tell from his tone that he didn't want her working, but that he'd play along because he respected her decision. "Let's go. But I'm driving you to and from. I don't want you driving. Deal?"

It was a fair compromise, so Lexi nodded. That settled,

Liam drove the Subaru to Lexi's in silence, each listening to satellite radio tuned to Liam's favorite alternative rock station instead of talking. Thankfully the station was not the type of channel that would play Damon's latest hit. When they arrived to Lexi's subdivision, she noted her street was clear. No cars lingered that she didn't recognize. A few kids played outside on the front lawns, their mothers holding glasses of what looked like iced tea as they socialized from the front porch. One of the moms waved as she and Liam drove by. This was normalcy, set in a safe and comfortable suburban neighborhood where people knew more than their neighbors' names, they knew each other. A jogger went by, AirPods visible in his ears.

"I've got it from here," Lexi said, hopping out when Liam parked in the driveway. "No need to walk me in. I'll be right back out. Five minutes, tops."

Back in LA, when she'd left the gates of her own place, she'd had photographers camping out to follow her. Once a fan had gone so far as to get on the grounds and tap on her kitchen window. That had been a disconcerting shock. The police had arrived and arrested the trespasser. After that she'd lived with the house alarm turned on at all times. Whenever she'd traveled, despite being on a secured floor, she'd wedged an alarm under her door. In Beaumont, Lexi could walk down the streets without being hounded or surrounded by bodyguards. She could eat at restaurants and wine bars, or go to the movies without having to be one of the only people in the venue. If Damon kept his word, she'd continue being able to do that.

She crossed her fingers, changed and joined Liam at the car.

Hours later, at six, Lexi noted that Liam had taken her

at her word. While he didn't park himself on a bar stool in front of her, he did wander in and out of the Esprit in his efforts to check on her. Because of Liam's constant drive-bys, she'd had to reassure Alvin that nothing was wrong or amiss, and that Alvin wasn't in any danger of being repri-manded for asking her to take on some emergency duty—especially for a shift that was to be hers originally anyway. With it being Sunday, the bar contained new travelers who'd stopped in for predinner drinks, along with a few wedding stragglers who weren't planning on leaving until Monday. They'd been either been playing eighteen holes of golf or taking the Clayton trolley to the various wineries.

"All good?" Liam asked on another one of his pass-throughs.

"Calmer now that Sunday afternoon happy hour is over," Lexi replied. "And the tips have been excellent."

"Okay." Liam stood for a long moment and watched her. She had no idea what he was thinking. All he said was, "Then I'll be back."

Alvin waited until Liam left the bar before approaching Lexi. "What is going on with you and Mr. Clayton? And don't say he's concerned about you because you passed out last night. I can see how he looks at you. That's not a boss-employee expression. And, you're far too casual with him."

Lexi sighed. "He's technically not my boss."

Alvin put a two fingers to the side of his face and puck-ered his lips. "Girl, I've got daughters. Don't try to pull one over on me." He dropped his hand. "You know you can trust me, right? Talk to me."

She stepped toward the back side of the bar and Alvin moved with her. "I met Liam the night of the gala. I didn't know who he was. We went our separate ways and then later that night we ran into each other while we were in town. We were both at the wine bar. The next day he learned he was taking over the wineries."

"But he knew you worked here." Alvin tilted his head and studied her.

"He did," Lexi admitted. "And I knew he'd been at the gala."

Alvin shook his head. "I take it things happened." He made air quotes around the word happened.

"You could say that. And those things will have consequences several months from now," Lexi admitted. "I'm having twins."

Alvin's mouth dropped open. "Oh honey. What were you thinking?"

"Clearly I wasn't thinking," Lexi told him. "And being pregnant is why I fainted. I found out last night. You can't tell anyone." She glanced over at the bar. The couple seated at the end shouldn't be able to hear her, and they weren't paying her or Alvin any attention.

"You know I have your back," Alvin said. "Let me know whatever you need."

"Time off when the time comes," Lexi answered immediately. "And just your support."

"You got it. But do you really think he's going to let you keep working? He's not happy I called you. He hasn't said anything, but you know I'm right. He's only keeping his tongue because of you, so I thank you for that. Whatever happens, he should step up and do the right thing."

"Do not say marriage. We don't love each other. We're having twins, not a love affair." Realizing she'd raised her voice, Lexi lowered it. "It's the twenty-first century."

"So they keep telling me. I meant money. He's a Clayton. They have plenty. Be sure he supports you."

She shook her head. "I don't want anything from him. Not now. Maybe ever. Money comes with strings. I've had enough of those to last a lifetime."

She'd already be paying the price by singing Damon's song. But at least singing would put her on solid financial footing. Allow her to face Liam as more of an equal. Speaking of her ex, Damon had sent her a text twenty minutes ago, but she hadn't had time to look at it. She dug her phone out. The bar was empty enough that she could take a moment to see what was going on. She swiped her phone open. The next words she read sent a chill through her heart.

It's all over the internet you're pregnant. Are you pregnant? How? Who? What the hell?

Damon had sent two links, each leading to gossip sites asking "Who's Melynda's baby daddy?"

Someone at the hospital must have overheard. Or maybe the couple at the bar, who were now openly staring at her as one of them slid an empty glass forward. Who had leaked the story?

At the hospital she'd been Lexi Henderson. Maybe after the debacle at the winery today, though, someone had put her identities together. As if proof the nightmare could get worse, another text slid into the display on her phone. Her father had texted:

I've tried to give you the space you needed, but if what's on the internet is true, that's done. We'll deal with this when I get there.

Lexi couldn't read the rest. As her phone slipped through her fingers, Alvin peered at her. "Lexi, you've paled. Are you okay? What's going on?" He stooped, grabbed her phone and read the message. "What does this mean?"

It meant her father was coming to Beaumont. The only question remaining was how imminent was his arrival.

When Liam wasn't checking on Lexi, he was sitting in Eva's suite. Even though his sister rented a condo out by the wineries, because she was part of the wedding party, she'd chosen to remain at the hotel through Monday—she'd joked that there had to be some perks for being a Clayton. She hadn't yet arrived from Jamestown, where she'd stayed drinking with her friends, but she'd texted that she was en route. She and Liam had been texting most of the day, especially once he'd sent her instructions to google Melynda Norfolk.

His sister's shock had been clear: The other half of Damon and Melynda? That's Lexi? Liam, she's famous. She has a Grammy. A CMA. A TV show.

Then Eva had sent something that shocked him:

Liam, she disappeared six months ago and hasn't been seen since. Social media is having a field day saying she's in Beaumont. I thought our brother was a PR nightmare. You need a plan. Have one by the time I get there.

Liam, known in his family as the list maker and the planner, had been doing nothing but planning for the past hour. Once he'd done his own scouring of social media, the urgency at which the decisions had to be made became even more critical. People were starting to put two and two together and getting four. They'd deduced that the girl who'd fallen and passed out at the wedding and the girl who'd run off with Liam Clayton at the winery were the same person.

Many social media sites had posted the headline "Is this the same person?" atop side-by-side images of Melynda at her last concert and the girl photographed leaving the winery. The *yes*es that Lexi-Melynda were the same ran three to one. Then came the speculation of why Melynda was in Beaumont working at Clayton Hotels, and the answers ranged from speculation that Melynda was undercover researching for her next movie to the idea that Melynda was having a mental breakdown over the fact that Damon's solo career had taken off and hers hadn't.

Liam knew what Lexi had told him, so he knew Lexi's version of the truth. He also knew she hadn't told him everything, but then he hadn't wanted to pry earlier and send her into another panic attack. Besides, the side-by-side pictures told a story. The Lexi who'd manned the bar and made love to him had a passion and a fire in her eyes that Melynda did not. Melynda's face, while pretty, had been too thin and gaunt. Her cheeks had hollows. Her hair might be in the style of how a pop star should look, but the bleached, straightened strands didn't have the natural beauty of Lexi's hair, waves he'd caressed and run through his fingers.

Whoever Lexi had been, she didn't want to be that version of herself any longer. Liam could understand. He'd left behind the Liam who'd been with Anya, the one who'd craved hiking more than breath itself. He was new Liam— vice president. Soon to be dad. People changed and grew. He would give Lexi the benefit of the doubt.

Liam had always had a strong protective urge, but the fact Lexi carried his twins made him even more determined to care for her and ensure her safety and happiness. He might not be able to love a woman deeply again, but he cared for Lexi. He would ensure that she and their children had their every need and whim met. Another text came in from his sister that contained a link:

I'm on my way to suite. You need to click this now.

However, his phone rang, and even though he groaned, he answered the call. "Hi, Mom."

"Eva says you have to talk to me and your dad. You know we came into town today, right? So lunch tomorrow? Anyway, you're on Speaker. What's going on?"

Darn Eva. Always sticking her nose into everyone else's business. He'd wanted to have a firm approach before talking to his mom and dad. Liam took a deep breath. "Well…" He didn't know how to tell them he was about to have two children out of wedlock. "Uh, the thing is…"

"I can't hear you," his mom said. "Are you there? This is as bad as when we try to call Edmund. We need a new phone."

"We don't need a new phone. Just spit it out, son," his dad said before Liam's mother got frustrated. "Eva said we should call, that there's a situation. I heard someone passed out last night. Is it about that? Or are you quitting early? You said you'd give me a year. I expect a year of work from you, son."

"And you'll get your year. I promised that." Liam heaved another sigh and decided he might as well rip off the Band-Aid. "The server who fainted? She's Lexi Henderson. Also formerly known as Melynda Norfolk."

"The pop star. I've heard of her. She was huge. We were

trying to negotiate a residency for her and Damon in Vegas. Why's she working in our hotel as a server?" his dad asked.

"That doesn't matter," Liam said. "It's all over social media that she's pregnant."

"Does this mean the paparazzi is going to be coming to our hotel? Is that the situation Eva's trying to control? We will, of course, do that for her. But why is she working as a server?"

"Her job is not what's important. It's the fact she's pregnant. With twins. Identical twins. They're mine." He ignored his mother's gasp. "Congratulations. You're going to be grandparents."

The wedding party was back in the hotel. Lexi had seen the bride and groom pass by the entrance to Esprit. Thankfully, they hadn't come inside. Taking her break, she'd texted Damon, asking him about her father. Since she hadn't gotten any response, she did the rare thing of scrolling social media. What she'd seen caused the panic she'd felt at the winery to return. The number of posts had exploded exponentially.

Alvin poked his head around the door. "You okay?"

"Yep," Lexi called back, trying to keep her voice light and chipper. She'd told Alvin about Liam. But she hadn't told him about Damon. She tried to formulate a plan.

Even if the proof and the speculation was on the internet, maybe denial could still be the best policy. Sure, pop stars changed their hair color—just look at Lady Gaga, Billie Eilish, or Dua Lipa—but that didn't mean Lexi was Melynda. Maybe she could pretend she wasn't Melynda. If someone said "Hey, aren't you Melynda?" Lexi could blow it off and say, "Oh, I get that a lot." While the fan would be disappointed, hopefully they'd believe her. People accepted celebrities had doppelgängers. Almost every sporting event showed those on the jumbo screen, and social media often did celebrity look-alike profiles. As long as she and Damon weren't in the same room, she had plausible deniability. And she was carrying Liam's babies, not Damon's.

Lexi wished she hadn't panicked today, or that hindsight wasn't that nasty twenty-twenty. So much for her strong self-control. She could have handled the situation so much better had she thought things through and been better prepared. Had she laughed off the accusations at the winery with an easy "I wish" or an "I get that a lot" to those girls, she wouldn't be in this situation.

Alvin poked his head around the corner. "Hey, FYI. Nancy is on her way."

Lexi smoothed down her vest and straightened as Nancy breezed in with a "Lexi, come with me." Saying Nancy had breezed in wasn't the best descriptor, Lexi decided. Unlike a breath of fresh air, Nancy had arrived with an expediency that announced her as a woman on a mission. Like the other day, she wore her blue pencil skirt, a suit jacket and a silk shirt. "I'm supposed to bring you to Mr. Clayton."

Lexi frowned. Liam had been dropping by the bar all day. Why hadn't he come himself? "He called for me again?"

"Yes. Quickly now." Unlike the designer heels that had clicked—how many weeks ago had it been?—this time Nancy's flats made no sound as she and Lexi wove their way through the corridors to the office. Liam met them before they reached the conference room. Like watching a movie, Lexi heard him thank Nancy. He then turned to Lexi.

"Hey," he said. "It's time to go. We found someone to cover your shift."

Lexi sensed an urgency to him that she hadn't seen before. "Is everything okay?"

He cupped her elbow, his fingers gentle despite their restrained tension. He guided her to the doorway. "We'll talk in a few."

"Really, I'm fine. I've seen the internet. We can say it's not me. Eva can spin some story about doppelgängers." Lexi resisted the childish urge to pull away—the sensible shoes she wore wouldn't give her a purchase on the tile anyway.

"Grab your purse." He'd accompanied her to her locker, and once she retrieved her belongings, he led her to the employee exit. "Do you have sunglasses?"

"Yes." Lexi dug into the oversize tote bag crammed with her stuff.

"Put them on. And add this." Liam pushed a ball cap onto her head before covering his eyes with a pair of classic mirrored aviators. He pushed open the exit. "Get ready. We have unwelcome company. Eva's trying to get rid of them, but they're media guests who were covering the wedding and Damon's concert."

"What? Oh no!" Despite the hat and sunglasses, Lexi covered her face with her hands as two paparazzi began shouting out questions and taking pictures. "Are you Melynda Norfolk?" one shouted.

"Are you researching a role?" the other called.

"Why hasn't anyone seen you for six months? Are you having a breakdown?"

"Melynda, what is your relationship with Liam Clayton?"

"Are you keeping the baby?"

Liam's arm draped possessively over her shoulders and shielded her. "Get in."

Lexi climbed inside the golf cart, and Liam started the electric engine. Soon Liam was speeding down the service path, but not in the direction of the Grand. He made a quick turn. Lexi hadn't been on this section of the service road before. "It's okay, Lexi. Breathe. You're clearly not okay, but it's going to be fine."

"No, it won't be. No, I am not okay. None of this is okay. I'm pregnant, my father is texting me, and people are shouting at me, and you're dragging me away."

"If it helps, there were more photographers in the lobby. We got you out in time. The bar's open to the public and people have phones."

Lexi clutched the front grab bar. "Why do they care? Can't they follow Taylor or Miley instead? They are so much more interesting than me."

"Maybe, but my guess is it's because Damon's here. That's one reason why you're viral on social media. The other is because you're with the reclusive Liam Clayton." Liam bit out his last name as if he detested it. "Someone at the hospital must have leaked that you're pregnant."

Lexi jutted her chin forward. "There are laws against that."

"Yes, and we can look into suing them later if you want, that is if we can even figure out who. An orderly? A tech? A nurse? Someone in the hall? Another patient? Their family? Who knows? Could be anyone."

"Not Dr. McMenamy." She'd liked the doctor, and he was way too kind.

"I agree. Not him. But whoever it was, for right now, we

need to get you out of Beaumont. With Damon here, it'll get worse. He's extended his stay."

"No." Lexi made a fist with her free hand. "Make him go. If he goes, I can lie. Say I look like her."

"Lexi, Damon confirmed it was you. The cat is out of the bag."

Her throat seized. "I texted him! I told him not to do that!"

"You texted him? When? Why? Anyway, maybe it happened before you texted him. Like when we were leaving. I'll ask Eva. She was there. According to her, he stayed at the winery for a while signing autographs. And in the grand scheme of things, does it matter who said what?"

"Yes. No. Maybe. I was building a life here." Her life had turned upside down and inside out. She hated it. She'd wanted calm and contained. This was anything but.

Liam sensed her tumult, for his tone soothed. "And you still are. But for now, we need a tactical retreat. That's what we're going to do. I just need you to trust me. Can you do that? I probably should have discussed this with your earlier, but time's been of the essence."

They'd reached the end of the cart path. Liam turned the ignition off, removed his sunglasses, folded them and set them on the seat. He reached over and gently pulled off hers. "You panicked at the winery, and what's out there is getting worse. People are speculating. We needed a plan and I made one."

"I'm not having a mental breakdown."

He tucked some hair behind her ear and then ran a finger along her cheek. "I know you're not. But you know the media. They publish whatever gets the most clicks. The best thing to do is retrench. If something is burning, you take it out of the oven or off the fire. You don't add more flame."

"That makes sense," Lexi admitted. "Do you know you talk in analogies sometimes?"

"It's what makes me so adorable. So trust me. Because at some point it will be obvious you're pregnant, and I want you safe and sound before that happens. I want you to be healthy and strong. Be the gutsy woman I couldn't resist in the wine bar."

Liam reached for her hand. Her body recognized his and desired the feel of his rough velvet skin on hers. "The sooner you and I come up with something, decide on which bone we can throw them, the sooner the paparazzi will move on and find more interesting people to hound. There has to be some other celebrity doing something stupid that will take the heat off you. Off us."

Lexi shook her head. That was what made this situation so terrible. "No, from experience I know they don't give up."

"Then maybe we should leak another story. Do you think that would help? I can run it by Eva. If she agrees, what should we tell them? That we're madly in love? That we've been dating these past six months and hadn't wanted to take our relationship public until now? That you're learning all parts of the hotel business because we're engaged and you're planning on joining my family business?"

"We are not engaged. We are not in love. I am not marrying you. The lies only make things worse." Lexi balled her fists in frustration as she bit back the tears. "I hate gossip. Social media. All of it. It exists only to destroy people's self-esteem. To destroy people."

Lexi's chest heaved as she fought the panic. She couldn't

have an attack now. She had to think. Be reasonable. She heard the *whomp-whomp* noise before she saw the cause. A sleek black helicopter came into view and began to lower onto the field in front of them. "Liam, what is going on?"

"Trust me, Lexi. We need a plan, and we can't make a good one here. So I made a temporary one for us. You, me? We're leaving. I'm hoping that works for you?"

She couldn't form an answer but nodded her assent.

"Okay. Let's go."

Liam knew he'd shocked Lexi with his exit strategy, but whatever else Lexi might have wanted to say was lost in the noise of the chopper descending. The blades whipped the dust and flattened the grass. For expediency of takeoff, the pilot would keep it running, so it was the copilot who jumped out and brought Lexi and Liam headphones, which silenced the noise. Liam rounded the front of the golf cart and helped Lexi out. He rushed her through the downdraft to the chopper, which soon had them airborne.

"Doctor's orders were for no stress," Liam said over the headset. "You've had two panic attacks today alone. This is the fastest way to get us out of here."

It had been fortuitous his parents had flown into town today. That meant the company jet had been nearby. Once he'd decided where they would go, the rest was easy. Liam had spoken with the ER doctor from the night before, and the doctor had told him about an obstetrics practice that he'd trust to deliver his kids. Using the power of the Clayton family network, Liam already had Lexi's new appointment scheduled. But Liam told Lexi none of this, for she gripped the seat tightly and looked straight ahead instead of at the green landscape below.

The chopper landed at Spirit of St. Louis Airport. Even though he knew she'd known the truth the moment they'd gotten in the air, the landing had confirmed that they were leaving Beaumont. "This isn't where I live," she said.

"No, it's not. We're going to take a vacation. It's the only solution. I have property in Estes Park. It's nothing but trees and snowcapped mountains. Clean mountain air. No photographers. We'd be out of reach of everyone, including my mother, who already is clamoring for a wedding. I told her about the twins this afternoon. I got the approval of the ER doctor, and he said it would be fine for us to travel. You'll have to adjust to the altitude before doing anything strenuous, not that you should be doing any heavy lifting. Believe me, the view is worth the trip."

He guided her up the stairs and inside the jet. "Let me do this for you, Lexi."

And maybe, in a sense, he was doing this for himself, too. He hadn't been back in two years. Not since he'd lost Anya. The house he'd built had sat empty, a ghost of the past waiting to be revived. Perhaps it was time for Liam to stop mourning for what would never occur and move on. He had children to think about, and it was the first place that had come to mind. He'd built the house for a family, so Lexi should be comfortable. The place wouldn't have any of Anya's personal effects. He owed Edmund big time for handling the removal of those once the funeral had ended.

Outside, the chopper pilot took off while the chopper's copilot had entered the plane and joined Chris, Clayton Holdings' main pilot in the cockpit. Once Chris flew them to Northern Colorado Regional Airport, a two-and-a-half-hour flight max, they'd make the hour drive west to Estes

Park. Liam glanced into the cockpit to see Chris sending the tower their flight plan.

Cheryl, the Clayton's long-serving flight attendant, greeted them. "Get her some water," Liam instructed as he settled Lexi into one of the comfortable chairs. He might have failed to protect Anya and their unborn child had he known she was pregnant…but he hadn't. A heavy weight settled on Liam's shoulders and his throat constricted. Even though it hadn't been his fault, and even though Anya had kept her pregnancy a secret from him—if she'd even known—this time he wouldn't fail. He'd protect Lexi. Keep her and the twins safe. He couldn't fail again, too much was at stake.

Lexi buckled her seat belt and stared around the opulent jet. From the way she didn't appear too awed, he knew she'd ridden on many a private plane. After all, she was Melynda Norfolk, pop star and icon. He never would have expected this strange twist of events weeks ago when he'd asked for some bourbon in the bar. Part of him wondered if he knew her at all. The other part knew he did, and better than the fans, the paparazzi, Damon, or the father she tried not to mention.

He saw the panic arrive again. "Liam, wait! I can't leave town. My life's here. My stuff. I haven't told my roommate I'll be gone. How long are we going? What will I do for clothes?"

"Shh. It's going to be okay. We needed a place to chat where they can't find us." He reached and took her hand. He liked the weight of her palm in his. "All those things you just mentioned, we can take care of them once we're in the air. Chris said we should have smooth skies for the next two hours, so relax. If we come back tomorrow, that'll be fine.

If we stay a while, that'll be fine too. But we can't talk or figure things out if we're under a social media microscope."

"True. Thank you." Her breathing slowed.

Liam had never quite understood his older brother's statement that being a Clayton meant one could work miracles, that was until Edmund had to bring Anya home. Today it was now Liam's turn to wave the magic wand that being a Clayton afforded, a power he held as a birthright. The engines whirred and the plane began to taxi to the runway. Within minutes, they'd be westward. By the time they'd get to the Estes Park house, it would be around eight thirty Mountain Standard Time.

"Liam…"

He reached over and placed a forefinger on soft lips he'd love to kiss. Maybe later, much later, when she felt better. "Let it go for now, Lexi. There's time enough later. The doctor said no stress, and I'd say today was pretty stressful. Please let me do this for you. I'm taking you somewhere special. Mountains. Fresh air. Open skies. You'll love Colorado."

Lexi's nose wrinkled and she sipped the water Cheryl had brought. "Colorado?"

Liam said the words that sealed their fate. "Yes. I'm taking you to my home."

Chapter Nine

Having spent most of her formative years in eastern Tennessee and Nashville, Lexi had seen mountains. Even LA had its version. But not like this. Pictures hadn't prepared her for the majesty of the Front Range of the Rocky Mountains. The white-capped, jagged peaks rose to the sky in an attempt to kiss the heavens. Liam's Range Rover bumped over a winding, well-maintained dirt road, Highway 36 having been left behind more than fifteen minutes ago.

She must be crazy to be agreeing to Liam's escape plan, but when Liam had asked if she trusted him, her instinctive thought had been a resounding *yes*. When she'd called Dawn to explain, her roommate had told her that there were several photographers sitting in cars outside the house and that they'd shouted at her and asked where Lexi was. Dawn had easily accepted the fact Lexi was actually a singer, but the fact there were photographers stalking the house was extremely upsetting to her. To make things right, Liam had gotten on the phone, and after promising Dawn a year's rent to break the rental agreement, and the equivalent of another year's rent to a local animal shelter to offset the inconvenience, Lexi officially became homeless.

Satisfied with the fact the reporters would be leaving,

Dawn had written down Eva's number. Eva would pack and ship whatever Lexi needed and that the rest could go to charity. It wasn't much, Lexi admitted. After six months, she had two suitcases worth of things. She leaned back against the seat. She and Liam had about an hour to sunset, and as the power he could wield began to settle on her shoulders, the beauty of the mountains reminded her that she was simply a speck in the huge expanse of time. Lexi thus caved to the inevitable and let him take over. It seemed easier, especially after Damon had texted that he'd come to find her at Esprit. He'd sent a message saying that they'd told him she'd left and asked what was going on.

Lexi hadn't responded. Instead, she marveled at the fact that protecting her was so important to Liam that he was taking her to his home—the one he hadn't seen for two years. She didn't know exactly what to make of that fact, but she sensed its importance. She recognized the sacrifice he was making.

Liam's Range Rover had been waiting in the parking lot—someone having driven it over while they'd been in the air. On the drive, he'd told her he owned 136 pristine acres. As they rounded a curve, the house came into sight. Surrounded by trees, the structure was snuggled high into the bosom of a smaller mountain. Late evening sun bathed the place in a surreal glow. Lexi gasped. "That's it?"

"All mine. I designed it." Pride laced his tone.

She didn't know that about him. "You're an architect?"

He appeared slightly sheepish at her light but accusatory tone. "Guilty. Did my undergrad at Stanford. Graduate degree at Harvard. My specialty is sustainable architecture. Then I created a tech start-up and sold it."

"And now you're in charge of the wineries." The thought boggled her mind. He was far more than met the eye.

"I am. I told my dad a year." He seemed resigned but then brightened. "You'd be amazed at how sustainable the Clayton Winery division is. We recycle and reuse bottles. We make verjus, which is the juice made from unripened grapes that's often used in cooking or mocktails. The Grand and the Chateau use geothermal heat and have solar panels that don't look like a solar farm. Costs a little more, but we believe it's worth it. This house was my pet project. It's all me, and I worked with a consulting firm to be sure the impact to wildlife and the land were as minimal as possible."

"It looks like you," Lexi admitted. For the house did, far more than his Third Street rental. The structure was made of stucco, log and stone that made his home fit seamlessly into the landscape. The edifice poked out of a small clearing and, like a bird perched on the edge of a branch, the building had a commanding view of the landscape below.

She found herself awed and impressed. He'd created something. Oh, she'd tried, once wanting to write her own songs, but each one of her ideas had been shot down. After that, she'd kept the notebooks filled with lyrics to herself. Her father had overseen the producing of Lexi and Damon's music, pushing producers until he'd been satisfied they had a hit on their hands. Liam had taken his vision and made it reality by himself.

"Tell me about building it," Lexi said, for Liam had grown quieter the closer they'd gotten. They'd hardly spoken on the plane, as once the panic had subsided, she'd taken a long nap. Now that they rode in his car and headed to his house, whatever this "vacation" was that he'd planned, it wasn't going to work if they didn't communicate. Co-parenting wouldn't work either. "It had to be amazing watching it go up."

"It was fantastic." Liam became slightly more animated as he began to tell her about his vision. "I wanted something off-the-grid but not rustic. It's fifty-eight-hundred square feet and has a commercial kitchen. I wanted to work in harmony with Mother Nature, not against her. Think of the ancient Greeks and Romans and even the Chinese and Egyptians. In Bolivia, there are ancient civilizations that used sustainable strategies. Many early cultures used the earthly materials that were nearby to build whole villages. We moved away from that when we discovered how to mass produce bricks and concrete. You'll notice the air out here is so much cooler. There's no urban heat island where those materials trap and hold in the heat."

They were still on the drive and took another switchback. The house nestled into the mountainside, its artfully arranged solar panels angled to capture the sun. They drove past more solar panels located in a clearing. Liam had a barn and several fenced yet empty pastures, and then the SUV climbed upward through two additional switchbacks until they reached the house itself. Liam drove into a four-car garage that contained one other SUV and two, all-terrain four-wheelers. "We're about five minutes from town. You can see the town of Estes Park from the deck. You can even see the Stanley Hotel. The incredible view sold me on this spot."

"I can see why. It's gorgeous." She took a deep inhale. "You're right, the air seems fresher. Better."

"Thinner, so you'll need to get used to the altitude." He helped Lexi from the vehicle, curving an arm around her waist. "It'll be the perfect bolt hole for us to plan and figure things out. And protest all you want, but I'm covering your bills while you're here, and if you want to enroll in online classes, I have satellite internet. Let me give you a tour. We're entering on the lowest level. It's built into the side of the mountain, so there are both stairs and an elevator."

Lexi discovered that this level had an indoor lap pool, workout room and sauna. They took the elevator to the main level, which had fourteen-foot ceilings. Wooden beams the color of warm caramel topped floor-to-ceiling windows that let in a three-sided view. A huge deck wrapped around the house. Liam led her outside, where she discovered a bridge that led to the top of a set of boulders, where a hot tub had been built in between natural rock outcroppings. He flipped on the lights. The setting sun created shadows on the surrounding treetops. Back in the house, the kitchen opened to the dining room and living room. All the rooms had breathtaking views of the Front Range and the valley below.

"I love it. It's you." Whereas Liam's rental had been decorated by his landlord Zoe, personal decorations flourished here. Photos of his family lined the wooden fireplace mantel. Knickknacks and trinkets—many from foreign countries—adorned tables. The contrast made the point painfully clear: this was Liam's home. The home he'd lived in with Anya. Anya, the reason Liam would never love again. She pushed the pang from her heart. One-night stands did not make relationships. He'd rescued her and given her great sex. What she felt for Liam had to be hormones, that was all, and best she remember that.

Liam opened the refrigerator, withdrew a pitcher and poured each of them a glass of water. "My caretaker and his wife live in the apartment above the barn. He maintains the place for me. Write down a list of everything you need from the grocery store, and I'll have him get it for you. I'll give you my PO Box. It has a street address, so anything not purchased in town you can ship there and someone will pick it up."

Lexi could see that two-story barn building from the window, as well as the parallel lines of the four acres Liam had fenced in. "He and his wife manage the upkeep and stock the kitchen. All you have to do is ask and they'll shop and deliver. But we'll do our own cooking. No one delivers restaurant takeout this far from town. You'll find out how good a chef I am."

"I'm not sure how serious you're being right now. I hope you can cook, because I can't."

His grin covered his face and lit up the room. "I'm not a top chef, but I'm not entirely helpless in the kitchen. It will be edible. And if you think I suck at meal prep, well, we can subscribe to some of those online, meal kit delivery services and be sure to pick it up in town the day it's delivered. I'm up for the challenge."

"I'll take you at your word." Lexi stepped out onto the balcony and drew in a deep breath of clean mountain air. Unlike in LA, no exhaust of city cars or the aroma of trash and a million people here. Nothing but pine, juniper and wildflowers. The sun was behind the mountain, casting the valley in twilight. She gazed out over the town of Estes Park, snuggled down below, the lights flickering in distant windows.

"Tomorrow you'll also be able to see elk and mule deer wandering through the property. They come through frequently. It's really incredible."

Lexi sighed. "I know this place holds sad memories. I'm sorry you had to bring me."

Liam cupped her chin and lifted her face. "The doctor said no stress, and this is the most stress-free place I know. Let's make some good memories here."

"I feel like an invader." She had to be honest.

He dropped his hand from her chin. "I will do anything to protect you and the twins. This is your home now. There are no traces of Anya. Edmund took care of that, for which I'm grateful. Besides, the accident is in the past. The babies are my priority, and by extension, you. If you haven't noticed, I'm the type of guy who does what needs to be done."

"I'm starting to realize that." Liam, not wanting to face Anya's things, had asked his brother for help. But still, this had been their place. Even if her possessions weren't in sight, she'd walked these halls, sat on the leather couches and slept in Liam's bed. Lexi watched as Liam gripped the wooden railing. He shrugged and rolled his shoulders, as if trying to free the hidden tension.

"I'd forgotten how much how I loved the air here. Crisp. Clean." He closed his eyes and inhaled a deep breath. "At some point you have to face your demons. You can't run away."

"Ironic, as that's why I'm here." Lexi couldn't help it. The words slipped out. "I'm running yet again."

Liam's gaze locked on hers. "You faced your demons when you bought out your contract and moved to Beaumont. Coming to Colorado with me is being brave. You're doing what needs to be done for the lives growing inside of you. They depend on you being stress-free. Consider this a strategic retreat rather than a surrender. A tactical maneuver, not an evasive technique. We'll let the media frenzy die down and we'll make a plan. One day at a time. One step at a time."

Six months ago she'd vowed to save herself and not let another man run her life. Modern-day Cinderellas didn't need Prince Charmings to make them whole. But Liam had a way with words, making her want to believe. Of course, she'd heard similar things before. And this wasn't some rom-com fantasy but the real world.

He faced her. "Would you mind if I went and climbed? I've missed tackling the mountains. Standing here, it's like an itch I must scratch."

"I'd be selfish if I refused you."

"But you could."

His answer surprised her and Lexi shook her head. She had no real claim over him. "That wouldn't be right or fair. I don't want you to control me, and I don't want to control you."

He reached for her hand and toyed with the finger that would wear an engagement ring, if she ever found Mr. Right. A vision of Liam on bended knee had her pulling away.

If he noticed her quick withdrawal, he didn't acknowledge it. "There's another SUV in the garage. That's yours to use. I'll drive you into town the first time or two, but after you know your way around, drive it as often as you want. Don't get cabin fever. While the doctor says no stress, you're not a prisoner. I don't want you to be trapped like one."

"I'm more worried that you and I will drive each other crazy the longer we're together," Lexi admitted. That's what had happened with her and Damon, and they hadn't even been intimate. But so many years on the road, surrounded by people, had taken a toll.

Silence fell as they studied the famous white Stanley Hotel, which was lit up and visible in the distance. Finally, Liam's deep voice broke through. "We don't have to be alone. Remember my friends from the wedding? Scott and Julia? They live nearby. We can visit them. You'd like Julia, I think. And it's a big house. We can find ways to occupy ourselves, even without sex."

A warm evening breeze teased Lexi's hair. Liam caught a strand and brought it to his nose. Lexi reached out and put her hand on his arm. "Liam."

He dropped her hair as if she'd scalded him. "Sorry. Ever since the doctor told me you're pregnant, and ever since the truth was out, I've wanted to kiss you. It's been hard keeping my distance and my hands to myself. But I will."

The doctor had told them that having sex was fine. And she couldn't get any more pregnant. And the light pressure of his palm on her arm was doing delicious things. Sex had been their fundamental connection. She'd had one night. Why couldn't she have more? Enjoy being Liam's lover for as long as it lasted, for Liam wasn't going to fall in love with her. But he could make love to her, teach her all the things he knew until the spark between them burned out and he moved on to someone else. As long as they remained friends and great co-parents, she'd be fine, even if that was a lie she told herself. "Liam."

At the sound of his name, his lips parted and his eyes darkened. Miles from everywhere, not even a high-powered scope could see this far. She fingered the buttons on her shirt. His breath hitched as she shed the garment, dropping the oxford cloth to the deck. Already her breasts were heavier, bigger. While not needing any kind of maternity bra yet, she would have to purchase new undergarments soon. As she'd fled with the clothes on her back, she'd shop tomorrow. For tonight, she wanted the magic the night promised.

"Lexi." He coughed, choked as he fought to maintain control over his body. "Lexi, what are you doing? You don't have to."

"Meet me halfway, Liam." She brought his left hand to her right breast, folding his fingers until they cupped and weighed. Now she was the one quickly losing control. "I don't break. You do want to keep me stress-free, don't you? Doctor's orders?"

"Yes," he rasped, drawing the bra cup down so he could flick a thumb unimpeded over her straining peak.

Lexi whimpered with pleasure as her nipple detonated and swelled. Somehow, she wouldn't let him divert her or regain control. Not yet. "I don't know why we have this chemistry between us, but I want it. It's a place to start, especially as I'm in a space you never meant for me or wanted me to be. A space you probably planned to sell."

"If someone had come up with the necessary millions. I admit I almost listed it. Had it out privately, but the deal fell through. In a way, I'm glad. It means we can come here. Get a chance to get to know each other."

"We did get interrupted," Lexi admitted. "I'm sorry this is hard. You're being exceptionally kind. You and I didn't intend to become parents. We didn't intend to even fall into bed."

"I liked being in bed with you. I wanted you. I still do. You don't love me and I don't love you. But we have passion and caring and two children between us."

They did. Could it be enough? She was realizing that her feelings for him were turning into more. Liam was so lovable. He was worthy of so much. She didn't like the idea of any other woman having him, touching him or loving him. But she didn't trust her burgeoning feelings, especially since she'd heard the stories about what pregnancy hormones could do. She was also realistic. Eventually they would each move on. They'd share children and manage to get along with each other's spouses. Even if the thought nauseated her, she'd make it work.

She let go of the negativity as Liam's hands found her bra straps and yanked them down around her biceps. He could make her forget, as he had the first night. Show her the sun, the moon and the stars in his lovemaking. He stripped her top half bare in the midst of the warm summer night. Her skin heated. She suppressed the moan and tried not to detonate.

"You're fighting me, aren't you? After you started this, you try and resist?" He chuckled and tugged at her jeans, sending a hand into her heat. "This isn't a battle you can win. I don't fight fair. Never have."

Lexi whimpered and let him take over. She leaned against the railing of his palace in the sky, until he carried her inside and made love to her in the huge king-size bed in a master bedroom with panoramic views of the mountains.

She awoke to find herself in the dark, surprised at how pitch-black the room was. LA and Nashville always had had ambient light, but out in the wilderness, the sky blasted a billion stars instead.

She found him in the kitchen, pasta boiling and sauce simmering on an eight-burner stove. "Sleep well? I'm making spaghetti. It's one of my many chef-inspired dishes. Just don't look in the recycle bin for the glass jar."

Her stomach grumbled. "Smells delicious."

"Food will be ready in a few. I'd call it dinner but it's like eleven. Midnight snack Beaumont time."

"That late? Huh." She felt oddly rested.

He grinned. "We were pretty active, and it takes a bit to get used to being at seventy-five hundred feet above sea level. Beaumont was a mere six hundred fifty. Perhaps we shouldn't have been so strenuous."

"I don't break," Lexi reminded him, leaning to sniff the tomatoey smell of spaghetti sauce. Her body ached in scrumptious ways, and she had missed Liam's touch. She would take the physical. But what would that make her? Was she a woman exercising her own agency? Or was she instead rather pathetic for settling for pleasure and substituting it for real substance? Was that using someone or being used? She didn't know.

This was uncharted territory, and she wondered if she might be passing on a chance of a real connection with someone by settling with Liam. Should she sacrifice that for her children? Could she live with always being second best—as she was with Damon and now Liam—to be found useful in the moment but not long-term? Perhaps life was a series of fleeting moments of happiness followed by second-guesses and regrets. She wished she had closer girlfriends. Did her coworkers count? They were probably gossiping about her. And she and Dawn had cohabited and cared about each other, but they weren't besties. In this decision, she was alone. She missed her mother more than ever.

Liam served spaghetti onto her plate. They sat at the kitchen table. "It's good," Lexi said as she took her first bite. Conversation stilled as she chewed. Then again, how did one communicate with someone when you knew each other as intimately as you could but still didn't know each other, or at least not in the ways that counted? Lexi understood sex was sex. Nothing more. Her stylists, makeup artists and others had reinforced that as they'd bemoaned their weekends or decried their relationships.

"I can feel you thinking from here," Liam told her.

She toyed with her spaghetti, wrapping it around her fork tines but not lifting the portion to her mouth. "This is new territory. I'd never had sex, much less casual sex before I met you. I liked what happened just now very much."

If he was surprised she'd been a virgin, he didn't show it. Instead, he concentrated on the present. "At the same time, it's messing with your head, isn't it?"

He could read her so well it was scary. "Somewhat," Lexi admitted. "Exactly what are your expectations? What does one day at a time mean? Do you want me to be in my own bedroom? Do you want me to share your bedroom? I don't know what's going on. Maybe we should talk about that."

"Why don't you tell me what you want?" Liam asked.

Had anyone ever really asked her that before? Next to her, like a prophetic sign, her phone buzzed with an incoming text. Automatically she turned over the phone and saw the name. Damon. She flipped the phone back over. "I don't know. This is where you and Anya lived. I feel like an interloper."

"It's just a house. You're the mother of my children. This is yours as much as mine."

She wished she believed him. She put some of the spaghetti in her mouth, chewing slowly. She wasn't certain what to say. "That didn't answer my question. Is there an intimacy to sharing a bed? Like, we're lovers but that's it. Friends with benefits. Although, that sounds sort of cheap."

Was she being illogical? Her father often told her she was.

"How can you feel cheap if you're the mother of my children?" Liam asked.

"I just can. This isn't a real relationship. We didn't want this. And while I said I need you to meet me halfway, I don't even know what halfway looks like."

He set his fork down. "Are you sure you don't regret what happened between us earlier?"

"No. Yes. I don't know. I don't understand the rules. I lived a sheltered life. Work. Be perfect. Be the good girl. And then with you, I was a bad girl."

"You are not a bad girl, Lexi. You're a woman with a healthy sex drive, and we have incredible chemistry. There is nothing wrong with you. You're great exactly who you are, and who you are is wonderful. You don't have to impress anyone, especially me. I like you exactly the way you are. If you're asking if I'm going to cheat on you, the answer is no. I'll marry you if you change your mind and want that. I'll sleep in your bed if you want that. I'll be yours if you want that. You tell me."

Yes, he might do all those things. But it wouldn't be enough because she'd never have love. He'd told her at the winery that he didn't think he'd ever fall in love again, that he considered Anya his soulmate. He'd said it wasn't even on his radar to try. He'd been truthful then, and she knew he was being truthful now.

"Thank you," she said for lack of something else to add. She'd long ago learned that when a decision had been made—in this case Liam's feelings—things wouldn't change even if she wanted them to.

He set his napkin on the table. "I get up early in the morning when I hike, like three or four o'clock, so I don't want you to feel you have to wake up with me. Maybe having your own space might be best so that you can sleep straight through if you want. Or if you want to have a place to go if you need to get away. There are three guest bedroom suites in this house. Take one if you want."

That sounded perfectly reasonable, which made the pang of heartbreak she experienced irritating. She had to be stronger than this where he was concerned. "Okay."

"It doesn't mean I don't want you less. The sex we have is incredible. What we just did proved that our one night wasn't a fluke." Liam had finished his food. Dinner had been a delicious salad and pasta, yet she had no appetite. "You didn't eat much."

"I'm not really hungry."

He nodded. "Might be the altitude. It can take a while to become adjusted. Drink lots of water. When you're hungry, the rest will be in the refrigerator. Help yourself. There's nothing in the house that you can't touch. I mean it, Lexi. Treat this like your home."

She rose and walked back outside. Across the valley, lights flickered, like friendly beacons far below. The mountains themselves were dark, reminding Lexi of that one time she'd stood at the edge of the ocean and gazed out into the blackness of the never-ending water. Above her was a different story. Without any light pollution, billions of white sparkly dots covered the night sky. She located the Big Dipper. Pulling her phone out, she used an app to locate Jupiter and Venus. Then she found Vega, Deneb and Altair. Her arm was still stretched and the phone held high when Liam approached.

"Learning something new about you every day." He

wrapped his arms around her and pulled her toward him. She enjoyed the touch. "What are you looking at?"

She pointed. "Scorpio now, my zodiac sign. Can you see Antares? It's red. It's about eight hundred fifty times bigger than our sun."

"It's a red giant," Liam added. "Which is why it's red."

"Yes, and in the tail are Ptolemy's Cluster and the Butterfly Cluster. The death of Orion, the mighty hunter."

"So you're a Scorpio." He dropped his chin into the little dip in her shoulder.

"Yes. November 12. You?" She lowered her arm and locked the phone screen.

"March 18. Pisces, I think."

"Yes. We're both water signs. All my stylists loved to share their horoscopes so I learned. To be honest, I really just love looking at the stars."

"Me too. I'll order us a good telescope, but we won't see those stars until October and November."

Would they still be in Colorado then? Lexi didn't ask. One day at a time, he'd said. She'd try to follow that advice. "Pisces is two fishes tied by a ribbon. Aphrodite and Eros. Mother and son. I love astronomy. I would like to have studied it formally. I'm not as much into astrology, but my stylists were." Lexi scanned the skies, looking for other stars she knew. "The mythology fascinates me though."

"I'm like an old sailor. Despite having GPS, I often use the stars to navigate before the sun comes up. In order to have enough daylight to climb Longs Peak, I like to be on the trail by three o'clock. It's fifteen miles each way and takes between ten to thirteen hours for me to hike to the summit and back. Leaving that early also means that I'm below the tree line before the afternoon storms start, which is key. In late July and August we get thunderstorms almost every day, so best be prepared. And no worries. I'm very prepared to deal with lightning when I'm hiking."

Lexi shuddered. "I'd hate for you to get hit."

"So would I." Liam chuckled low and drew her backside closer to his front. His arms rested on her still-flat stomach. "I have a lot to look forward to. Thank you for that."

"It's strange to think I'll be huge soon. I…" Before she could tell him about her previous eating disorder, a ringing sound shattered the night. She fumbled for her phone, only to notice it wasn't hers. However, she had two more messages, both from Damon. She frowned as Liam stepped away. He held a phone to his ear.

"Hello?" He stepped into the living room and closed the sliding door behind him. Lexi swiped her phone open and studied the heavens for a few more moments. Then she sat in a chair and opened her phone. She deleted Damon's first text, which was the one telling her he'd come to Esprit to find her. His second one was much more to the point: Where are you?

His next one was an all caps: CALL ME.

Lexi glanced at the time. Beaumont was Central Standard Time, meaning it was an hour later there. But his text had been sent twenty minutes ago, meaning Damon would still be awake. She pressed the bar containing his number and the phone immediately began to dial. "Lexi, what the hell?" Damon said as the call connected.

She tightened her grip on the phone. "Hello to you too."

"Where are you? I've been worried sick."

She highly doubted that. Damon's only worry was his career and his next hit. "Don't worry. I'll be back to do your song."

"When? And you still haven't told me where you are." His tone was more accusatory than understanding.

"I'm in Colorado."

"What the hell?" Damon said again, which Lexi knew was his favorite phrase to use whenever he was frustrated. "Do I need to come get you?"

"No, especially since I just arrived. I'm staying with a friend."

"Liam Clayton." Damon practically spat out the words. "The one they're calling your baby daddy. Well, besides me. And we know it's not me."

"I didn't want to see my father," Lexi told Damon, circumventing the entire conversation. "You told me you wouldn't tell him I was in Beaumont."

"Lexi, he's worried about you. He can read social media like everyone else. I didn't have to say anything. I'm going for new management, remember?"

Lexi could always tell when Damon was lying. His voice hitched on the last syllable or last word. She heard that inflection and sighed. He hadn't changed. Neither had her father. She was the ticket to their careers, nothing more. Damon filled the silence. "Lexi, everyone is worried about you. You had a huge career and you walked away. Do at least one more song and go out on top."

"I said I'd do that song, Damon, but I'm not dealing with my father. That's nonnegotiable. He sued me. His own daughter. What kind of man does that? Tell you what, you figure out a recording schedule and let me know. I'll see if I can make it work. Until then, all you need to know is that I'm fine, I'm safe, and it's no one's business but mine why I'm here or who I'm with."

Jabbing the red end circle felt good. In the past she

wouldn't have dared or been brave enough to cut the call short. She rose and noticed Liam silhouetted in the doorway. "Damon?" he asked.

"He went into Esprit to talk to me and discovered I was gone. He's been texting. I told him I was fine. I told him I was in Colorado."

"But you didn't confirm who I was."

"I didn't think it was any of his business."

"I overheard that part. That's about where I came in. You can tell people you're with me. I'm honored to be the baby daddy to your twins."

Lexi shook her head. "I don't think you understand. The moment I issue confirmation, they'll find a way to fly helicopters out here. They won't leave us alone. If you thought what your brother endured after he went viral when Veronica broke up with him was bad, well, you've not seen anything yet." She shuddered. "I can't begin to tell you what I've gone through. They nitpick everything. I'm featured in thousands of reels, stories, you name it. Everyone wants a piece of me."

"The only piece I want of you is this one." He gathered her in his arms. "Lexi, I'm a Clayton. There are huge perks. I will keep you safe."

She prayed that was true. But at what cost? How much hard-fought independence would she have to give up? She realized Liam was still speaking. He'd drawn her closer.

"But I do have to warn you. There is one person who knows how to find us, and she's worse than the entire media machine put together."

"Eva?" She agreed with Liam's assessment that his sister was a force of nature.

He shook his head. "My mother. And tomorrow she's on her way."

* * *

"Well? What did he say?" Laverna Clayton demanded of her daughter as Eva lowered the phone.

"Liam knows we're coming out there sometime tomorrow. I told him to prepare the guest rooms." Eva set her phone on the dining room table of her mother's hotel suite in the Beaumont Grand. Even this late at night, her mother dripped with class and charisma.

Eva had always marveled at her mother. While born in Texas to a cattle rancher, Laverna was the epitome of an East Coast socialite. She'd fit right in with any of the Gilded Age matriarchs or easily hobnob with British royalty, which indeed she had. Laverna had shimmering silver hair, a wide smile—which she bestowed generously whenever her children did the right thing—and a frown that could make grown men quake in their boots. Never one to dress down, she still wore a pink sundress and the matching cardigan she'd worn to dinner. Unlike her mom, Eva wore a short-sleeved button sweater and jeans. She tried to remember a time her mother had worn jeans but failed. Liam, Michael and Edmund had gotten their height from their father, as their mom stood five foot two, same as Eva.

"I've texted Chris that he's to be on standby any time after noon tomorrow." Eva mentioned their pilot. "We'll take a chopper out from the airport to Liam's to save time."

"What do you know of this girl?"

"Lexi Henderson is a musician and an actress. Liam seems to like her." Enough that he'd fallen into bed with her, Eva thought but didn't add. That part was obvious. Eva still marveled that her brother had gone from celibacy to fatherhood, and with a virtual stranger. When she'd told him to stop wallowing, she hadn't meant like this.

"How's the construction going?" Eva switched to a safer subject, and listened as her mom began to describe the house she and Eva's dad were almost finished building in the same million-dollar subdivision as Eva's aunt and uncle. Eva's phone buzzed and she looked down to see the caller. "Hey Mom, I have to go meet someone in the lobby. Do you mind?"

"No, I'm going to change and go to bed. I'm still on Portland time. I'll see you downstairs for breakfast in the morning."

Eva gave her mom a kiss and headed downstairs and into the Grand's bar, which resembled a wood-paneled, nineteenth century British gentleman's club, complete with a fireplace in the corner and original artwork from local Beaumont artists. It was the kind of place that screamed old money but without any of the pretension or exclusivity.

She found Damon Stevener in a booth in the back. She slid in across from him. "Thanks for coming," he said.

Eva tilted her head, a movement she knew made her diamond stud earrings twinkle. For a brief moment after the wedding, she'd considered Damon a potential, but she'd dismissed the idea once he'd gained a few hangers-on. Eva didn't compete for male attention. She shoved a few strands of her bob behind her ear and waited. "So you know your employee at the Chateau, Lexi Henderson, is Melynda Norfolk."

"Despite all my internet research, I learned that at the same time everyone else did, at the winery." Eva had discovered that, when dealing with celebrities, sticking to the truth whenever possible worked best. "Until then I didn't know who she was."

"Did your brother? Because that's who's in the viral video. She told me she's in Colorado. I assume she's with him."

"I can confirm nothing," Eva said.

Damon scoffed. "Oh come on, Eva. You and I both know she's with him. He ushered her out of here like precious cargo. And now she's in Colorado? Only someone really rich has the power to do that. I did my own research. If she's pregnant like the gossip says, it's his."

"Again, I can neither confirm nor deny. And if she is with him, which I cannot confirm, then you should be reassured she's in good hands." Eva twisted her hands into her lap, rubbing the palms on her jeans. "My brother is the best human being on this planet."

Damon shook his head, sending floppy hair across his face. He shoved it back. "You should know that she bought out her contract. She's estranged from her father. She's broke, which is why she moved to Beaumont to become a bartender." He practically spit out the word.

"There's nothing wrong with that." Eva defended Lexi easily. "She's learning all aspects of our family business. In fact, Liam was behind the bar for a while at the wedding."

Damon tapped a finger on the table. "Lexi is a star, not a lackey. And now that the press has found her, they'll come for her. Does your brother really want that? He had enough press after the earthquake on Everest."

Even though she inwardly bristled, Eva remained calm. "If you researched my family, you'll know I'm the VP of Communications and that our family has handled far worse. I'm sure nothing will be as bad as you make it out to be."

"Have you seen this?" Damon reached for his phone, swiped and brought up a clip. The social media influencer had inserted a video of herself into the corner of the video of Liam and Lexi leaving the winery. What she said about Melynda was in no way flattering.

When the clip ended, he lowered the phone. "Melynda is as famous as Miley, Olivia and Taylor. Her walking away from fame has made her even more of a target. I can take her away from this. I can make it appear as if she's the victim, not me. She's agreed to sing one more song, a duet with me. She'll go out on top because the song's killer. You're in PR. You know we can fix this. She needs to return to LA, with me. If you see her, tell her I sent her father away. He came into town this evening and I told him to leave. There's bad blood between them because of her mother's death and her eating disorder."

"Her what?" He'd caught Eva off guard, and she'd reacted without thinking.

Damon leaned forward, conspiratorial tone locked into place. "You didn't know? That's only because her father hid it so well from the media. Lexi is an anorexic and bulimic. She's binge and purge. She's had both inpatient and outpatient therapy because when she's stressed she won't eat. Her panic attacks make it worse. I'm really worried this could send her back over the edge and give her a complete mental breakdown."

Not much shocked Eva, but this did. Still, minus her earlier lapse, she kept control over her emotions and her expressions, schooling her face into neutral as she had that one time her ex had blindsided her by having another woman in their bed. "I'll take that under advisement."

"Please do. I only have Melynda's—Lexi's—best interests at heart. You've got my number." With that, Damon slid out of the booth.

Eva watched as multiple people stopped him for selfies and autographs. She opened her phone and sent one text to her brother: We need to talk. Now.

Chapter Ten

"**S**hould I be worried about your mother?" Lexi asked Liam as she walked into the kitchen late the next morning. Following their respective phone calls, Liam had decided tugging her back into bed had been the best option. This morning, when he'd called his sister in response to her cryptic text, Eva had unsettled him by what she'd revealed about Lexi's past, which had also made Liam even more determined to protect her. Lexi had fallen asleep after their morning lovemaking, which last night had exceeded their first time at the inn, something Liam hadn't thought possible.

Liam poured the eggs into a serving bowl as Lexi took a seat at the kitchen island. "All my mother's going to want to do is prod us to get married. Be prepared for the spiel. Don't worry, though, I've got your back. No wedding."

"I've been thinking about that. Maybe we should marry."

"What?" Liam almost dropped the bacon he was transferring to a plate.

"Yeah. Maybe. The idea had popped into my head overnight that your mom might have a point. It would solve many problems."

"It would create many as well," Liam pointed out. He wasn't opposed to marriage. But Lexi was recovering from an eating disorder. She'd started on a new life. With her being pregnant, nothing was going as planned. Like breakfast. After the little she'd eaten last night, he wanted to get some food into her. "We don't have to rush things."

"I'm not. I just don't want to rule out the idea."

Liam gestured, indicating she should start filling her plate. "You really want us to get married?"

She shook her head. "No. Not really. Not yet. I'm saying we should leave marriage on the table as an option. I want to hear what your sister and mother have to say when they get here. You said last night that you would protect me, protect our children. Well, I want to do the same. I come with a lot of baggage, so let's listen to Eva and your mom with an open mind. Then you and I will talk about what we want to do and go from there."

"I would be faithful to you," Liam said.

"I know." Lexi nibbled some bacon. "But you wouldn't love me. I have to consider that. I'd be giving up the idea of finding my own soul mate."

Liam's hand stilled as he had the sudden image of another man with Lexi. He set the pan aside, his back to her so she couldn't see his troubled expression. He didn't like the thought of her with anyone else, whether it be Damon or some unidentified man she'd met in the future. He'd seen how some of the men at the wedding looked at her. He smoothed the hackles, calmed the jealousy and diverted himself from that train of thought by settling onto a counter stool next to her. He began serving himself. His phone buzzed. He lifted it. "They've landed. We've got about an hour. How are the eggs?"

"Delicious. I'm hungry. Must be all our nocturnal activities."

She grinned at him, and he noted that Lexi had finished her eggs and was munching on a strip of bacon. Satisfied that she'd eaten enough, Liam watched as she left to change clothes. He cleaned the kitchen and gave the living area one last once-over. The caretaker had left the place spotless, so Liam didn't have much to do. He stood with Lexi on the deck and watched as a SUV wound its way up the mountain. "There they are." He gazed at Lexi. "Are you okay?"

"I think I'm going to be sick," she said as she rushed off. When she reached the bathroom, she slammed the door in his face.

"Are you okay?" he asked, listening to her retch through the door. "Are you sure I can't help."

"It's morning sickness. It'll pass."

As the doorbell rang, Liam made a mental note to ask the doctor. He didn't believe she was purging because Lexi wouldn't do anything to harm the twins, but surely the sickness should have passed?

"Where is she?" his mother asked as she entered. "I want to meet her."

"Hello to you, too, Mother," Liam greeted her. It amazed him how his mother was the queen of etiquette and comportment, with the exception of her sons. "She's in the bathroom."

A few minutes later, once the caretaker had dropped off the suitcases and driven back down the hill, Liam watched as Lexi walked into the room. He moved to her side.

"Hi," Lexi said. "Sorry. Morning sickness."

"The worst," Laverna said. She planted a kiss on each of Lexi's cheeks. "But we women are far tougher than we look, aren't we, dear?"

"I'm trying," Lexi said. To Liam she appeared fatigued,

and he handed her a bottle of clear electrolytes and guided her to the couch. She took small sips.

"I see Liam is taking care of you," Laverna said.

"He's doing a great job." Lexi shifted uncomfortably and Liam sat next to her. Eva sat across from him. Laverna's gaze shifted back and forth from Liam to Lexi. "You two are getting married, yes? Liam. Lexi. That's the only course of action. You are getting married."

Liam had to give his mother credit. Her tone never changed, but he knew she expected an answer. "We've talked about it," Liam said smoothly, trying to keep his mother's feathers from becoming too ruffled. Protecting Lexi came first. "Lexi and I are discussing what steps we want to take."

"It's a great idea," Eva said, throwing her lot in with their mother. "Solves all the problems. You and Lexi— Melynda—met and fell in love and that's why she hasn't been seen for six months. Explains everything. I'm ready to spin it."

"Brilliant," Laverna said. She smoothed a piece of silver hair that didn't need it since it wasn't out of place.

"Except it's up to us to decide," Lexi said, and Liam turned to look at her. Lexi lifted her chin and he was proud of her for taking a stand. "As Liam said, we're still talking. What he and I want to do is up to us."

"Not when you're carrying his children," Laverna said, her matter-of-fact tone not even considering a counterargument. "He's a Clayton."

"That might be so, but it's my choice," Lexi returned as the two women sized each other up. Somewhere in the last few minutes, Lexi had found her backbone and Liam found her magnificent. She was a warrior, and he wished she could see herself as he did.

Laverna backtracked. "I wasn't insinuating otherwise."

"You didn't have to," Lexi said.

Liam worked to check his grin. His Lexi was no push-over. His Lexi. Oddly, he liked the sound of that more and more. Especially once she said that marriage was still one of the options.

His mother shifted. She wasn't used to being thwarted. "Eva and I are only trying to help. The best way to have the press die down is to feed them a story. I've got a wedding planner on standby."

Lexi rubbed her jean-covered thighs. "Which is moving way too fast. Liam and I haven't yet discussed what we want for a wedding, if we want to marry at all. For all I know, he could want to do an Elvis chapel in Vegas. Time is of the essence."

"It would certainly be faster and more efficient," Liam agreed. He captured Lexi's hand.

She nodded at him. "Like running off to Gretna Green."

While Liam had no idea what that meant, from his mother's stunned expression, it must be something terrible.

"You wouldn't dare. Liam. You wouldn't," his mom protested.

"I'll do whatever makes Lexi happy," Liam said, watching as Lexi used her free hand to bring the clear Gatorade to her lips. She took a long sip. He gave a little squeeze on the hand he held, letting Lexi know he meant the words. He didn't lie. He wanted her happy. "She and the twins mean the world to me. Not some pomp and circumstance so you and father can outspend your friends and throw the social event of the decade and get the press off our backs."

"Liam," Eva protested. "Seriously."

His mother scowled, a rare show of negative emotion. Usually she could cajole her way into getting what she wanted. "You always were the troublesome one. I thought they'd have to do a C-section to get you out. Your older brother slid right out."

"I do things my way on my timetable," Liam confirmed. "Always have."

"But certainly not Elvis." Laverna shuddered. "I was thinking the Chateau. But first, your father and I want to hold a small family dinner. We'd like to welcome Lexi to the family."

His mother's idea of small started at thirty-plus people. "Lexi and I will discuss it. Same as a wedding. We're a team. When we decide what we want, we will let you know."

His mom sniffed her disapproval. "Fine." She studied Lexi again. "You're going to be family. I do want us to be friends."

Lexi, to her credit, nodded. "I would like that too. You will be the twins' grandmother. I was close to mine before she passed and hope that you're as close to them as I was mine."

Liam knew Lexi well enough by now to know she meant every word. He gave her another gentle, reassuring squeeze. After setting her drink down, she put her other hand over their joined ones.

"I will be the best grandmother," Laverna said.

"I hope so. But my being pregnant is all very new, so Liam and I would ask you to respect our privacy and let us make our own decisions."

Laverna gave a small huff. "Well, in case you change your mind, I brought my engagement ring with me. Liam,

I thought Lexi might like it when the time's right. There's a lot of love behind the ring, and since Edmund gave Lana your grandmother's, I thought creating a tradition by using mine might be nice. You never wanted it before, but it would be perfect."

Liam felt Lexi hands fall away. He'd donated Anya's ring to a charity auction. Anya, who slipped further and further from his mind whenever he was around Lexi. He could see the differences between the two women clearly. Lexi had an inner core of steel and a determination to make her way in the world. She'd overcome adversity. He was worried about her eating, especially after what Eva had told him when she'd called from the plane. But his gut said Lexi wouldn't put herself or the twins in danger, and he trusted his gut.

As for Anya, she'd let Liam's mother walk all over her, calling it "humoring your mom." Anya had enjoyed being wined and dined and molded into a style befitting a Clayton wife. But Lexi had made Laverna, the human steamroller, pause in her tracks. Liam let go of Lexi and rose. "Mother, let me show you and Eva to your rooms. I've arranged for us to have dinner in Estes Park."

He'd booked his mother's favorite restaurant. Laverna didn't blink an eye as she stood. "That will be lovely. Lexi, it was nice to meet you."

"Thank you, Mrs. Clayton," Lexi began.

His mom paused. "Call me Laverna, dear. We're going to be family."

After getting his mother and Eva settled, Liam found Lexi still seated on the couch. "Sorry about that. I warned you my mom can be a lot."

"I'm sure she had to be, with raising four children."

Liam chuckled. "Don't let her fool you. Don't make her

out to be a martyr. She and my father love us dearly, but we also had nannies who did much of the heavy lifting."

"That sounds almost tragic."

"Perhaps. We grew up into strong, independent thinkers. Don't get me wrong. We have a strong family loyalty. I'd lay my life down for them. When my mom says you're her family now, she means it. You'll be a daughter to her. Hell, Eva will be thrilled she won't be the only female. I hope you and my sister will be fast friends. You did a great job standing your ground. I can tell my mom already respects you."

Lexi bloomed under the compliment. "I can see where you get it, the difficult one."

Liam laughed. "Oh yes. I'm praying our twins will not be the same handful I supposedly was. So big wedding or small?"

His teasing tone earned him a smile. "I haven't said yes. And just so you know, I happen to like Elvis, a lot. I can even sing my top three favorite songs of his."

"Say the word and I'll get Chris to fly us to Vegas. We can be married before the sun goes down." Seeing her sober rather than laugh again like he was doing, he held his hands up in surrender. "Joking. Sort of. Let's do it, Lexi. Let's marry and make our children legitimate."

"It's a crazy idea, marriage."

"One you were thinking about earlier. I'm game if you are. But one thing. If you say yes, as for the how? The where? That's up to you. The when? That's before you are seven months along. That's my only condition. I'm old-fashioned that way."

Lexi nibbled her lip. "I said I'm keeping the idea on the table. I'm very serious about wanting to work and do school. I can't sit idle any more than you can. I don't want to be hanging around Beaumont or be like some mistress in a romance novel who never wins the man."

"You aren't a mistress. You are your own person. If you want, you'll be my fiancée."

She arched a brow. "Are you proposing?"

"Not until you know you want to say yes," Liam said. He didn't want to rush her or add any stress. "Just know one thing. Whatever you decide, we will make things work."

Lexi was assured of one thing. While it seemed she might have won Liam's affections, it didn't mean she'd be the love of his life. That important piece would be missing. It was the one piece that kept her from telling him she was ready to say yes, let's do it, let's get married.

"So you were engaged to Anya." He hadn't told her that part and in a way, the revelation stung. Anya—the reason Liam wouldn't love again. Not that Lexi wanted that. Or did she? Her heart grew more and more confused.

"Let me guess. Her ring was at least three carats," Lexi said, making her voice as casual as she could.

"A two-point-one solitaire in Tiffany's proprietary setting. She'd told me what she wanted." Liam seemed far away, remembering. A special smile stole across his face, one that told Lexi how much the woman he'd loved had meant to him, and it tore at her heart. "I spoke with a man on the phone, and he put it together for me. When I got there, it was perfect. I'd planned to give it to her once we returned from Everest." Liam shook his head as if to clear the memory. "I donated it, and the charity sale funded clean water infrastructure systems in a developing country. She would have liked that."

He rounded on Lexi, and his eyes gleamed as he raked his gaze over her. "I liked waking up with you today. And the way you stood up to my mom turned me on."

Lexi scoffed. "That's all it takes? Standing up to your mom? You're a cheap date."

His grin widened. "Maybe, but no one has ever stood up to her like that. Not even Anya."

"Really?" Lexi felt a jolt of pride as Liam nodded his head.

"Yeah, and I liked it. She needs to know she can't boss you around."

"I'm not going to let her. No one's ever going to boss me again."

"Good. You're fierce. I like that." He tugged her to him and peered down at her. "How's your stomach?"

Lexi studied his face. He wore an odd expression. "Fine. Settled. Why?"

"No reason. Sadly we have company so we can't be naked all day. I'm making sure you're ready for shopping and heading into town."

"Did I hear shopping?" Eva had returned.

"I need clothes," Lexi said. "Minus what you brought me in my suitcase."

"Oh, those. Yeah. I left those at Liam's house. You need summer stuff. Mom's going to take a nap and since I know all the good places, let's go have some fun."

"That sounds like a plan." Lexi smiled at Eva. Once she got her money from Damon, she'd pay Liam back. "I'm all yours."

Eva and Laverna stayed one night and left the next. Once his mother had discovered she wasn't going to get her way with an immediate engagement, she'd stopped asking. After that had occurred, everyone had relaxed and Lexi had discovered she liked Liam's family.

She also liked Liam and being in Colorado. Over the next two months, she and Liam developed a rhythm. They slept in the same bed. However, because he'd gone back to hiking, she'd often wake to find his side of the bed empty and Liam already gone. If he wasn't working on Clayton Holdings business, Liam would hit the trailhead no later than four o'clock in the morning as a round trip to the summit and back on a fourteen-thousand-foot peak took at least ten to twelve hours of hiking. Liam hadn't been kidding about the late afternoon storms, and more than once he had thrown wet clothes into the washer, having changed into dry gear upon reaching his car.

Lexi worried, but what could she do? Liam seemed hardwired to climb the same way a racecar driver couldn't stop putting his foot on the gas. Mother Nature must be conquered, but Lexi decided that the more Liam fought the challenges of the Front Range peaks, the farther he slipped away. Sure, they found each other in the throes of passion, but even that time together had dwindled, especially with Liam rising early to tackle the mountains.

Lexi didn't know what to do. Liam worked and counted down the days until his year was up. When he climbed, Lexi wondered if he exorcised demons. She didn't know. What she did know was that Anya shared this love of climbing with him. Lexi didn't climb, and she couldn't anyway as she put on weight and grew round.

As the days ebbed shorter she saw him less and less—a climb meant when he returned, he'd eat dinner and crash into bed, his body physically spent. As Colorado had approximately fifty-eight 14ers, as those peaks over fourteen thousand feet were called, Liam seemingly could disappear for days at a time. She started to wonder if he was avoiding her, which bothered Lexi. To keep occupied, she filled her days with online college courses and meal planning.

"Where are you going?" she asked on a rainy day after they'd returned from the doctor. Her pregnancy was progressing perfectly in the eight weeks they'd been in Colorado.

Liam's knuckles tightened on the door handle to the gym. "Working out."

For some reason, today was the day Lexi picked a fight. Perhaps it was because Damon kept texting about his song. Perhaps it was the helicopters that had flown past, reminding her of the paparazzi. Perhaps she was simply becoming bored with no common interests between them minus astronomy. While she'd seen Julia once or twice, she hadn't warmed up to her. Julia had been Anya's friend, and the contrast was obvious. "You keep disappearing," she accused.

Liam's jaw twitched. "How? I'm in the gym."

"Only because it's raining and you can't be out there somewhere."

He peered at her, trying to read her. "You sound like you're spoiling for a fight."

That was Liam. Ever observant where she was concerned. "Maybe I am. You're never here."

He stared at her blankly. "Why does that matter?"

She couldn't tell him she missed him. Or that she hated how he handled her with kid gloves. While eight weeks ago she'd thought of marrying him, once his sister and mother had left, Liam hadn't brought the subject up again. Instead, he climbed, which reinforced that if she took away the physical, she and Liam really had nothing in common. "Is this what our lives are going to be? You gone all the time and me juggling twins by myself?"

Liam blinked. "I told you I'd be here every step of the way. We'll hire a nanny if managing two kids gets to be too much."

Lexi didn't want a nanny. Or an assistant. The elevator door opened and she stepped in. He followed. He pressed the button for the main level. "What do you want, Lexi? Just ask. We don't need to fight for you to get it."

"I think I'm tired of being roommates with sex benefits, which lately have tapered off."

"You heard the doctor. Your condition…"

She cut him off. "Pregnancy is not a death sentence. You are never here. When you are, you avoid me as if I have Covid, not pregnancy. I'm feeling fat and unattractive."

"You are not fat. You're pregnant and perfect."

Lexi felt irrational. The doctor had told her that her hormones could be all over the place. "An absent partner is not what I want for my future. For my children's future. Neither is one who counts my calories and makes sure I'm eating. I'm not a child. I'm a woman. I have needs."

Liam ran a hand through his much shorter hair. "Okay, then tell me what you do want."

"I've decided I want it all. I need love, Liam. I want the entire thing. I don't need another caretaker. I've had enough of those. Dawn was my roommate. You, Liam, need to be more."

When he shook his head, her heart broke. "Don't ask me for the one thing I can't do. I will be faithful. I will come home every night. Sleep in your bed. Protect you with my life. Watch all those silly romantic comedy movies you keep downloading. Vote the way you do. I will do whatever it takes."

She'd rattled him, but it wasn't enough. "Except for the thing our relationship needs the most to make it survive. Love."

"I can't give you that. Not the way you see it in those movies. That's not real. It's a fantasy."

"Why? Why is it you could find it with Anya and not me?"

When he didn't answer, Lexi's heart tore. Such a stubborn man.

Anya remained the ghost that stood between them. Another sliver of Lexi's heart shredded as they entered the great room. She'd grown to love the expansive, all-encompassing view of the mountains. "When are we going back to Beaumont?"

"We can go anytime you want." He shoved his hands in his front pockets. "If you need me to stay home more, say so. You aren't to have stress. It's upsetting me to learn that my climbing is causing you stress."

"It's not about the climbing. It's everything else." She blew out a harsh breath. "Forget I brought anything up. It's doesn't matter."

Even though it did. Proximity did something to a person. In her case, seeing Liam every day had made her fall hopelessly in love with him. What she wanted most was for him to figure out he loved her. To realize that they could perhaps figure out how to love each other, grow their relationship into something that could go the full distance. But as much as he cared for her, he couldn't bring himself to let Anya go.

Every day she lost herself—she couldn't live in something one-sided. She had done that before and barely survived unscathed. At least at the Chateau, she'd worked. Now she sat around and did little. Protection had become a cage, like she feared. No way could she marry him.

"It's not enough. I want it all. The happily-ever-after," she suddenly blurted out.

Liam blinked once. "You don't love me."

She would never tell him that she did. When was the moment she'd fallen for him? Was it one? Or a series of small things that told her Liam was a man worthy of being loved?

Whatever or whenever it was, her heart wouldn't ache or her soul feel so stomped on if she didn't love him. She wanted to reach for him. To start unbuttoning her top, but as he touched her less and less the more her stomach protruded, her insecurities over her weight had crept back in. Was he afraid she'd break? Or was he disgusted by her body? Sex had been a time when they came together. When barriers between them seemed to vanish and when she hoped they could be more. Daily the walls between them thickened like her waistline. She had no idea how to tear them down.

When she'd been searching for some small kitchen tools, she'd discovered a set of framed pictures in an obscure drawer in the storage room. Edmund must have missed them, but Lexi hadn't. There was a five-by-ten of a parka-wearing Anya laughing—a mountain in the background. Liam's and Anya's arms were wrapped around each other on some summit, the sky a slab of robin-egg blue. Another picture showed the two of them in formal attire, the slip of a gown showing off Anya's willowy arms and dancer thin, lithe figure. Lexi had shoved the drawer closed. Shut off the flow to her bleeding heart and cooked without the tool.

"Are we still fighting or can I go grill those steaks?"

Liam asked suddenly. "You're probably hungry. I can work out later."

No point in continuing the conversation. "I'll prepare the salad," Lexi said.

Food prep was simple, and Lexi washed the romaine lettuce and put it in the salad spinner as Liam fired up the grill. How did she reach a man so closed off? So afraid to love again? She'd told him everything: her dad's betrayal. Her history with Damon. He remained closed on what had occurred on Everest. He'd shared little, shutting her out.

She lifted the lid of the spun lettuce. Paused. Frowned as her body trembled, as if a ghost blew on her neck. The quickening sensation came again, and she pinpointed the location. Grew excited. While she'd felt little flutters here and there, today was the first time she'd truly felt the babies move. "Liam!"

He set down the grill brush and rushed inside. "What's wrong? Are you okay? Do we need the doctor?"

"No. The baby's moving. Or maybe they both are. I can feel them kicking." She pressed his hand to her abdomen. "Can you feel anything?"

He shook his head, clearly disappointed. "No. Nothing."

She covered his hand with hers. "Maybe it's not strong enough yet. But it will be soon. Especially with two of them moving around in there."

His chin came up and his wondrous gaze caught hers. "Hey, wait. Did you feel that too?"

"Yes. That's them. They're moving." She brushed away the tear. "Why am I crying? I'm happy, not sad."

"Hormones." He kept his hand on her stomach and grinned wider. "They are active."

"Don't even say boys," Lexi reproved, her tone light.

"We don't know. We told the doctor we didn't want to know the gender."

"As long as they're healthy, I'm good with two adorable girls like their mother." Smoke poured from the grill.

"Go get that fire under control before you burn the deck down." Lexi giggled as he lifted her off her feet and spun her around. "Go. I'm hungry."

"Your wish is my command."

She wished he loved her. Still, as he cooked dinner, an odd sense of peace settled. Maybe they could make things work. Maybe like some arranged marriages, he would grow to love her, at least a little. If that was the case, she could plaster on a happy face and pretend all was well, let a sense of calm reign.

The doctor had told her no stress. But she couldn't hide here forever. She walked out onto the deck. "Liam, I want to go back to Beaumont."

"Okay," Liam said. He turned off the grill and plated the cooked meat. "I've got things I need to wrap up that I can't do remotely. We'll come back next summer. We can have a designer convert one of the bedrooms into a nursery while we're gone."

Of course they could. "Liam…" She began to tell him what she'd decided about making things work, but he slid his hand under her shirt.

"Remember our first night here? Because I do. You came out and began stripping for me."

"Yes. I remember it." She was glad he did too. At his touch, her body sent rivers of pleasure through her. A baby moved. "They seem to like my body's reaction."

"I've missed you. Missed this." He bent her over the railing. Gently let her breasts fall into his hands. The breeze picked up, but the heat he created kept her warm as she quivered. He scooped her up, took her into their bedroom.

"I've missed you touching me," she told him as he began worshipped her body. Food was forgotten and clothing disappeared as he kissed her.

"I've been a fool."

"Yes," she agreed.

Whatever he'd been about to add, he lost the thought as he settled her down onto him, her body ready to join with his. He kissed her stomach and Lexi closed her eyes—the intimacy with the man she loved being too much, too intense as she tipped over the edge.

After their lovemaking, he cradled her to him later, the fire he'd built in the fireplace making the room warm and cozy. They ate dinner much later in bed.

"I met Anya in high school," he told her suddenly. "She was this wild girl with diplomat parents who had lived all over the world by the time she was fourteen. You might not believe it, but I was the socially awkward, book smart one. Edmund knew he'd take over from birth, but I was the spare. My father took me to the company too, but I like building things. Being outdoors. We did the mandatory, upper crust summer camp experience, and I loved it. Edmund hated the smell of bug spray. I fast-tracked Eagle Scout and still Anya picked me. Shocked the hell out of me that I was the guy she chose. Maybe that's why I loved her."

He shifted Lexi and drew her closer. "The reality is that there are those men who have to display their power by being dominant, those men who simply enjoy sex and using women, and then there are the men who fit somewhere in between who don't want to become either of those stereotypes. I can get what I want, but I don't want to be an asshole to do it. Win-win is always better. Not that I won't crush someone like a bug if they harm what's mine. When your life seems to go in one direction and then suddenly it's thrown in a complete ninety-degree turn and thrust onto another track, you question everything you once believed. Anyway, Anya understood that and she liked to be outdoors with me. We fit together. It was comfortable."

She was grateful he was finally opening up. "I understand. My mom stood between me and my dad, who was my and Damon's manager. My dad had this vision for our career and I followed along because it was easier than fighting for what I wanted. Besides, he was my dad. When she got sick, it was like being between a rock and a hard place. My safe harbor was gone."

"Now look who's talking in metaphors." He ran his fingers over her shoulder. "I'm sorry that happened to you."

She sighed. "It's okay, well, it is now. Since we're being honest, you need to know that I had an eating disorder."

"I already know," Liam said simply. "Damon told Eva. She told me."

Lexi shook her head. No wonder Liam had watched her every bite, relaxing only once the morning sickness had stopped. "I would never harm the twins. When I was performing, anorexia and bulimia were a way to make sure I was thin enough to please everyone. My father controlled my life and my career. I had no power over what my nutritionist and trainer let me eat, but I could control whether it stayed down. I know, that's warped logic. Took me therapy to figure out my attempt at control wasn't healthy control, but desperate control. Healthy control meant facing those who controlled me, and it meant taking back the power I gave them. My singing career was what I did, not who I was.

Realizing that difference was so freeing. A turning point. When I ran away to Beaumont and disappeared from the limelight, I did so to find myself. That's what makes my being with you a struggle. Control matters to each of us. I can't lose control, and fate stole your control from you when I got pregnant."

"That day on the mountain was the worst of my life." Liam dipped his head to suck a nipple. "You walking into my life was a bright spot. We're good together. You turn me on like no other." He palmed her breasts. "These are so heavy, sensitive."

Her response to his attentions was a pleasurable groan. She'd always crave his touch. Crave him. Love him.

"When we return, let's find a way to stay on the same page," Liam said as he planted kisses down her neck. "You can stand up to my mother. Let's both of us stand together against the world. Be true to ourselves. Let me make you happy. I'm going to try."

Time to tell him what she'd decided, one of the reasons she wanted to return to Beaumont. She wanted some closure in one area of her life.

"By the way, I've decided I'm going to do Damon's song. Most likely this month." She'd decided that a few days ago. She simply hadn't texted Damon the news yet or made the arrangements. She'd do that later, once Liam stopped tracing his fingers over her skin.

Liam stilled, but then slid a hand between her legs. "You don't have to do that."

But Lexi did. All this time in Colorado she'd been dependent on Liam. Even when he'd been gone, she lived in his house. He bought her clothes. He prepared the food. Took her to her doctor appointments. Sure, Lexi had read books. Lounged. Went on long walks. Swam in the indoor pool. Completed several online classes. Hung out with the caretaker and his wife. Rested and watched movies and binged TV shows. Her routine was the same. Get up. Figure out what to do. Go to bed.

Certainly, she was far more relaxed than when she'd been under Melynda's nonstop daily agenda. But the fact remained that no matter how little she did and how much Melynda had been on the go, the situations Lexi found herself in were similar. She was beholden. Once showbiz had been the driving factor of her life. Now it was Liam. It might be different if he'd loved her. But she was simply another one of his responsibilities. The mother of his twins. The VIP of his life. But he'd never love her, not as he had Anya. She had to reassert control. Find her independence. As Liam's fingers worked their magic, Lexi pushed the negative thoughts aside.

"Give us a chance, Lexi," Liam said as he slid inside her. "Give me a chance."

She wanted to do nothing more. But the words disappeared because already she had tipped over the edge as his lovemaking tended to make her do. Sighing against his neck afterward, Lexi chose the inevitable. Chose the path of great sex and least resistance. She could do this. Take healthy control. Be her own person. When they got back to Beaumont, she'd sing one more song. Put herself on equal footing with Liam. Then make him see reason. Show him they could rewrite the script and he could love again, love her.

"I promise I will make you happy," Liam whispered as he stroked deep inside her. How could she resist? Liam was an addiction. A drug. She couldn't fight him any longer. "Marry me. Be mine. We will be happy. I promise you that."

Her body clutched his as she let go of her last bit of control. She prayed he was right. "Yes. Yes, Liam. I will marry you."

Chapter Eleven

When they returned to Beaumont a few days later, Lexi realized she had never seen Beaumont in the fall. However, she'd heard tales of Winery Road and the blaze of red, orange and yellow colors once the trees turned. But as she and Liam returned in early September, nothing much had changed. Green grass still needed to be cut. The temperatures remained warm, although most people had put away their shorts. School had started. Beaumont had two fall festivals forthcoming, the second of which was the annual balloon race. The only difference was that the days were growing shorter instead of longer. That fact made Lexi sad.

Liam hadn't wasted much time after she'd agreed to marry him. They'd conferenced with his parents and picked a date at the end of October. While a normal forty-week pregnancy would come to term in early January, the thirty-four week mark came around Thanksgiving and the thirty-seven week mark closer to Christmas. Eva had leaked the story onto social media, which had sent a few more helicopters over Liam's Estes Park house. But Eva had been right—the announcement of their engagement had changed everything. Minus a few of the haters who said Liam was only marrying her because she was pregnant, most of the media attention died down. Drama sold, and a love match didn't have quite the headlines of "Melynda Scorns Damon for Baby Daddy Liam Clayton." Besides, Damon had been seen at a film premier with the supporting actress, so media speculation claimed he was getting over his broken heart.

Liam drove the Subaru into the carport of the house on Third Street. "We'll need to find a place to live," he said. "We can also commandeer one of the suites at the Grand if you'd like. It's two thousand square feet and comes with staff."

"This is fine for now," Lexi told him as they walked inside. "I like the house. It feels right."

The one-hundred-year-old bungalow did. She'd lived in suites before and had no desire to go back to that lifestyle. Besides, the house had been Zoe's postdivorce home where she'd raised her daughter. The house had good energy, good karma. Liam set her suitcase down.

"Shall we walk down to the Fall Festival?" Lexi asked. They'd left Colorado early, so it was around three in the afternoon. Lexi had slept on the plane, so she wasn't tired. "I'd like to stretch my legs and I've never seen it."

"Sure. Since it's Saturday, the booths are open late tonight and there should be a good band playing. We can grab some food."

A few minutes later, after they both had donned ball caps and sunglasses, Lexi and Liam made their way down to Main Street, which had been shut down for the event. Booths lined both sides of street, selling everything from soaps to quilts, to knickknacks, to books, to clothing and high-end art. Kids could get their faces painted at the Makerspace, or they could pluck yellow plastic ducks from the duck pond located in front of the Blanchard Inn. They strolled through the large crowd, going mostly unnoticed. A few people did a double take every now and then, but when no one approached, Lexi relaxed.

"Want a turkey leg?" Liam asked as they walked past a food booth. Some of the roasted turkey legs appeared as large as a small child's arm.

Lexi laughed. "Think I'm good. Been to a few county fairs. No need for those or funnel cakes. But that kettle corn smells really good."

"Do you want some?"

"Yes, but let's grab it on the way back." It was still early afternoon—they had plenty of time.

They passed La Vita è Vino Dolce's outdoor wine garden and made their way down to the riverfront. A magician had finished performing. Children climbed on the red caboose that was a permanent feature and a band set up its gear on the main stage. The entertainment was always local to the St. Louis area, and this time was no different.

Liam picked one of the barbecue food trucks and returned with two paper plates filled with brisket burnt ends, coleslaw, and macaroni and cheese. "Think this is the healthiest fare they have down here," he said as he and Lexi sat on one of the picnic tables. He passed her plastic-ware. "Enjoy."

Lexi dug in. "You know, this is a first for me."

"What? The burnt ends? It's a Kansas City thing that's been adopted by pretty much any BBQ place in Missouri."

"No, I mean sitting on a picnic table in the middle of a crowd and eating food without being surrounded by body-guards. It's one reason I chose Beaumont."

Liam lifted his fork. "My parents love it here. But they would never be caught eating food from a truck."

"They don't know what they're missing," Lexi said. "It feels normal."

The band began to play, and four songs in, Lexi turned to watch. "This is my song," she told Liam. She'd finished her food and she rose and threw her waste away. "Well, mine and Damon's. They're not doing a half-bad cover."

"I can't imagine you up there. If you hadn't shown me that concert footage, I'd hardly believe it." Liam reached for her hand "You ready to head back? We can grab some of that kettle corn on the way. You can treat yourself once in a while."

Since she'd been taking care of herself, Lexi had gained the required amount of weight but not much more. The doctor had told her she was doing everything right. She definitely appeared pregnant though. She and Liam made their way up the sidewalk and back toward Main Street, where they joined the short queue for the popcorn. Liam, ever protective of Lexi, stood a half pace ahead.

"Are you Melynda Norfolk?"

Lexi turned. It was bound to happen at some point. But as Lexi went to say, "I'm sorry, I get that a lot," she found she couldn't do it.

The young girl standing there and her friend couldn't have been more than fifth or sixth graders. "My dad says you live here now. He and my mom fly the town balloon. Will you be coming to the balloon glow in two weeks? You should. Our balloon is Playgroup. It's the best. I'm Anna. This is Brinley. Want a cookie?"

After speaking without taking a breath, Anna held out a white bag from the town's famous cookie store, Aunty Jayne's. Zoe, who was Liam's landlord, owned the landmark bakery. As a test of her new healthy eating, Lexi had tried the cookies once during an event at the Chateau. The nibbles had been delicious.

"Thank you, but you keep your cookie. I'm full from eating burnt ends." Lexi glanced around. Was Anna allowed to roam free? Lexi had been surrounded by people from age six on. "Where are your mom and dad?"

Anna pointed to a booth a few down. "They're working the duck pond. As long as I'm with Brinley and stay on this block, we can wander around. We're big now. We know about stranger danger. But this is Beaumont. Nothing happens here and you're famous, so not a stranger."

"Okay then." Flummoxed by Anna's assertiveness, Lexi watched as a tall man who was clearly Anna's dad headed in their direction.

"Anna, are you bothering these people? Oh, Mr. Clayton, hey. I'm sorry she's bothering you. I'm Luke Thornburg. My dad's on the city council. I own the Makerspace."

Liam shook Luke's hand. "Nice to finally meet you. Call me Liam. And she's fine. Lexi and I were going to grab some kettle corn and head home."

"Dad, she's pregnant like Mom was." Anna munched on the cookie she'd first offered Lexi. "Do you need a babysitter? Because I babysit my younger brother and sister."

"I'm sure we will need one at some point," Lexi said. She tried not to laugh. Anna was so serious and Lexi didn't want to disappoint her by taking her offer frivolously. Would one of her twins be that way? Serious? Forthright? Precocious? Lexi patted her stomach and felt a kick in response. She'd find out their genders and personalities soon enough. "Tell you what, Anna, how about we get them born first?"

Anna nodded. "Sounds good. Your songs are in my music library. Are you going to go solo? Because you should. Damon's cute but you're better. You should make your own record."

Lexi was flattered. "Why, thank you."

Anna nodded. "My mom's a photographer. She could shoot your album cover."

"Okay, Anna," her dad interrupted. "Let's leave the nice people alone."

"Can I have a selfie first?" Anna asked.

"No," Luke said at the same time Lexi said, "Sure."

Anna held out her phone, and Lexi pulled off her sunglasses. "Here, let me." Lexi took the phone from Anna and held it out. She took a photo with just Anna, then one with Anna and Brinley. When Anna asked her dad if he wanted a selfie, he passed. "It's because my mom's a famous photographer," Anna announced. "He likes to say famous people are just ordinary people with interesting jobs."

Luke was clearly embarrassed. "Anna."

"It's fine," Lexi said. "I happen to agree with you." She turned to Liam, who'd bought a two-foot-long and six-inch-round bag of kettle corn.

He shrugged. "What? This is the size they sell it in, and it doesn't go bad for a while."

"Hey," Luke said, his tone holding a warning note, "you two are starting to attract some attention."

Lexi shoved her sunglasses back on her nose. A small crowd, sensing something was happening, had begun to form. "Follow me," Luke said. He led them a short distance to the duck pond, and they darted under the tent cover. "If you go out the back, you can walk alongside the inn to the alleyway, then walk that to the cross street and head up to Third Street."

"Thanks." Lexi and Liam followed the path. "This brings

back memories," she quipped as they darted off the main path and rounded the building. They walked behind the cars parked in the lot. But Liam said nothing.

"What's wrong?" Lexi asked. "You've gotten quiet."

"That could have been a situation," Liam said, the bag of popcorn bumping against his leg. He shifted it to the other side.

Lexi didn't understand. "What? Nothing was going on."

"It was about to because of your selfie. If Luke hadn't had an escape route for us, we would have been quickly surrounded. When you took off your sunglasses, people recognized you."

"They're going to do that," Lexi said. "It's Beaumont, though. I would have been fine."

Shifting the popcorn again, Liam placed his hand on her arm, turning her slightly so she faced him. "You can't say that. It might not have been fine. People could surround you in an instant and then what? You have to take care of yourself. You have to take care of the babies."

Lexi bristled. "I am taking care of them."

"Not if you're putting yourself in danger." Liam guided her though the crowd gathered on the corner as they reached the cross street.

"Melynda! Are you Melynda?" someone called.

"No," Lexi yelled back, quickening her pace. Her legs began to burn as they walked up the hill. Thankfully the hangers on dropped off as she and Liam reached Second Street. Another block and they'd reached Third. A quick right and they were on final approach to Liam's rental. However, Liam stopped. "What's it now?" Lexi asked.

"I'm making sure we're not followed." He craned his neck and glanced over his shoulder. "Okay. We're good."

The street was empty, so they began to walk again. Lexi understood Liam's hesitation. Last thing they needed was anyone knowing where she lived.

"We're going to need to find somewhere else, though," Liam said as they went up the front walk. "Eva's on it."

"You're having Eva find us a place?" Lexi asked as Liam ushered her quickly inside.

He locked the door behind them. "Did I overreach? She loves doing that stuff. I needed a place anyway and she volunteered while we were in Colorado. We could build in the same subdivision as my parents if you want, but I'd rather find something more move-in ready. Maybe with some land. What do you think?" He led her forward, not waiting for an answer.

Liam went into the kitchen, put the tube of popcorn down and poured her a glass of water. He handed it to her.

Lexi sat on the couch as her head began to pound. She twisted the ring she'd put on her left hand, the one Liam had handed to her after she'd caved and said yes. She couldn't stay in Colorado any longer, but Beaumont was no longer safe either. Worse, Liam had entered protector mode. "Liam, this isn't going to work."

Liam sipped from his own glass. "What do you mean? If I overstepped, we can look for houses ourselves. Eva was doing the preliminary stuff."

Lexi took a deep breath. She could do this. Lexi 2.0 was strong. An advocate for herself. "It's not about the houses. It's everything. You can't put me in a glass case. I don't break."

"I'm protecting you," Liam protested.

She kept her tone gentle. "Which is the last thing I want.

I've been surrounded by people my whole life who did that. I put up with it in Colorado because…"

Because she was weak. Because she'd fallen in love with him. Completely and totally in love. Because carrying twins was new to her and she was overwhelmed.

Lexi removed the ring that suddenly seemed too tight on her finger. She held it out. When he didn't take his mother's engagement ring, she set it on the coffee table. "Liam, I don't know if I can marry you. Not if things are like this. Not until I'm on equal footing."

"How are you not on equal footing? I don't see it that way." She could tell she'd shocked him. Liam shook his head. "Lexi, we have a good thing. We came to an agreement."

But love was more than that. She knew he couldn't understand. At times she didn't either. But she had to trust herself, as she had when she'd chosen to walk away from fame and being Melynda. "I have to do this for me. It's time. I let Damon know that I'm ready to sing his song."

"Lexi." Liam set the glass down.

"It's time to deal with my father and give Melynda her exit." She crossed her arms. "And while I do, you need to deal with Anya."

"How? She's dead."

Her finger felt bare. Her heart was heavy. Lexi sighed. "Yes, Liam. She's dead. I'm not unsympathetic to that fact. But you didn't die with her. Instead, you carry the grief around with you like a shield and let it taint everything good you have. I'm always second since you won't let her go. I thought I could accept that, but today I realized I can't. When I quit my contract, I wanted to be my own person. Having children doesn't mean that I'm okay with trading one gilded cage for another."

Agitated, Liam rubbed his jaw. "I'm not trying to cage you."

Lexi wanted to hug him, to tell him she loved him. Instead, she worked to reach him. "But you are. And I can't do it. I want it all and I thought I could settle. But I can't."

"You don't understand. I have to protect you. Anya… she…" Liam's grief was palatable. He yanked a hand through his hair. "She was pregnant, Lexi. I don't know if she knew she was. Or maybe she did and decided she didn't want to deny me my dream. But that day on the mountain, when the avalanche happened, I lost them both. I lost my baby, Lexi. I can't lose you. I can't lose anyone else, especially you or the twins."

As Lexi's face drained of color, Liam wished he hadn't said anything. He didn't want her sympathy. He wanted her to understand, to put her ring back on and tell him everything would be fine, even if the word was a blatant lie. "If I'd known about the baby, I wouldn't have taken Anya up the mountain with me. When I've been protective of you, I took those actions because I can't lose anyone else. You are carrying my family. I couldn't handle it if I lost anyone else."

Lexi's phone began to shrill. She glanced at it, shook her head, and said, "I'm sorry. I have to take this."

An extreme sense of loss hit Liam as she went into the kitchen and talked in hushed tones. He'd shared his deepest secret, his greatest fear, and she'd walked away. Did she understand? Did she realize it was his fault Anya had died, his selfish dream that had been the reason Anya had been on the mountain that day?

Dread added to the sense of loss, and before he could

make sense of his feelings, his security system beeped. Checking the feed, he went to the front door and opened it before his mother rang the bell. "Not now," he said far too sharply.

His mother frowned but bustled in anyway. "I was in the neighborhood."

"You can't just drop by," Liam told her. "This is my life."

Laverna's eyes narrowed. "I'm not planning on staying. I brought Lexi some bridal magazines and some portfolios of wedding planners. Why is my ring on the table?"

"Mom, this really isn't the time," Liam could hear Lexi, who was still in the kitchen, moving about. She rounded the corner and stopped as she saw Liam's mom.

"Mrs. Clayton. I mean Laverna."

Liam's mom rushed over and gave her a big hug. "How are you, dear? I come bearing gifts."

Lexi hardly glanced at the magazines Laverna thrust at her. "That's nice. Thank you."

Lexi turned to Liam "Liam, "I need to go out of town for a while. I was going to leave tomorrow, but tonight will work. There's a car coming to get me in about fifteen minutes."

"What?" Both Liam and his mother seemed to say the word at the same time. "Where?" Liam asked. "What about the wedding?" his mom said.

"LA," Lexi replied. "We start recording tomorrow. Time is money."

"Do you need Chris?" Liam asked.

Lexi shook her head, and Liam sensed he was losing her. "No, you're not the only one who can hire a pilot. There's a plane ready to leave as soon as I get there, and someone will get me once I land. I need to go pack."

MICHELE DUNAWAY   237

"What are you doing there?" Laverna set the package of magazines on the coffee table. She reached for the ring. "Don't forget this."

Lexi reached for the ring and slid it on her finger. "I have some music business to finish."

"When will you be back so we can start planning?" If Laverna sensed the tension in the room, she dodged it artfully. "Please tell me you won't be long."

"My plans are open-ended, but I should be back for my doctor's appointment."

That, Liam knew, was two weeks away. She wasn't going away forever, but she was leaving him. At least she'd put the ring on. "We'll talk when I get back," Lexi said.

"Mother, let me walk you out," Liam said, ushering her to the door. "We'll talk later," he told her before she got in a word edgewise. "Later," he said with emphasis.

Ten minutes later, Liam carried Lexi's suitcase to the waiting car. "Please take care," he told her. He dropped a kiss on her forehead. "I'll miss you," he said. "Can we text? Talk? Will that be okay?"

"Yes, of course. I'll always be your friend," she told him.

He captured her hand. "I'm glad you put this on. Give me a chance, Lexi. Please."

"We'll talk when I get back. While I'm gone, I want you to think about what I said."

"I will," Liam promised. He gave Lexi a long kiss on the lips, shut her safely inside, and then watched the car until it disappeared out of sight. And wondered why it hurt so much.

Chapter Twelve

Some things never changed, and LA was one of them. The town and the industries it contained thrived on making deals. The region loved the hustle and the glamour. The place manufactured dreams, but at the same time, the town could also be dirty, gritty and the place where real dreams died. The studio system had taken her, sucked her in and spit out someone she didn't recognize. But a year after leaving, Lexi was a different person, and not simply because her stomach protruded.

She'd not only started taking college classes online, but she'd completed many and had a straight A average. She had a large, antique diamond sitting on her left hand, one that felt right despite the lack of fanfare in its delivery. The diamond flickered in the glow of the streetlights. The gold warmed her finger and the band's weight was ideal—not too light and not too heavy. Perfect. The only thing missing was Liam's heart and soul. She had his affections. But not his love. She hadn't wanted to leave and hoped she'd made the right decision.

"Thanks for coming," Damon wove the six-figure sports car through traffic. He'd picked her up at the Santa Barbara airport for the eleven-mile drive to Montecito, where he'd purchased a lush estate. "You're looking well. Pregnancy suits you."

"You don't need to flatter me. I'm here, so let's get this over with," Lexi said. She'd flown from Chesterfield to Santa Barbara, so she was also jet-lagged even though she'd gotten some sleep on the plane. Sensing this, Damon turned up the radio volume and they fell silent.

He drove through the gates. The front of his gigantic house blazed with lights and multiple cars were parked in the driveway, including the Bentley for Lexi's attorney, Carl. Carl's car idled, and he turned off the engine and stepped outside once Damon parked. "Hello, Lexi," Carl said. He was a thin, willowy figure with a shock of tufted white hair.

Even though it was late Sunday evening, he wore a full suit coat and dress pants. He'd told her once it was a throwback to how things used to be done.

"Thanks for being here, Carl." She knew it wasn't a hardship, not with what he charged per hour for his celebrity clients. After all, in this town, deals could be made 24/7 and anywhere from the boardroom to the bedroom, the golf course to the bathroom sink.

They watched as one of Damon's entourage grabbed her carry-on suitcase and toted it inside. Damon followed behind.

One of Carl's bushy white eyebrows lifted the moment they were alone. "You sure you want to be doing this?"

Lexi shifted her purse to the other arm. "Actually no. But I need to. Just as long as you ensure this doesn't come back to haunt me. Get me the maximum with me doing the absolute minimum. I'm ready to sing, but nothing more."

"I'm going to try. Considering they want you more than

you need them, it's a definite possibility you'll get every-thing you want from the deal. If I'm not being too forward, you're looking far better than you did when you left. You look happy. Beaumont must agree with you. Dare I venture to say that being engaged to Liam Clayton might have something to do with that?"

"I'd say it's more being healthy and being my own free agent. But he's definitely part of the plan." Lexi left it at that since they'd reached the door to Damon's house. Inside waited Damon, her father, Damon's attorney, recording executives and whoever else Damon needed for this deal.

"Ready?" Carl asked as they stepped through.

"Ready," Lexi said.

An hour later, the negotiations were over and the contracts signed. Carl had once again worked miracles. He'd pushed back. He'd demanded concessions, such as no touring. He'd secured her a massive amount of money. On her side, Lexi had agreed to make a music video so long as it wasn't obvious she was pregnant. She'd also agreed to attend and perform at any award shows for one year, but only if the song was nominated. She would not join Damon for any surprise performances. No publicity would link her and Damon in any romantic capacity. She would not do any media, such as morning or evening talk shows. Carl had been thorough.

Damon hadn't minded. He wanted the song. So did the studio executives. Her father had fumed, growing silently angrier as Damon had agreed to whatever Carl asked, which then forced his team to cave. Her father's posture had never changed from being closed off, eyes narrowed.

"Since we're in agreement, we can start recording tomorrow. You'll have five business days," Carl said as he locked his briefcase. He turned to Lexi. "Are you sure you'll be okay here?"

Lexi nodded. Damon didn't scare her. He never had, and she'd known him since childhood. She'd stay in her own suite, in her own wing. The recording studio was in a separate building located on the estate. The musicians and producers would arrive by nine tomorrow morning, and the long days would begin until the song was done. As part of the contract, her father had been banned from the studio the entire time Lexi was recording. She'd be fine in Damon's house, especially as her father lived elsewhere. If her dad bothered her, she had the right to walk away from the deal.

"I hope you got what you wanted," her dad said as he prepared to leave. He gave her a glance that once would have had her quaking in her designer pumps. Today her tennis shoes remained grounded and solid. "You're at least not showing too much."

Lexi shook her head. She didn't want to fight with him today. "Dad, I'm sorry I can't be who you wanted me to be. But I'm my own person and I'm happy."

His expression dripped derision. "How could you not be happy? You had it all."

"But I didn't have what I needed. I don't regret what you did for me. Being away from it has given me insight. I'm sure being a mother myself will give me more perspective. But one thing I've learned is that family isn't defined by blood. It's what you make of it. You and I—we can't work together any longer. You sued me. You have my money. I hope it keeps you warm. I'd like to have you in my life, but not yet. Not until you realize that you can't control me. To have a relationship with me, you can't have my soul. You have to let me go."

Her therapist would be so proud, Lexi thought as her dad walked away. Part of her would always love her father, but it was time to banish this part of her life and leave it behind. If she and her father found a way to become a family again someday that would be good, but Lexi wasn't going to compromise to do it. She was done with toxicity. She had other priorities and responsibilities.

Damon hovered in the foyer. They were alone, if she didn't count his housekeeper and a few of his friends who lived on the property. "Shall I show you to your room? I figured tomorrow we'd have a working breakfast on the terrace by the pool. We can go over the lyrics and talk about some of the arrangements by ourselves before we have to meet the crew. I've got some ideas, and I want to run those past you while everyone sets up in the studio."

He'd never asked her opinion before, and Lexi nodded. "Sounds good."

After saying good-night, Lexi went into the bedroom, locked the door, and threw herself on the bed. Then she called Liam. Despite the lateness of the hour, he answered immediately. She reassured him she was fine and told him about the negotiations. They stayed off topics relating to them and finally, when Lexi started yawning, they hung up with a promise to talk again.

The next day, after the breakfast meeting, Lexi realized that maybe at least Damon had changed somewhat; he'd listened to her ideas. As for her singing, the recording portion came back naturally, almost like riding a bicycle. Despite not having done any singing besides in the shower, her voice hadn't failed. If anything, her vocals were stronger than ever.

Over the next two days, she recorded her portions both

separately and in duet with Damon. When with Damon, they fell back into the easy pattern they'd developed over the years, but this time her emotions didn't come into play. She wasn't in love with him like when she'd been a star-struck young girl with rose-colored views of her future as his wife. Those had been the wishful hopes of a studio system bent on cranking out the next hit from its young stars.

Each time they sang, she faced him as an equal. She pushed back when she didn't like something, using the backbone she'd developed over the previous year. While she wanted to get home, she also wanted to get the song right and do it justice. This was her literal swan song, as she'd texted Liam. Her exit from the limelight. She had new goals—one of which was to be the best mom ever.

As for Liam, she missed him. She'd grown accustomed to sleeping in his bed and seeing him daily, even if that time in Colorado had been limited by his being on the mountain. In this case, perhaps time apart did make the heart grow fonder. However, she discovered Liam wasn't a texter.

Instead, they talked on the phone. She loved the soothing deepness of his voice. Lexi liked how their conversations, where they couldn't see each other, allowed them to be open and honest. But she didn't allow herself to lower her guard. Even though he ended every conversation asking when she'd come home and also telling her he missed her, those three little words—I love you—never came. She didn't say them either. But she told him she missed him—for she did. He told her he missed her, and she heard something in his tone she hadn't before that gave her hope.

"We're listening to the final cut tomorrow," she told him. "If it's good, I'll be home after that. Since I don't know what time, I'll take a rideshare and text you once I land."

As she drew the covers to her chin, Lexi realized she was ready to be back in Beaumont. She wanted to see Liam, to set things to right as they'd failed to do the night of the fall festival. If only he could love her. Part of her believed he did. She'd give him one more chance before she walked away.

The next morning, Lexi went to the studio. The room was crowded. "You ready?" Damon asked. Lexi noted her father was there, but he stood a way off and didn't approach.

The producer pressed a button and the song's opening began to fill the air. Lexi closed her eyes and listened. The notes soared. The vocals harmonized. The effect was ethereal. The musicians had hit everything perfectly and the vocals became seamless to the track.

When the silence fell at the end, for a long moment no one spoke. Lexi opened her eyes and her gaze caught Damon's. Then everyone burst into applause. The producer spoke first. "Lexi, I know you're not going to like this, but you're going to have to be ready to walk the red carpet. That song has Grammy winner written all over it."

A surge of confidence joined the shiver of delight that made the gooseflesh rise as the giddy feeling took hold. Lexi knew a hit when she heard it, and they'd done it. This song would be number one. She'd go out on top, fully in control of her destiny.

"Thank you." She accepted the congrats. Soon after, the group began to disperse. As her father and Damon moved off to chat, the producer approached Lexi and handed her his business card. "You ever want to record solo, you let me know. I want to be first in line to work with you."

Lexi fingered the cardstock and put it in her purse as a rush of possibility traveled through her. "Thanks. I'll let you know."

Solo? Wow! Did she even want that? For once in her life, she could take it slow. She didn't have to decide today. The future was what she made of it, and what she wanted to do was get home to Beaumont and see Liam. The babies clearly agreed as they began kicking her in earnest.

Damon approached. "You already packed?"

She nodded. "You know it."

"I've got business to finish here. Called you a car. You good?"

She nodded. "I'm good."

"Don't be a stranger. And Lexi? Thanks for this."

Lexi reached out her hand and shook Damon's. "See you on the red carpet."

"Looking forward to it. Can't wait to meet Liam when he's not trying to push me out of the way." Damon indicated her stomach. "Let me know when they get here. Liam's a lucky guy."

She wished that Liam knew that. That they could have everything if he'd let down his walls and figure out that he could love her as he had Anya. She had to break through to him. She'd give it one more try.

As the plane landed at Spirit of St. Louis Airport, the words of Damon and her new song came back: "say how you feel."

Yes, that was something she hadn't tried. She'd told him that she wanted it all, but she hadn't told him she loved him. She'd never said the actual words to him. She gave her engagement ring a twist. The flight had taken four hours, and it was twilight. The driver transferred her luggage from the plane as Lexi climbed inside the car. She sent Liam a text: Leaving the airport now. See you soon.

She took a deep breath. All in. She'd tell him she loved

him. Maybe then they could break through the impasse. If not, she'd have to let the chips fall where they may.

"Ready to go home?" the driver asked.

"I am." She was ready to see the man she loved.

Except that thirty minutes later, a pair of deer seemed to drop out of the sky. As the buck bounced from the hood and shattered the front windshield, tires screeched and all went black.

Chapter Thirteen

When Liam got the call, he'd never known such raw panic, even worse than when he'd been on the mountain. He made it to Beaumont General and to Lexi's hospital room in record-breaking time. "Hey. There you are. We really need to stop doing this."

"What?" She hadn't passed out, but for some reason her brain was fuzzy. Lexi blinked, and Liam moved to turn the lights off, plunging the room into a darkness lit only by various machines. Lexi screwed her eyes tight, her fore-head forming tiny wrinkles. Liam wanted to smooth each of them but resisted. "My arm hurts."

"You sprained your right wrist. The doctor put it in a brace. And don't worry, the babies are fine."

"Oh my God!" Lexi pried her eyes open and tried to place her hand on her stomach, but she couldn't move. "Why can't I remember?"

"Probably because you fell asleep. Give it a few minutes. Everything's going to be fine," Liam soothed. Unable to help himself, he stroked her hair back from her forehead. "You have a sprained arm and a mild concussion. The car swerved and hit a tree. Luckily the airbags deployed. The driver of the car is okay. A bit beat up from the airbags but okay. You're lucky you had your seat belt on. But you still hit your head on the passenger door window."

"That poor man."

Liam loved how Lexi was concerned for everyone else. "He's shaken. Luckily a couple was driving behind you and saw the accident. He's a first responder. He took care of everyone until the ambulance came."

"I remember that. I must have blocked it out." She shuddered, and Liam gripped her hand.

"Lexi." Liam's voice caught. "I've never been so afraid."

"Not even with Anya?"

In the darkness, he couldn't see her face well. Her words felt like a lance though his soul. "No. This was worse. When I heard what happened..."

He couldn't continue. Liam lifted his hand and rose. Sitting by Lexi showed him how inadequate he was. He'd failed to protect her. She would have been better off had she stayed in LA rather than coming home to be with him.

"You were right all along. My motives, they've been misguided. You were hurt today. It could have been so much worse."

"I'm fine."

"No, you're not, and it's my fault. I told you I can't have someone else hurt because of my actions. Lexi, I failed to protect Anya. I should have stayed at base camp. She'd vomited. Said it was altitude sickness. Told me it was nothing, to go ahead so I could get things ready for when she climbed the next day. But she never intended on climbing."

"Liam..."

He couldn't let her talk him out of his decision. He couldn't be selfish. He couldn't let anyone else get hurt because of him. Anya had never wanted to climb Everest. If he hadn't been so selfish...

"You were right to leave me and go to California," he said, biting out the words. "I've been a beast. I've trapped you. You were right to snap and leave. I've made you hate me so much that you'd rather be anywhere else than with me. I can't trap you into a marriage without giving you the love you deserve. I'm heartless, but I'm not a monster. I refuse to be that man. Lexi, and you deserve to have it all. I can't let you marry me and shortchange yourself. We can't get married."

Whatever Lexi thought might happen when she woke up in the hospital, it wasn't this. Liam was setting her free. But her love for him made her want to reach out. To comfort. But her arm was in a brace.

"Lexi, I can't live with any more injury or death on my conscience, especially yours."

Her head hurt and the cause came from more than the car wreck. "Liam, accidents happen. You must let go of the guilt. I was coming home to you."

The words, though, weren't enough. She could read that truth on his face, revealed in the low light by the door.

Liam shook his head. "When we first met, I told you the choice was yours. I told you to say no and I'd respect it. That I won't do anything to make you uncomfortable. You're right when you say I've controlled you. I've tried to run your life. Monitored your food. I've done everything wrong. There's only one way to fix it. It's to let you go. To let you be that person you wanted to be when you came to Beaumont. The one you were becoming before I came into your life. I can't cause anyone any more pain."

Oh Liam. Lexi's heart broke. His greatest fear, of her being hurt, had made him retreat rather than embrace the truth of his feelings. His guilt over Anya's death had driven him to all the wrong answers.

The doctor appeared, ending conversation. As the doctor moved forward, Liam slipped out the door. Eva and his parents waited. "They'll be keeping her overnight for further monitoring. The doctor is in with her now and giving her the news. Then she's to be on bed rest. I'm going to move into a hotel. Give her space in the house on Third."

"Liam," Eva gasped. "Don't."

"Son." His father gripped Liam's shoulder. "I've been watching you now for two years. I might be all business most of the time, but I know when you say you're moving out what that means. I admit, I wasn't sure about Lexi, but I see the way you care for her, and I'm not sure you going is the right thing to do."

"I'm not going to discuss this now." He needed to leave, to nurse his own wounds. The fact she'd been coming back to him when she'd been hurt made it worse. He hurt the people he loved.

They were better off without him.

His dad lifted his hand. You know I lost someone before your mother. I've always been open about that. It can be good again. You can love more than one person in your life. Let's talk soon, okay?"

"Sure." That was the crux of it. The reason he'd panicked was rooted in how much he loved Lexi. Liam had learned that lesson, that fact, too late. He loved her. "Dad, sure, we can talk. But she'd never believe it if I did tell her. There are too many ghosts."

Two weeks later, Lexi found herself bored out of her mind. Streaming offered plenty of movies and TV programs to binge watch, but she'd oversaturated herself the first few days she'd been on bed rest. She'd also read enough books to fulfill her Goodreads yearly challenge three months early.

She played games with Liza, whom she'd dubbed her keeper. Liza, whom Liam had hired, served as Lexi's cook, nurse and housekeeper. For the two weeks Liza had lived in, Lexi had to admit she'd needed her. With her dominant arm in a sling and wrist brace as her muscles healed, Lexi had struggled with basic functions immediately following the accident. Even though she could do more things for herself each day, Liza remained a constant companion.

To her disappointment, Liam had been true to his word in giving her space. He'd moved into a suite at the Beaumont Grand. Minus several texts and a few stilted phone calls to ensure she was okay, she hadn't heard from him. She hated it.

Unlike her time in California, where the old adage "absence makes the heart grow fonder" had been true, this time that adage would be better written as "absence makes the heart grow angrier." He'd walked away. But the majority of her anger she directed at herself, for she'd failed to confront him. She'd let him go. She hadn't told him she loved him or fought to get through that thick head of his.

"We really are a pair," she grumbled.

"What's that?" Liza asked from where she was dusting.

"Nothing." Lexi tapped on her laptop. She checked her sparse email—Damon had sent one telling her the song was doing fantastic. Then she watched kitten videos. Maybe a pet would help. An older cat from a shelter could use a home. Dawn could help her find one. "Liza? Do you like cats?"

"What?" Liza asked.

"Never mind." Lexi moved to the living room couch after lunch, which was where she was when Liza announced she had a visitor. Liza opened the door to admit Eva.

"Hi, Lexi, I figured it was time for us to really talk," Eva greeted her. She surveyed the room. "At least I'm not finding you up to your elbows in takeout containers."

"No, I have Liza. She keeps me from overindulging my misery. And let me guess. Liam doesn't know you're here."

"No, he doesn't. So since I know how he is and I can see how you are, I figured it was time to take matters into my own hands. First, if you haven't realized it, my brother is dumb and stubborn. He's also miserable. I've never seen him like this, and I comforted him years ago when Anya died. You need to go see him and knock some sense into him. I can't have him wallowing around any longer. Not when he loves you and is too proud to tell you."

Liam didn't love her. "He said he'll never love me. That Anya was his soulmate."

Eva sighed. "What Liam knows about soulmates could fill a thimble. Trust me, he does love you. He figured it out and now he thinks you won't believe him if he tells you. But he's crazy about you. I saw him with Anya. I've seen him with you. It's you, Lexi. He just needs to figure things out on his end and get his priorities straight. He needs to let the guilt go and stop believing he hurts those he loves."

"I'm not appreciating the irony."

"Me either. You're feeling fine?" Eva asked.

"Bored out of my mind," Lexi admitted.

"I can imagine. Well, when you're ready, I've got an offer for you. I think it's one you'll like."

"Thanks, but no. Because of the song, I don't need to work. Besides, everything always comes with strings."

"What if those strings were for your eternal happiness?" Eva's eyebrow rose in challenge.

"Not even for that. That's why I have a hit song. I'll be fine. No need to sell my soul."

"Fair enough. I knew there was a reason I liked you. And it's a good song, by the way." Eva got right back to business. "So now that you're on equal footing with my brother financially, what do you really want? If it's the love of my brother, then you need a plan. A big gesture. Clayton men are stupid and stubborn. You should have seen Edmund." Eva rolled her eyes and pushed her longer hair behind her ear. "He was so clueless it was almost embarrassing. Anyway, my brothers don't know what love is unless it hits them in the face. Metaphorically, of course. Although I'm sure hitting him might be fun."

That made Lexi smile for a moment. Then she shook her head. "He doesn't love me," Lexi told her. Then doubt crept in. Eva was so insistent. Did Liam love her? Could he?

Eva read Lexi's debate. "He does. At his core, my brother Liam is integrity and goodness. His motivations come from a deep-seeded need to protect those he loves and cares about, and he can't tolerate himself when he fails. Believes his failures make him a monster and those he loves are better off without him. He left you because he didn't want to pressure you into marrying him. He also doesn't know how to win you back."

"Why are you telling me this? Why are you not telling him?"

"Because he refuses to listen every time I try. Question for you? How does one walk on eggshells without them breaking? How do you handle being damned if you do, damned if you don't?"

254 ROOM FOR TWO MORE

"I don't know," Lexi admitted. Loving someone was a tightrope. One misstep could cost you dearly.

"Well, you think about that because that's my brother to a T. And maybe think about some grand gesture to get his attention. I can think of one, but you might need my help to execute it. Liam is my brother, and I want to see him happy. You make him happy."

"Really?" Lexi loved Liam. Because she'd been put on bed rest, she'd backed away from telling him how she felt. Where was the girl who'd gone to his hotel room? Who'd been bold and brash on a deck in Colorado? What about the one who'd faced her father and had a hit song?

That woman deserved it all, and she'd told Liam that. "I'll think about it."

"Do. And when you're ready, ask. Besides, I'm going to be an aunt. I promise you no strings attached except to make me a godmother. Which you will because you and me, we're going to be great friends. Hopefully like sisters." Eva pointed at the backgammon board Liza had brought in. "You play?"

"Not well," Lexi admitted. Eva grinned and Lexi liked her even more than she had in Colorado.

"Me either. But like you, I've got some time to kill."

"What's the emergency?" Three weeks after he'd left Lexi in the hospital, Liam stepped into his parents' four thousand square foot house. They'd moved in once construction had finished and were constantly calling Liam to come hang something. A degree in architecture did not make him a handyman, but here he was. Well, he had been an Eagle Scout and had done much of the finishing work at his house in Colorado. "Bates, what's going on? What's it this time?"

Upon getting the 911 text message from his mother that had been followed by a directive to come straight to the house immediately, he'd rushed out of the office and out into the gated community where they lived. Thankfully it was late afternoon on a Friday. He'd had to weave around a bunch of cars—the neighbors were having a Halloween party of some sort, he guessed.

"You'll have to ask her," the expressionless butler said. The man had been with his parents as long as Liam could remember and had relocated from Portland. With his stiff demeanor, Bates would fit right in at the neighbors' costume party as a throwback to the past. "She's waiting in the salon."

"Bates, you know everything in this house before even my parents do," Liam said. He fingered a Halloween figurine. "Why aren't you giving me a clue? Don't tell me it's because a screen fell out again. She can call the builder for that."

"She's waiting in the salon," Bates repeated, his face a mask.

"Fine." Liam wouldn't get anything from the man. In a constant state of irritation from missing Lexi, Liam made his way back to his mom's favorite room. At least Lexi was healthy. Eva had visited twice and said she was, and the few times he'd spoken to Lexi, she'd sounded fine. He missed her. Missed her voice.

Liam pushed the door open and strode toward the light-filled room that overlooked the side gardens. Everything outside was dead for the winter, but the landscape simply matched his heart. "Mother, what is going on? Why did

I need to rush out here on short notice? I had work to do and…" He stopped as he saw her.

"Hello, Liam."

"Lexi. What are you doing here?" He drank her in. She wore a soft cream maternity gown that accentuated a generous bump. "You're supposed to be on bed rest. The twins…"

"Are growing leaps and bounds. The doctor said I can go places, just not exert myself." She rose from the sofa. "We've missed you, and I thought it was high time we talked. A few calls and texts are not enough. You've been avoiding me and I don't like it. Not when I want more."

"I'm sorry." He was, but mere words weren't enough. A lump formed in Liam's throat. Lexi's brunette hair was pinned into a French knot accenting her high, pinked cheekbones. She glowed with an angelic, pregnant radiance. Pride surged through him. She'd be the perfect mother. How had he gotten so lucky as to meet her? "Congrats on your hit song."

"Thanks. It's gotten tons of award buzz. You know, once the song aired, I realized some hard truths. The first was that I was right to run away and leave behind Melynda. She was not doing well. Then I came here and found myself. Found you. Being with you changed me, so much so that when I was in California, I realized I wasn't afraid anymore."

Through the fabric draped over her, Liam could see a bulge. One of the twins was pushing against her. "They're moving."

"All the time," she said. She patted her stomach. "They know you're here."

He made no move to touch her though. He didn't have that right.

Lexi seemed to understand his reluctance. "But something I hadn't realized is that sometimes we do have to face the past before we can move forward. Even though I'd started healing here in Beaumont, I still held back. I was hiding the fact I was Melynda. I was still caring what people thought. I worried what you would think. You know what doing that causes? Fear. And fear means we're not living our best lives. The constant worry that we have to please others keeps us from taking risks that are needed to live fully, to love fully. Why do we live in fear?"

"Because life can be painful. Full of hurt. Soul crushing," he asked.

"Yes. It can be all of those." She came toward him and took his hands in hers. He loved the soft texture of her skin. "Anya would rather have died on that mountain knowing you loved her than being hidden away in a protective cage. Deep down, you know that's true."

Liam shook his head. "I never should have insisted we climb Everest. I should have been at base camp. She told me to go ahead, but I…"

She interrupted with a "Look at me." He did, staring into brown eyes that he could swim in forever.

"Life is full of *shoulds*. We can lose ourselves in what we should have done. That's why we have to forgive ourselves. Losing my mother hurt. Her loss shook my foundation so much that I threw away my financial future to be free. Broke, I ran to Beaumont, which in hindsight is the best move I ever made as it brought me to you and the lives we're going to bring into the world. Liam, the accident I just had taught me something. When our time's up, it's up. Yours wasn't up. Mine wasn't up. Do you think Anya would want you to live the rest of your life in fear? Doing so doesn't honor her memory. It does the opposite. She'll always have your heart, Liam. But if you can give me even the tiniest sliver of it, then that will be enough for us to have a future. Because I love you and I can give you all of mine."

She was putting it all on the line, Liam realized. She loved him and was risking his rejection with every word she spoke. He wanted to give her everything. He just had to tell her and hope she believed. "You deserve more."

She wove her fingers into his, and he took comfort in the pressure. "Do you know the thing about cracks? Of course you do. You climb mountains. Time makes cracks widen. All the love and hope you've been trying to keep inside is busting through the seams you keep trying to keep closed. The tiniest trickle of water can burst a dam. I love you. I've been remiss in saying it because I've been afraid. But no longer. It's okay if you don't love me. We've wasted enough time, though, don't you think?"

He lifted the back of her hand to his and kissed it. His Lexi was so wise. He'd been a misguided fool. "Yes. Far too much time. I'm miserable without you. You being gone in California was the worst week of my life. These past few weeks have been even worse than that."

"You're a good man. You'll be a good father. You've got my heart. I love you, Liam."

"You love me." He savored those words. Hearing them acted as a balm to his battered soul. "You love me. I don't deserve it."

She squeezed his hand. "That's why love is a gift given freely. I'm not asking for but a sliver in return. I think you do love me back. Which is why I'm here. Risking. Taking control. I will never be Anya. But we can be happy. This time the choice is all mine. And I choose to love you, completely and without reservation."

Hope took flight. Played in the sunlight pouring in the windows, the weather clearing. "I will make you happy. I will spend my life doing that," he promised.

Before he could say more, she said, "I believe you. I'll never ask you to let Anya go. She'll always be part of your past. But I'm your future. Me and these twins."

She moved his hand to her stomach where he could feel them kick. The emotions powering through him were unlike anything: love, joy, promise.

"And any others we decide to have," Lexi continued. "I was an only child. I like the idea of being part of a huge family. A big, normal family."

"My head is spinning," Liam admitted. His heart filled and ran over. "I haven't even told you how I feel."

"I'll take the sliver."

The crack widened. The dam burst. He felt whole. Healed. Loved. "It's not a sliver. It's a mountain. Like standing atop a mountain. The air is thin. You're lightheaded as your body works to breathe. The adrenaline pumps. There's no feeling quite like it, except for being in love. I've been so foolish. From the moment I first touched you, I had to have you. The connection between us was primal. Elemental. Basic. Pure. I complicated it when I began second-guessing. Rationalizing. Denying myself. Allowing my guilt to consume me."

"You don't need to punish yourself. Her death was an accident. No one could predict an earthquake. You might not be here if you were with her. I might never have met you."

"I know. I realize that now. I've spent the last week traveling to the other wineries out of state. While I was gone, I made side trips to see places from my past again. I was exorcising demons. Saying goodbye. I had to banish the past. During my journey, something became crystal clear.

While I was letting go of the past, it solidified that you are my future. I'm a different person with you than I was with Anya, and you complete the new person I've become."

She still held his hands in hers, and he lifted her left hand to his lips and kissed the flesh of her palm. "I love you, Lexi Henderson. And it's not a sliver either. It's all of my heart. I love you and am not afraid to say it."

Tears rimmed her lower eyelids "Enough to love me forever?"

The love in his heart overflowed its banks. Joy pounded in his ears like snowmelt pouring its way down a mountain. "Yes. I love the idea of being with you until death do us part, which I hope and pray is decades from now."

She smiled like Mona Lisa about to reveal a long-kept secret. "Good. Because they're all waiting for us out back."

"Who?" It registered that his mother's engagement ring sat on her finger. "You're wearing your ring."

Lexi freed her hand. Brushed away tears. "Yes. And thanks to your sister and the power of the Clayton name, I've got a marriage license with both of our names on it, ready to be signed, sealed and delivered."

"All those cars?"

"For us. Our guests are waiting, if you say yes. There's a minister and everything. All you have to do is say 'I do.' I hope you will, because I'd rather not stand up there by myself."

Joy transformed his face. "We're getting married."

She nodded, laughed, and he drank her in. "In less than an hour. If you'll have me."

"I want nothing more." Liam cupped her cheeks and brought his lips to hers for a mind-drugging kiss that seemed to wash him clean. Dazed, he drew air. "We're getting married. Like now. And this is the wedding you want."

"Yes. It's exactly what I want as I arranged it. Technically, we're eloping. I don't want to waste another day."

Droplets formed at the corners of her eyes, and he reached and flicked them away. "Don't cry. It's all going to be okay from here on out. I love you and you love me."

She nodded. "Yes."

"Then we won't waste another minute. But—" Liam glanced at his jeans and black Henley "—I'm not dressed."

"That's what I'm here for." Dressed in a black tux with black bow tie, his brother Edmund stepped into the room. "Can I take him now? Our mother's out there getting nervous."

Tears brimmed in Lexi's eyes and she laughed as she dabbed at them. "Yes. Please do. If not, I'll be all puffy in the wedding photos. Eva will have a fit."

"And that's why we've got you, Lexi." Dressed in hats and formal dresses, his mother and sister entered the room. Lana poked her head in as well. Laverna pointed. "Go, Liam. We've got forty minutes to get everyone dressed and ready. Seriously. Go. When I told you it was an emergency, I wasn't joking."

"You're a lucky man," Edmund said as he stood next to Liam inside the conservatory forty minutes later. Twenty guests sat in the white chairs strategically placed around a floral-covered dais, and a white runner covered the stone path of the indoor garden.

"Trust me, I know how lucky I am. I met her wearing a tux."

"Well, now you'll marry her in one," Michael said.

"You ever going to settle down?" Liam asked his younger brother.

"Let's get out there," Michael said instead.

Which was why Liam found himself standing to the minister's left as the string quartet began Modest Mussorgsky's "Pictures at an Exhibition: Promenade (Part 1)." Trust his Lexi—he loved the sound of that—to pick a song so perfect and different from the traditional wedding march.

Unadulterated emotion caused Liam to quake in his polished black leather shoes as both his heart and smile split open when Lexi came down the aisle on Liam's father's arm. She was beautiful, the mother of his babes-in-womb and the love of his life. She was generous, kind and everything he'd not known he could hope or wish for. A dream realized. A promise of a life of happiness to come. She stood beside him, and he took his hands in hers. "I'm so grateful you came into my life," he whispered for her ears only. "I love you."

Lexi's designer stilettos had her eye to eye with him. "I love you right back."

Epilogue

"Then we went to the dinosaur exhibit at the science center."

"Really?" Lexi sat cross-legged on the floor next to the child-size seat at the table where three-year-old Emma colored. Lexi had been back one day from her overseas trip with Liam. "It sounds like Grandma kept you very busy while Mommy and Daddy were gone."

"She did," Erika replied. She sat across the table. "She loved babysitting us. What do you think?"

Whereas Emma's neon color choices verged on eccentric and outside-the-box thinking, firstborn Erika opted more for traditional reds and greens. "Just like me and Edmund," Liam had observed once his and Lexi's twins started crawling. "Opposites in the best of ways."

Her husband loved his twin daughters. Spoiled them rotten, as did the girls' grandparents. Even Lexi's dad had come around, though the relationship was still tenuous.

Erika held up her picture for inspection. "Grandma said you were gone a week on vacation. Normally you take us."

"We had to go dedicate a school. We wanted to be there in person, and sometimes adults need to have adult time."

"In Nipple," Emma said matter-of-factly.

"Nepal," Lexi corrected. "Someday we will take you there, Daddy and me. When you're older."

"Maybe I'll climb mountains like Daddy sometimes does," Emma announced.

"Did I hear my name?" Liam entered the playroom of the Beaumont house he and Lexi had purchased a month before the girls' birth. An old farmhouse on five acres with a view of the Missouri River valley had become available and they'd snatched it up, remodeled it, and created a warm and loving home.

"Daddy!" Both twins raced to him and he scooped them up, one in each muscular arm. "Are my girls coloring?"

"We are." Emma wiggled to get down and brought back a picture of a half-colored teddy bear whose head was a shade of bright neon green. "Pretty," Liam admired. "I love it." After complimenting Erika's red rose picture, he drew his wife to her feet. "Do you know how much I love you? I missed you at work today."

Liam was still a VP at Clayton Holdings, but with Edmund and Lana's return, Liam oversaw Clayton's philanthropic endeavors. Lexi loved being a full-time mom, but she'd discovered she loved fundraising for the foundation and she took an active role in that.

"Eww," Erika said with an exaggerated point before breaking into a fit of giggles. "Daddy's going to kiss Mommy again."

"Yes, he is." Liam dipped his lips to Lexi's as his girls squealed and raced around the playroom.

Later that night, once the girls were fast asleep, Lexi and Liam sat in bed. Liam's arm was draped around her, and he leaned to nuzzle her neck. "Did I tell you how much I appreciated you going to Nepal with me?"

Lexi tilted her head to give him better access. "I wanted to honor her, too. I think she'd be pleased with what we've done."

"I know she would."

They'd dedicated the Anya Morrison School, which Liam had designed and which the Clayton Holdings Foundation had funded. Built to withstand earthquakes and provide education to all no matter their family income, the school was one of Lexi's first fundraising duties, and she had recruited Laverna to help raise a huge endowment.

Together, the amount she and her mother-in-law had raised had exceeded their expectations, and with a trusted headmaster and governing board in place, Lexi and Liam had high hopes for the school, which had opened to much local excitement. The experience itself had been eye-opening, standing so near Everest, the mountain that had claimed so many lives yet still stood as a beacon of fulfillment and hope.

Liam had gazed up at the summit, let go of that dream, turned to Lexi and grasped another. As for Lexi, she currently had the number one pop hit on the charts, thanks to being asked to sing solo on a box-office smash movie soundtrack. Three years ago she'd walked the red carpet with Liam. He's been the first person she'd thanked from the stage when she and Damon had claimed another Grammy. There were rumors she'd be nominated again. As for doing an album, she hadn't decided. She knew she wouldn't tour though. If they took the kids anywhere, it would be to Colorado, which was their bolt-hole and the place they'd first fallen in love.

"Any news on the other front?" Liam asked as he planted

kisses along her neck. His doing so reminded her what was really important.

"It's too soon to tell. And since we don't know for sure if I'm pregnant, it can't hurt to keep trying."

"I hope it's another girl," Liam said between kisses. "Edmund took care of passing down the Clayton name to his son. The firstborn gets the boys. The second can have the girls."

"You want another girl? I'm okay with that," Lexi said before she pounced on him.

Nine months later, with much excitement and fanfare, Lexi and Liam welcomed eight-pound, ten-ounce Elena Joy, adding another bundle of pure love to their growing family.

* * * * *

HARLEQUIN
Reader Service

Enjoyed your book?

Try the perfect subscription for Romance readers and get more great books like this delivered right to your door.

See why over 10+ million readers have tried Harlequin Reader Service.

Start with a Free Welcome Collection with free books and a gift—valued over $20.

Choose any series in print or ebook.
See website for details and order today:

   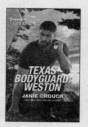

TryReaderService.com/subscriptions

RSBPA24R

HARLEQUIN

Reader Service

Enjoyed your book?

Start with a Free Welcome Collection with free books and a gift — valued over $20.

TryReaderService.com/subscribe today